THE HIDDEN SHIP

Other Books By MWM

Scrapyard Ship Series

Scrapyard Ship (Book 1)

HAB 12 (Book 2)

Space Vengeance (Book 3)

Realms of Time (Book 4)

Craing Dominion (Book 5

The Great Space (Book 6)

Call To Battle (Book 7)

Tapped In Series

Mad Powers (Book 1)

Deadly Powers (Book 2)

Lone Star Renegades Series

Lone Star Renegades
(also called 'Jacked') (Book 1)

Star Watch Series

Star Watch (Book 1)

Ricket (Book 2)

Boomer (Book 3)

Glory for Space Sea and Space
(Book 4)

Space Chase (Book 5)

Scrapyard LEGACY (Book 6)

The Simpleton Series

The Simpleton (Book 1)

The Simpleton Quest (Book 2)

Galaxy Man Series

Galaxy Man (Book 1)

Ship Wrecked Series

Ship Wrecked (Book 1)

Ship Wrecked 2 (Book 2)

Cloudwalkers Series

Cloudwalkers (Book 1)

The Hidden Ship

The Hidden Ship

THE HIDDEN SHIP

MARK WAYNE MCGINNIS

Published by Avenstar Productions.

Paperback ISBN 978-1-7335143-3-0

Visit Mark Wayne McGinnis at http://www.markwaynemcginnis.com

To join Mark's mailing list, visit http://eepurl.com/bs7M9r

prologue

There are a number of outlying buildings on my family's property; a massive barn, a bunkhouse once occupied by a team of ranch-hands, and several long and narrow chicken coops. The house itself is large, far too big for a single occupant—*me*. Hell, this sprawling ranch-style structure has no less than six fireplaces, twelve bedrooms, a ridiculously huge ballroom, a library, and a kitchen larger than those found in most hotels.

Unless you knew exactly where to find the concealed room, and the specifics on how to access it, you wouldn't come across it—not on your own, anyway. Family members as far back as 1919 searched the grounds for the subterranean vault hidden somewhere in the house. You see, my great-great-grandfather, Robert Polk, a prominent and successful Colorado cattle rancher at the time, was no fan of the 1918 Volstead Act, more commonly known as Prohibition. Back then, the local constable, along with a team of police, searched for the vault where it was well known Robert was storing illegal stockpiles of liquor. Far more recently, Earth's alien occupying invaders also searched for it. Neither ever found it.

I now sat in the voluminous, not to mention dank and musky, vault sipping my eighty-five-year-old scotch from one of Robert Polk's fine cut-crystal tumblers. Only a single flame flickered within a lone gas lantern in the muted darkness. The vault was so large, only the nearest of the room's four interior walls was visible beyond the lantern's limited glow. Three thousand square feet of space that once contained hundreds of oaken barrels of liquor, stacked up to the rafters now contained a different sort of contraband. Military surplus supplies of every kind from all over the world were packed inside a significant cache of stacked crates. That contained a broad assortment of both new and used war supplies. Everything from pull-pin grenades, to night-optics headgear, to never used M-16 fully automatic rifles. Even laser-guided missile launchers. An arsenal of weaponry and ammunition that took me years to assemble. Procuring each piece had become so time consuming, along with my other, also highly deviant activities, that I had little time to do much of anything else.

Sitting at a wood plank table, I powered-up on my circa 1950s RCA vintage Ham radio transmitter and waited for the old glass tubes to sufficiently warm up. A minute later, I spun the dial up to the high 9,000 kHz range. Slowing through the frequencies, I heard ghostly clicks and sounds of static. Then I heard his far-away sounding, heavily accented words.

"Polybius . . . are you there? Hello, hello?" This is your friend . . . this is Sopravvissuto. Hello, hello . . ."

I smiled, hearing the old man's voice. *Sopravvissuto,* his code name, was Italian for *survivor*. An eighty-three-year old, he walked with a cane and owned a small corner grocery store somewhere in northern Italy. Specific locations were never used over the air, just as our actual names were never spoken aloud.

"Good morning, Sopravvissuto . . . I trust you slept well?" I asked. Now was our prearranged day and time to reach out to one another—about 9:00 p.m. in Colorado, and around 5:00 a.m. in Italy.

I silently listened to an extended pause—fluctuating background noise became an ominous precursor to his next words.

"To be honest, I am scared, my friend, even more so than usual. My daughter . . . lives nearby, in a town about sixty kilometers away called—"

I keyed my mic—"Don't say the name! No names, Sopravvissuto. They may be listening . . . Please, be careful."

"Yes . . . yes, thank you." Following another long pause, he said, "Polybius . . . I cannot reach her by telephone. Three days now. Neither can I reach others who live in that same northern Italian town. Not one person. The phones ring and ring, but no one answers."

Today was not the first day I'd heard news regarding that same Italian village. Other rebels, like Sopravvissuto and me, from all around the world spoke of a town in Italy that seemingly no longer existed. Only through shortwave and Ham radios were such illicit communications even possible. Cell phones were a thing of the past. The internet was long gone. Landline telephones were operational for the most part, but often monitored. I knew even this—transmitting by shortwave radio—might not be safe. I'd constructed a shortwave radio antenna some two hundred yards from the house; screened from sight within thick branches of towering oaks flanking both sides of my long driveway. But now radio tubes fitting my old radio were nearly impossible to find these days. Even worse, they were burning out more and more quickly lately.

"Sopravvissuto . . . I'm sure there is a good explanation. Perhaps the antenna was discovered, or a cable was severed. Do not lose faith, good friend." I tried to sound upbeat, even though in my heart I knew the situation in Italy was dire. His daughter had probably been killed. The alien invaders were beyond ruthless. But a whole town being eliminated was most alarming.

chapter 1

I turned onto Plum Creek Road and found three mounted lizards smiling back at me from the side of the road. The billboard, relatively new, had a nostalgic quality to it—reminded me of the old 1960s' TV show, Bonanza, where the characters, Ben, Little Joe, and Hoss, galloped across the plains of the Ponderosa on horseback. That fond image had been replaced with three Reptilian Gaps, wearing chaps, spurs, and oversized cowboy hats. The same questions arose—for me as they did for everyone else—*why were the invaders here? What did they want from us?*

It was still early enough that I had no trouble finding an open parking spot right out front of the greasy spoon, called the B&B.

I shut off the engine and climbed out, avoiding my three-year-old bloodhound's melancholy stare. Leaving the pickup's driver side and passenger side windows wide open, I scolded, "Don't be so dramatic," then stood there, feeling guilty anyway. *My life shouldn't revolve around the emotions of a damn dog.* "You want scraps, Mort? Best I don't hear any barking coming from this truck."

Pocketing the old Ford's keys, I headed for the entrance. Proprietors were busy decorating their storefronts. All major streets were already adorned with flags and banners depicting the annual Friends Unite Day in bright colors of orange, purple, and brown. A god-awful combination nobody quite understood, but went along with, since they had little choice but to do so. Tomorrow, the festivities would begin: an afternoon parade marching right down Wilcox, then the Friends Unite Day Carnival held at Castle Rock's fairgrounds. Throngs of people would attend. Was it mandatory? No. But missing it was the sort of thing that could get you noticed as one who could possibly be a dissident, someone non-compliant with the dictums of the new order. Yes, tomorrow was supposed to be a day of celebration—the two-year anniversary when everything on Earth changed. When, in truth, virtually every man, woman, and child would inwardly mourn the loss of someone—those taken from them that fateful night. But sure, we would wear our forced smiles and try to act jovial, as if nothing had changed. Life as usual. It was only by sheer chance that the invasion took place one week after the 4th of July. Now orange, purple, and brown flags replaced America's patriotic, and now forbidden, red, white, and blue flags.

A tiny overhead bell chimed as I stepped inside. Murmured voices suddenly quieted—eyes from the fifteen or so seated patrons rested upon me for several long beats. It was a routine reaction. Something we all tended to do in these volatile times. Being careful was the new norm. I spotted Donny and Matt in a nearby booth. Three booths further on, I made eye contact with Ronald Gant. One would think the only real foe around here were the obtrusive alien invaders who had so abruptly shattered everyone's lives here in America, and across the entire world. Just as they had right here in what was once a good and decent small town. But there was another enemy, perhaps one even more insidious, living among us: those fully embracing the enemy and their forced lifestyle changes and mandates. They have become—more or less—one of them. They sided with the aliens rather than uphold the very survival of the Human race. Ronald Gant was one such person. Once neighbor, friend, and someone I would have gone far beyond the extra mile for, was now one of my worst nemeses. The chief problem was that he was methodically bringing other Humans around to his sordid way of thinking. A kind of *if you can't beat them, join them,* philosophy. Ronald Gant was the founder of the *Friends For Friends* directive, a new neighborhood watch program. A gang of men and women who twice weekly held meetings and scheduled either late evening or early morning patrols. Its sole purpose was to keep any and all subversion out of Castle Rock. Sure, their reasoning was compelling; how many more decent people had to go missing, be tortured, and even executed, before *something* was done? The problem with their way of thinking was that someday you're going to want your freedom back. You're going to wake up and realize that hardship, even death, is the price one may have to pay for freedom. Ronald Gant and I were on opposite sides of that debate. Sooner or later, there would be a reckoning.

"Coffee, Brian?" Wendy asked, standing behind the cash register.

I answered with both a nod and a wink as I slid in beside Matt.

"You look like shit," Donny said.

"Good morning to you too, asshole." I retorted, reaching for a menu wedged in behind the condiments caddy.

"You've been coming here your whole damn life . . . what are you going to see on that menu that you haven't seen a thousand times before?" Donny asked. "And you always order the same thing, anyway," he continued. "Oatmeal and a side of bacon."

I gave Donny a sideways glance. Donny Kuruk was my best friend. Just a tad over six feet, his dark hair and dark complexion bespoke his Apache Native American heritage. Like me, he, too, was tall, broad-shouldered, and muscular from his in the military. Multiple tours fighting in hellish places like Helmand, Kandahar, and Logar Province. While Donny had battled on the ground as a Marine, I, Captain Brian Polk, had flown jets—piloting U.S. Air Force F-16 Fighting Falcons. We both grew up in Castle Rock, a bit more than a thirty-minute-drive south of downtown Denver. Once back stateside, three and a half years ago, I was teaching history three days a week at Colorado University, in Denver. That was back when Denver was an actual municipality, not a bombed-out shell of a city.

"Well, today might be different," I said, still perusing the menu. "Never know, maybe I'll surprise you. Get scrambled eggs, or maybe a short stack."

Wendy arrived at our booth, not bothering to pull the notepad from her back pocket. "Usual all around?" she asked, her neatly penciled brows raised high. She shot a quick warning glance at Donny, who smiled up at her.

"So help me, you start that grab-ass shit today and I'll punch you in the face. I swear to God, Donny, I'm in no mood for it."

Donny raised his hands in mock surrender. "Hey, I'm just here for the huevos rancheros." He shook his head, looking dismayed, but then added, "Look, calm down . . . you're like old enough to be my mother."

"Oh, screw you," Wendy shot back, looking ready to kill him.

I held back a laugh; I knew she wasn't more than a few years older than him, at thirty-two. She turned her attention to Matt. "Breakfast burrito, hon?"

"Yeah . . . and bring me a Coke, too."

"You got it." She abruptly spun away, not bothering to take Donny's or my order. Wendy knew what we wanted. No different today than yesterday, or the day before that.

I looked over at Matt, also ex-military, but six inches shorter and a good fifty pounds lighter than either Donny or me. Balding on the top of his head, he was the quiet one of our trio. He returned home from his last tour of duty missing one leg, although no one would suspect he wore a leg prosthesis by the agile way he got around. He'd been in the Army EOD: Explosive Ordinance Disposal. But the loss of his leg didn't occur while doing his job, but in the course of taking a crap—somewhere in Kandahar province. He didn't like talking about it.

"You see the '*Friends Fucking Friends*' breakfast club gang?" Matt asked.

I nodded back, not caring to get into it now.

"Tell me you've made some progress. Time is running out," Donny said, in a hushed voice.

I blew out a breath. "Hey, you want me to take a wrench to

an F-16's Pratt & Whitney power plant, no problem. But *this* isn't that. This thing . . . defies the friggin' laws of physics!"

"Okay, okay . . . keep your voice down," Matt interjected. "He was just asking. We have a strict timetable, so we're all uptight."

"Well, it doesn't help knowing we're constantly being watched and followed," I said, gesturing with a jerk of my chin toward the group of men sitting three booths away.

Just then the little bell above the café door chimed, then chimed again. The patrons quieted, everyone looking over to see who was entering the establishment. This time a pregnant silence prevailed as three beings entered. Their heavy footfalls made the old oaken floorboards beneath them creak. I put a smile on my face that didn't reach my eyes. Donny and Matt, plus everyone else in the B&B, nodded back. They were the EMS—Earupitan Marshal Service. The alien version of the Gestapo. All three still had what Humans referred to as their *ear pucks* still activated. About the same size and shape as a typical hockey puck—they're metallic with series of intricate concentric rings and tiny blue lights that flickered on and off seemingly at random. The ear pucks were amazing technology—for one thing, they seemed to defy gravity. Bring the device up anywhere close to one's head, let go of it, and it seems to know precisely where to go—to lock onto the location of a Gap's ear and position itself right above it—hover there all on its own. The apparatus was multi-functional—first being a kind of EMS communications device. Second, it can be activated to provide a virtual 3D heads up display that encompasses the Gap's head and shoulders where eye movements are tracked—and used to make virtual menu selections and so on. And thirdly, the ear pucks can be used as a kind of 360-degree energy shield for a Gap's head and upper torso. All in all, the devices were amazing tech. Each of the three Gaps took this opportunity to remove their ear pucks and place them into their pants pockets.

"Morning guys!" Wendy said, from behind the register.

The three *Gaps* headed for the counter, where the seating would better accommodate their substantial girth. Before taking a seat, one of them glanced our way. Nodding, he tipped the brim of his Stetson cowboy hat, in a *howdy-there* folksy gesture. I followed suit, tipping down the brim of my own baseball cap. Each of the alien marshals wore gunslinger-style, holster belt rigs, only they weren't armed with old six-shooters. Instead, they were armed with what today was commonly referred to as a *mistmaker*—because any area of someone's body struck by a mistmaker's energy bolt, instantly vaporized—turned to bloody mist. I watched as the three, seven-foot-tall aliens shuffled about, getting their ungainly legs situated somewhat comfortably into the limited space beneath the counter top. I stopped myself from shaking my head in wonder. Why they felt compelled to always wear Americana western garb, I had no clue. Like Trekkies attending a Star Trek convention where everyone dressed-up like Bones, Spock, and Captain Kirk, these three lizardy guys were excited to dress up like Roy Rogers and the Lone Ranger. They wore oversized blue jeans, cowboy boots, and different, brightly colored—red, blue, or green—long-sleeve, snap-button shirts with embroidered swirls on their collars. All three wore cowboy hats that didn't quite fit their oblong, lizard-shaped, heads. I silently wondered what the Gap invaders were now wearing in Moscow, or Vienna, or Mexico City. I tried to mentally picture a Gap lizard wearing an oversized sombrero. It was almost laughable, how hard they tried to meld into their preconceived slant of local cultures around the world. But if they really wanted to be accepted, maybe they should stop interrogating, torturing, and killing so many of the Human masses.

I watched as Wendy sauntered up before them, her notepad and pen poised to take their order. Making a mistake, while either taking their order, or when preparing it, could cost her her life. "What'll you have, boys?" she asked, playing up to their TV cowboy personas.

The Gap in the middle spoke up, "Lobster Rolls for the three of us."

I saw Donny make a revolted face. The Gaps around here tended to speak in an adopted Texan-like twang that sounded disgusting. The phlegmy gravel sounds emanating out of the reptilian's voice box had the unique ability to instantly sour just about any nearby Human's stomach. I watched Wendy's face as she turned her head toward the open window leading into the kitchen. Her eyes desperately conveyed her silent query: *Do we even have anymore fucking lobsters?* Gaps— the nickname given the alien invaders was coined after noting they all had a wide gap between both front teeth. Each Gap tooth was easily five times the size of the average Human tooth. Over the course of two years, nicknames for the green aliens were not limited to just a single derogatory term. There was Phlegmflams, relating to their gurgly-phlegmy voices; Sackdraggers, relating specifically to the Gaps' reported enormous genitalia; Bug Suckers, relating to their preference to abruptly suck out the insides of a lobster; and Shitshots, pertaining to the first Gaps arrival on Earth and their inability to utilize Human toilets. They often gave up in frustration and simply shitted upon a closed lid. The assumption that an interstellar invader, such as the Earupitans, would be far more intelligent than the society they invaded, namely now Earth's Humans, was debatable.

I always thought it interesting that most people were under the assumption one's brain size was the major contributing factor relating to intelligence. But elephants and whales have much bigger brains than Humans. Scientists long ago came up with something called the *Encephalization Quotient* to determine a species actual *smarts*. Something to do with the ratio of actual brain mass relative to the predicted brain mass for any given species' size—all based on the assumption that larger animals required a bit less brain matter, relative to their overall size, in comparison to those of a tinier species. By this metric, Humans came out on top on Earth, with an EQ metric of 7.5, far surpassing the dolphin's 5.3, and the mouse's measly 0.5. Word was, although I certainly had no way to confirm the findings, the average Gaps Encephalization Quotient was somewhere in the neighborhood of 6.2, a little above that of a dolphin, and certainly higher than that of a common yard pig.

The three Gaps seemed to be in a jovial mood today. The one on the left reached a claw-like hand across the counter and gave Wendy's left breast a painful squeeze. Crying out, she pulled away, clutching her notepad to her chest. Tears welled in her eyes as she stared back at them perplexed.

All three Gaps laughed uproariously. The one on the right began to slap his hand down repeatedly onto the marble counter top. Apparently, her reaction was just what they were hoping for.

Matt, leaning closer to me, whispered, "There has to be a way to move up our timetable . . . ," but then looked up.

The *Friends Fucking Friends* contingent of five men, now obviously finished with breakfast, were striding past us. Bringing up their rear was Ronald Gant. Giving me, and the others around our table, a contrite smile and nod, he then—as though a second thought had occurred to him—turned back and stopped at the counter. He leaned in close to the middle EMS Gap who was perched high on a stool, and whispered something into his ear. As he departed, he gave the big alien a conspiratorial pat on the shoulder.

chapter 2

Huddled together, Matt, Donny, and I stood talking along the passenger side of my truck. Mort's head still hung outside the truck window so Matt scratched the loose folds of skin around the dog's neck. Directly across the street was what used to be the town's government center and the DMV office. Now it was just one more Gap Oversight and Enforcement Center, more commonly referred to as an OEC.

"Where you off to now?" Matt asked.

"Elizabeth," I answered, referring to another, even smaller town than Castle Rock. "I'm running low on crustaceans. Might have a new underground source there. We'll see."

Neither Matt nor Donny said anything, but their silence spoke volumes—they disapproved of my food source and its intended purpose.

I said, "Look, Matt . . . I need you to talk to your sister again—"

Matt, already shaking his head, said, "I told you, no. She's not the slightest bit interested in any of this, in what we're doing. In fact, she's tried to talk me out of it."

I was well aware Karen had lost her husband in Earth's short-lived battle against the aliens. That she wasn't about to sacrifice herself, or Gwen, her five-year-old daughter, by going against the strict dictums now in place under the alien occupation. But she, like myself, had once been a pilot, and a damn good one. Her bird of choice was an AH-64 Apache helicopter. We really could use Karen's help now.

Matt said, "Anyway . . . same time tonight?"

"Um, best make it around ten. I have a few things to take care of. As always, make sure you're not followed," I said.

Donny rolled his eyes. "Oh . . . thank you so much for reminding us of that. I would totally have forgotten to check my rearview mirror, or to check the skies for distortion wakes."

As if on cue, a Milonge Bi-Hull transport suddenly thundered above into Castle Rock's airspace. The presence of the twin, side-by-side cabined spacecraft caused everything below it to vibrate. I felt the disturbing turbulence deep within my chest. Talking would be impossible until the craft moved on. It hovered, completely blocking out the sun from view, directly over the OEC. It slowly began to descend onto the four-story building's rooftop. We watched its four landing struts lower. The big ship gently rocked back and forth as it touched down onto the makeshift landing pad above.

Donny strode off, walking south down Wilcox, while Matt headed north. No sooner did I climb behind the wheel, giving Mort another pat on his head, than the town's public address system crackled to life. I looked at my watch. Eight o'clock on the dot. With all their faults, the Gaps were nothing if not punctual.

"Citizens . . . Good morning, and a fine morning this is . . ."

Right then every television channel, every radio station, and all the newly installed PA systems recently installed around the world, were transmitting local versions of this same message. The voice belonged to one Sleept Vogthner, the Gap's Chancellor of Communications. He ranked somewhere up there, amongst the higher echelons within the alien command structure. I watched the local Castle Rock pedestrians meander on, going this way and that, seeming not to listen to the all too familiar morning broadcast.

". . . today, I would like you to breathe in this wonderful Colorado air. Fill up your lungs and give proper acknowledgment and gratitude for the bounty provided to you by our kind eminence, Overlord Skith. '*No worries* is our motto. Strife is a thing of the past, citizens. Food, shelter, and healthcare are provided to each and every one of you. Also, a monetary supplement is offered to one and all, with no strings attached." The voice droned on and on. I caught sight of Wendy through the B&B's large, street-facing window standing behind the counter. She gestured comically, shoving two fingers down her throat and mimicking the act of throwing-up.

I offered her back a courtesy smile. *She needs to be more careful*, I thought. I started up the engine and put the truck in reverse, then backed out onto Wilcox Ave. Checking the traffic behind me, I noticed the same three Gaps who'd been seated at the B&B's counter now heading across the street.

Grasped securely between two of the Gaps was a man I knew: Barry Larson. He owned *Fishing Rods and Bait*, two streets over. Struggling to free himself—his feet gyrated two-feet above the ground. A fourth marshal strode into view, approaching from the opposite side of the street, and I did a double-take. The sheer size of the alien bordered on the impossible. The average Gap tended to be in the seven-foot-tall range—sometimes a tad taller or shorter than that. I turned around in my seat and looked out the truck's rear window. I wanted to make sure I was actually seeing things as they really were. Mirrors could sometimes distort reality. But this was no distortion. The Gap marshal really was *that* big, easily eight feet tall. And built like some kind of steroid-infused wild creature. His biceps were the size of soccer balls; the breadth of his shoulders would demand he turn sideways before entering a standard thirty-inch doorway. And he'd have to duck down real low to avoid hitting his head on the door's frame. His cowboy boots, beyond all doubt, had to have been custom-made. Had to be at least size twenty-four, compared to my own boot size of eleven and a half. The towering Gap marshal, intersecting with his fellow officers, took physical possession of poor Barry Larson. Using a clawed hand that almost spanned the size of a trashcan lid, the big alien plucked the struggling Human up by the top of his head and raised him to eye-level. The Gap marshal's words, spoken in a deep baritone voice, resonated all the way into my truck's cab: "If you don't stop struggling, I'll crush your cranium, Human."

Barry Larson did as told. His arms went limp by his sides. His legs stopped gyrating. I could see humiliation written on the man's petrified face. And then the Gap marshal's head, swiveling around, looked directly toward my truck—at me.

I put the truck in drive and sped away. I doubted Barry

would survive the night—fifty-fifty odds he'd never see his family again.

It was a twenty-minute drive to the town of Elizabeth, which wasn't really much of a town. About six hundred registered inhabitants lived there. Mort kept his head draped out the window as we drove, staring out at mostly open-range grasslands. I remembered back when hundreds of head of Angus cattle grazed these same pastures. Thing was, you'd need actual living ranchers still around to support such endeavors. Even from the street, I could tell that two out of three ranches were uninhabited. Falling into lonely decrepitude. I checked my rearview mirror often, since it was not uncommon to find myself tailed by the EMS, or even by one of Ronald Gant's *Friends For Friends* jackass members.

I slowed, approaching a cluster of curbside mailboxes. One mailbox, bowled over, lay broken apart on the ground—like a fallen soldier left for dead.

Seeing the street number I was looking for on one of the still upright boxes, I turned down the dirt drive. A brown dust cloud billowed out behind the truck's tailgate. My approach certainly wasn't a secret.

I pulled up at a ramshackle residence that looked like two separate single-wide mobile homes, butted-up to one another from end to end. One was white, with a tan horizontal stripe running across it; the other, a faded light-blue, had no stripe.

"Stay, boy," I said to Mort as I climbed out. I shut the door gently, rather than slamming it. It was so quiet around here, I felt compelled to make as little noise as possible.

The front yard, composed mostly of dirt with a few patches of crabgrass here and there, accommodated a lone, rusted-out

Maytag washing machine. Its bottom panel was torn off, exposing the appliance's drive motor and wiring harness. I approached the front door, which opened before I could knock. I couldn't see anyone standing inside, just a gloomy haze.

"What do *you* want?" came an old woman's voice.

Lowering my gaze down a foot, I saw her standing by the threshold of the door. Scowling up at me, the small elderly woman's silver hair was pulled back into a tight bun at the rear of her head. Her loose-fitting dress had a repeating floral pattern on it—an old schoolmarm's dress. A lit cigarette drooped down from the corner of her two thin lips.

"Whatever you're selling, I don't need . . . don't want. Now get the hell off my property!"

The crude welcome took me somewhat by surprise. "I'm . . . here to see Randy . . . um, is he your son?"

I didn't think her expression could turn any more sour, but I was wrong. Ma Kettle came to mind, from the old Beverly Hillbillies TV Show.

"Who are you . . . what are you doing here?"

"I told you, I'm here—"

"We don't take kindly to strangers around here," she cut in. "Not in these times." *Shit*, say the wrong thing to someone and you end up in one of those crazy *centers*. You don't come back from one of those places. Not alive, anyway. She continued to appraise me, giving me the once-over from head to toe. "Randy's out back. But let me warn you right now, I have a double-barrel shotgun nearby, and it's loaded . . . buckshot, not birdshot . . ."

"Thanks, I'll just head around the side—"

"I don't need to hear your life story . . . just git off my porch!" The door slammed shut in my face.

Doing as told, I moved alongside the connected mobile homes, wading through a mélange of old washers and dryers in various stages of disrepair. I figured Randy probably had some sort of side-business going on, which clearly wasn't doing that well. I pushed through a seven-foot-tall chain-link gate, covered by a lopsided sheet of corrugated steel. A heavy chain with an attached open padlock hung down, clanging as I pushed my way through. Entering the backyard, the odor stopped me in my tracks as my eyes took in the expansive space before me. In sight were no less than two hundred, brand new metal troughs—each about five feet long and two feet tall. Some sort of metal mesh covered their open tops. Small-motorized pumps were positioned between clusters of the troughs. Their low humming noise, the sound of churning water, created a calming effect.

I saw a dark shadow appear on the ground beside my own. It was massive. I swallowed and tried to think of a fast excuse for being there. *What could I say that a Gap would believe?*

"Quite the operation, eh?" a Human's voice asked, instead.

I turned my head and took in the mountain of a man standing next to me. Probably six-foot-eight in height, or close to that, he certainly was as tall as the average Gap, but not even close in size to the giant lizard I'd seen earlier on Wilcox Avenue. Wearing knee-high rubber boots, and filthy Farmer John overalls—his Rockies baseball cap was flipped backward atop his big head. A grisly black beard covered the entire lower portion of his face. But his brown eyes were kind and had a mischievous twinkle to them.

"You Randy?" I asked.

Randy smiled. "And you must be Brian . . . looking for a constant supply of bugs?"

"Bugs?"

Randy shrugged. "What most of us in the business call them . . . Lobsters are the cockroaches of the sea . . . scavengers. They eat just about anything put in front of them."

I gestured toward the numerous metal troughs. "Can I ask who exactly your customers are for all this?"

Randy licked his lips and hesitated. "Well, you know this is the primary culinary staple for the Gaps. They love 'em."

"But they're very particular from what I hear," I said.

"Yeah, they like their bugs real fresh. And only from the deep blue sea."

I nodded. "Probably only limited resources available for such an in-demand supply. What's a restaurant or supermarket to do?"

Randy smiled and took in a deep breath. "God, I love that smell."

"But they're right out in the open," I continued. "There must be alien ships crisscrossing overhead all day long. As impressive as this operation looks, you've done a miserable job concealing it."

"Why would I want to conceal it?"

"Because this isn't the deep blue sea. This bounty is contraband. You could be hauled into a center. You'd probably be executed."

Randy slowly nodded. "Who do you think paid for all

this?"

I considered the question. "You're telling me the Gaps did?"

"Humans aren't the only species capable of larceny. Racketeering, I would add, seems to be an interstellar phenomenon. This three acre plot of land is off-limits. Ships' geo-scans pass right over this property; no records kept in the aliens' databases."

"Or so they say," I said, wondering what turnip truck the big man had fallen off of.

"I know. Why believe any of them? But I didn't exactly have a choice. They had something on me. But the Gaps who came up with this scheme gave me a way out. One that could keep me and my ma alive, while making a few extra bucks in the process."

I considered that. "So you sell a few of these lobsters . . . bugs . . . on the side then, to someone like me?"

"Like you said, and to restaurants . . . supermarkets. I don't know what you need them for . . . and I don't want to know," he said. "But I am Human, and my loyalties will always be with my own kind. Now, how about I give you the grand tour . . . let you pick out a few of your own bugs?"

chapter 3

Even Gauz Za Chiv, a Commander Level 2 of the Earupitan Landing Forces, had to admit the countryside landscape before him had a certain appeal. He watched as the first of the flat, open air, disk-shaped troop carriers dropped from the sky and sped toward the outcropping ridge lying just above the northern Italian town of Valle d'Aosta.

He was forced to yell out his commands over the desperate pleas for help. He shook his head; no one would be coming to the aid of these Humans. Not today. Not ever. *What a strange, overpopulated world this is,* he thought. With all his experience, so many campaigns behind him now, he was somewhat taken aback by how docile this species seemed to be. *Pathetic*. And there were far too many of them to easily count. Yet this was supposed to be a smaller township than most. *Not to worry,* he thought, *the droids will take care of the accounting.* Yes, he was sure today had been a good day's work—an excellent round up, all in all. His superiors would be pleased. If things continued to go well, he would be able to get the whole lot of them transferred over to the atomizer dome by nightfall. He turned his gaze upon the distant structure, just now being erected.

Chiv stood erect within his little HovBB—a one-man hovercraft that required the pilot to stand upright at the controls. Chiv did not like the ridiculous scooters. As an officer of his importance, his stature, he should not be asked to preside over a roundup like this in a tiny *fucking* HovBB.

He glanced over at the nearby makeshift pen, at the huddled masses confined within it. The prisoners continued to moan, sob, and wail, as Chiv throttled closer in order to breathe in their scent. Drawing a deep breath of scented air into his lungs, he held it in until his lungs burned, then slowly exhaled. Their scent was distasteful to him but a necessary evil. He saw the despair in their eyes. "Shut up! All of you, just shut up!" he barked, exhibiting his ever-increasing annoyance with them. Suddenly lashing out in anger, he kicked the nearest human—a bald-headed elderly man. The hard heel of his boot tore open a ragged gash just above the silvery wisps of his brow. A crimson flow streaked down the wrinkled skin on the old man's face. Chiv kicked him again for good measure, then chided himself: *Stupid of me. A dead Human can't walk to the atomizer dome. Is the reason for my annoyance related to the fact I haven't slept in thirty-six hours? Or am I starting to feel my age?*

Chiv's earpiece squawked: "This is LT 231, arrival confirmation, sir."

"LT vessel . . . Set your vessel down atop the northern high ridge!" Commander Chiv barked back. "Hurry! Move it along, 231!"

Chiv tracked the *GravForce* drive's glowing white ring centered at the craft's perimeter. Both its pitch and volume noise increased as the straining craft resisted the increasing pull of gravity. But Chiv had to smile. The idiot of a carrier pilot had descended way too fast—much too abruptly. He could see the troops flopping around. Tossed this way and that, like the inanimate dolls several of the humans' small offspring held tightly clutched to their chests.

Chiv tapped at his console, bringing forth a heads-up display. He reviewed the virtual list of small town names appearing before him. His long tongue snaked out, as he wiped grit from an eye with it. He already knew he had been transferred elsewhere. Out loud, he said, "North America Sector," then ran a clawed finger down the new list before him. He tried to pronounce several of the townships and their state names: Armonk, New York . . . Castle Rock, Colorado. They were only the first of the locations scheduled for Phase II—*Extermination*.

Behind the nearby chest-high mobile barricade—a transparent energy field that provided shocks whenever touched—Commander Chiv noticed a girl child staring up at him, probably no older than four or five. He briefly wondered where her parents were. *Perhaps already hoofing it over to the dome*, he mused in self-satisfaction. The little girl was now reaching out to him—reaching out with small, grubby, dirty hands.

Chiv had been saddled with a lazy eye since birth, it was often confusing, even disconcerting, for those in his presence—not knowing the intended direction of his true gaze. Chiv narrowed his cockeyed eyes at her. "Did you really think our takeover would be the end of it? Then what? We'd all just live peacefully here on Earth together?" He chuckled as the small child gazed up at him, clearly not understanding a word he said.

The commander waved her angrily away for distracting him. Throttling up his little scooter, he sped away without looking back.

chapter 4

During the drive back to Castle Rock, I scratched between Mort's ears as the dog sprawled lazily across the center console, his head resting upon my lap. Unconsciously, I reached for the radio then stopped short just before my fingers reached the dial. Music was no longer broadcast over the limited airwaves, and the same went for the news. Both were deemed detrimental to the newly established, far more positive and cohesive society by the chancellor of communications. Which was, of course, total garbage. I knew for a fact, from first-hand knowledge, that Gaps liked Human music—especially country music. *God, I miss the way things used to be . . .*

Two years ago, the first of the strikes began; an attack that had occurred in the dead of night. I remembered waking-up to the rumblings, the familiar sound of distant exploding ordinances of war. It took me a moment to remember I wasn't still based in southern Afghanistan. I was home in bed, where air strikes just didn't occur. One glance at the nightstand clock told me it was three o'clock in the morning, the moment when every major city on the planet was under alien attack. An attack that was so thorough, so well instigated, that it was all over within a matter of days. A great many spacecraft dropped from the sky that night. Some were large, seemingly immobile craft—like the humongous dreadnought warships called *Situational Command Ships*—while others were small yet blazingly fast—the two-Gap *Shredder* crafts. There were thousands upon thousands of the latter. Their primary weapons included gravity-disruptor cannons that were like dropping bombs, but without the hardware or explosives. And then there were the smaller, wing-mounted plasma guns—weapons capable of precision hits on military installations and government offices. Media outlets were targeted, including most network and cable news companies, radio broadcasters, and many world newspaper headquarters. The hits were incredibly precise and ingeniously strategic. From Los Angeles, USA to Saint Petersburg, Russia, the world's population was thrown into chaos and an information blackout.

The Human race never had a chance. These interstellar invaders traveled cosmically for a mere seven days: *Seven fucking days to travel and then a few to completely humble and overtake a neighboring planet.* Loss of life was relatively small, at least during their initial invasion. One hundred million souls gone in hours—most of those killed were either military or law enforcement personnel, local and national politicians, or anyone unfortunate enough to be in the wrong place at the wrong time—like those living within the larger cities, which were hit harder. Earth, it seemed, had been of studied interest to the invaders for quite some time. Apparently, faster than light, *FTL*, space travel is not a real possibility. But that was not to say traveling to the farthest reaches of the galaxy wasn't possible. Not only possible but commonplace by a means our own astrophysicists would attribute to something called a Einstein-Rosen Bridge. Discovering and then procuring infinitesimal amounts of antimatter was the key—more accurately, the raw energy antimatter produces was the key. Apparently, many alien societies have mastered multi-dimensional physics. In overly simplistic terms, this is where two corresponding, fully entangled protons—even light years apart—are brought together with unimaginably high-energy manipulation of repelling quantum graviton fields. Whereby the precise folding of space-time not only can occur, but must occur, and does so with tremendous accuracy. The aliens refer to it as G-Hops, or Gravitational Hops.

Gaps, or more accurately, Earupitans, claim to be a planet's saviors, not her invaders. Wars were now a thing of the past. No country had a surviving military. Diseases, and most illnesses, were quickly eradicated. The highly advanced aliens were Earth's generous 'benefactors.' Like big brothers, they were here to keep us safe—safe from ourselves and from hostile beings in outer space. That was as far as their limited explanations went in justifying the real reasons they were here.

For a long while I had hoped they would just pack-up one day and leave—realize that Earth wasn't all that exciting a planet to hang out on. That they'd become bored out of their lizard-friggin' minds and depart the same way they'd come—disappearing into the dark sky in the dead of night.

But that was not to be. The Earupitans were here to stay.

For the past two years, both aliens and Humans had settled into some kind of mutual acceptance. Sure, there were uprisings on Earth, quite a few in fact, especially in the U.S., where many of its private citizenry were well armed. The alien invaders, the Gaps, lost thousands of their own brethren too. Perhaps that was one aspect of the invasion they had not anticipated. But in the end, their ruthless means of dealing with troublemakers succeeded in quelling further uprisings. Gaps made it a point to know exactly who their new subjects were. Used friend against friend and family member against family member to weed-out any subversive behavior. The means of gaining information, from anyone, went well beyond using solitary confinement or waterboarding. The Gap lizards were experts in the application of pain. They'd brought its effectiveness up to a virtual art form. *Ah, the wonders of advanced technology.*

It was after dark when I turned onto my own long dirt driveway. A quarter-mile later, I saw the lights in my ranch-style home—along with some in a series of smaller outbuildings—and in the large, faded red barn. The ranch had been in the Polk family for a number of generations. My parents, John and Lidia Polk, were on vacation on a cruise to the South Pacific at the time of the invasion. Most, if not all, of the large sea-going vessels were destroyed. Apparently the Gaps, not understanding the concept of pleasure cruise ships, sank all such ships thinking they were military in nature. My older brother, Glen, taken into custody a year ago for reasons still unknown to me, hasn't been heard from since.

I veered left toward the barn and parked next to Donny's Jeep Cherokee. Turning-off the engine, I glanced over and found my friend still sitting behind the wheel. I climbed out, quickly followed by Mort. The dog immediately ran off into the dark, undoubtedly needing to relieve his bladder. I heard Donny's footsteps coming around the bed of my truck.

"Why didn't you just go on inside, wait in the barn?" I asked, even though I already knew full well why.

"Ha ha . . . you're funny," he said.

I knew Donny was afraid to venture into the barn alone—afraid of what was inside there.

"What took you so long? I've been here close to an hour."

"My meeting in Elizabeth took me longer than anticipated," I said, lowering the truck's tailgate. "Can you help me with this stuff?"

"Holy crap, what is all this?"

"A more sustainable means to keep our guest properly fed."

A full moon provided just enough illumination for Donny to take in the truck bed's assorted contents. "Explain . . ."

"Well, I figured buying bugs only one or two at a time was sure to attract more attention than we wanted—Hey, grab that end, will you?"

"Sure."

"This here is a brand-new aluminum breeding trough," I said.

Once Donny got a firm grip on the trough he began walking backward. Together, we got the thing out of the bed. "Let's set it down over there, by the barn doors."

"And what's all this other crap?" Donny asked, now sounding intrigued.

"Municipal tap water won't cut it. And getting real sea water, which would be optimum, isn't realistic since the closest ocean is a thousand miles away."

"Okay . . ."

"So in there is a circulating pump, some hoses, various cleaning tools, chemicals . . . a large container of salinated water, and a big bag of baking soda to help in maintaining the proper pH level. Breeding these bugs, I found out, is a complicated process."

Donny threw a glance toward the barn doors. "And you got the lobsters . . . the bugs . . . to put in this trough?"

I nodded. "I bought six full-sized lobsters; they're in the coolers there. I also bought bug larvae. Enough that this little operation should stay self-sustaining for quite a while."

Donny shook his head. "All this for just one—"

Twin headlights coming down the driveway interrupted our conversation. We peered toward the approaching vehicle. "That doesn't look like Matt's Subaru," Donny said.

"No, it doesn't," I agreed.

"If it's a Gap patrol, you won't be able to explain having this stuff."

"Thank you, Donny, but I already know that."

"Or what you have locked-up in that barn, either."

I let out a relieved breath. "Looks like Matt got a ride. With his sister."

An old Bronco braked to a stop on the far side of Donny's Jeep. Matt and Karen climbed out, then made their way over to where Donny and I were standing by the doors into the barn. Almost a year had passed since I'd last seen Karen. The two of us had a shared history and it was good to see her again. I wondered if she felt the same. She wore skinny jeans and a tucked-in white T-shirt, its sleeves torn-off at the shoulders. Her exposed tanned arms were well-toned. Her long chestnut hair, cascading down her back, was secured in place by a loose scrunchy.

"Hey," Matt said.

"Hey," Donny said back.

Karen perused the trough, then looked into the bed of the truck. She finally turned to me. "Not a bad idea."

Of course, she'd figured out what all this stuff was for. She was the smartest person I knew—a hell of a lot smarter than me.

"Thought you didn't want any part of this," I said.

Karen shrugged. "Maybe I still don't, so don't push it. I'm here, aren't I?"

It took every bit of willpower to keep a smile off of my face.

chapter 5

I unlocked the double barn doors, slid them apart and went inside with Matt, Karen, and Donny following behind me. I relocked the doors and only then flicked on the light switch. A single light bulb came on overhead, providing little illumination into the rest of the barn. I watched Karen's face as she took in the dim expansive space lying beyond them. One horse, and then a second one, whinnied somewhere in the distance.

"I'd forgotten. Seems even bigger on the inside than on the outside," she said.

"One of the largest, still-standing barns in Douglas County," I offered. "Word has it, a hundred years back my forefathers held the county's annual livestock auction right in here . . . for three days, a few hundred local ranchers, along with all their farm animals, passed in through the barn's rear doors. Then came all the haggling and bartering."

Karen, both hands on hips, continued to stare into the mostly unlit darkness lying beyond the cone of light we were standing within. She crossed over to the wall and, one-by-one, flipped up the other six switches. The rest of the barn brightened beneath the big, industrial-sized, hanging lights situated high overhead. There were eight enclosed horse stalls, two of them occupied, situated along the far right wall. Tarp-covered farm equipment took up a good amount of space in the center of the barn. But Karen wasn't looking at the stalls or farm equipment. Nor was anyone else. Ten paces to the left stood a lone figure. A structural overhead beam cast him into dark shadow. Beyond him, positioned up against the wall, lay a thin mattress atop an army cot. Next to the cot sat a metal bucket. A chain jangled, metal against metal, as the figure tried to adjust his off-kilter stance. He was unused to standing. He wore overalls that I had to special order from a big-and-tall store to fit his oversized frame.

"So . . . what? You just keep him chained up like this? Day after day?" Karen asked.

"That's right," I said.

"Make him piss and shit in that bucket?" she asked.

I didn't answer.

"And he's helping you with that?" Karen pointed to a nearby workshop area where *something* was covered by a large green tarp. "And no, Matt hasn't told me exactly what you have hidden in here . . . other than the Gap prisoner."

Keeping their distance from the chained alien, Donny and Matt strode over to the workshop. Together, they pulled the tarp away from what it covered. The metallic surface of the sleek-looking Earupitan Shredder Craft gleamed brightly beneath the overhead lights. The two-person craft was about three-quarters of the size of the F-16 Fighting Falcon, the jet I flew in that dustbowl warzone, half a world away. The alien craft's fuselage, a mix of soft and hard edges, conveyed something both sleek and menacing at the same time. Two stubby wings angled back from the fuselage's midsection, while the six aft curved fins—like saber swords mounted in a circular configuration—protruded outward. Everything about the craft forewarned of ominous outcomes—power and destruction unleashed: *A harbinger of death.* Various crevices here and there, and along structural ridgelines, glowed a soft blue. I'd visited the vessel every day for the past two years, yet even to this day it still evoked within me a sense of mystery and wonder. And I couldn't wait to fly the damn thing.

"We can talk about the ship later . . ." Karen said, turning back toward the tall looming Gap, standing within the shadows. Glancing over at her brother, she asked, "You gave him one of your old legs?"

Matt said. "I only wear the new composite one," referring to his latest, state of the art, prosthetic leg. "I don't wear that old thing anymore."

Karen nodded. It was clear the alien was far too big for the much too small artificial appendage he now was wearing.

"It was his choice," I said. "Either use that, or crawl around on the floor with the rats and roaches."

"You could have given him a crutch or something instead," Karen offered.

"Bad idea . . . a crutch could be used as a weapon," Donny interjected.

Karen rolled her eyes.

"Look, Karen, Gaps are not like the diaper heads we once fought over back in the sand box. These aliens are fast and mean; and those massive jaws . . . those teeth, could tear off an arm or leg with no problem," Donny said.

"Couldn't he just use the prosthetic leg as a weapon?" she asked.

I raised a hand: "Enough about the leg. The important thing is, he's helping me. He doesn't complain. He doesn't ask for anything other than having me empty his shit bucket twice a day. He's a means to an end."

Karen took a step closer to the alien. "Does it . . . he . . . have a name?"

I settled my gaze on the prisoner Gap. He was perfectly capable of speaking for himself.

A phlegmy-gurgled voice answered her. "In Human phonetics, my name would be Jhall Doulk Hargoth. Brian calls me Jhall . . . sometimes Jhally."

Karen, looking somewhat bemused, said back, "Okay, then Jhally, it is. I'm new to all this." But her expression quickly turned to that of disgust. She turned to me. "Never could stomach the thought of being in such close proximity to . . . the ones that ripped our world apart. Not to mention, stole the love of my life. You'll have to excuse my resentment; my . . . growing hostility and anger."

It was subtle, but Jhally's head lowered some. Then his shoulders rounded down. "I am sorry. Truly. I know my words are meaningless. I know what I have done, what my kind has done, and continues to do across the galaxy. It is horrid."

"Yeah, he does that. Makes pitiful apologies, but don't

believe 'em. It's not in their makeup to care about us," Donny said, moving over to Karen's side and puffing his own chest out. By clenching his fists several times in rapid succession, it evoked the tendons and pronounced muscles along his large forearms and biceps to bulge. The Marine had his own reasons to hate Gaps. There wasn't a Human being alive who didn't have his, or her, own horror story concerning these alien invaders.

"This isn't about Jhally's feelings, or even ours, for that matter. Again, this setup is a means to an end," I said. "Karen, you're free to be here. You know we are coming up short with qualified pilots, but I can't tolerate anyone standing in our way. Or the possibility of someone around with loose lips."

Karen whirled around to face me. Seething, her eyes narrow, she asked, "Who made you the fucking general around here, Brian? If you think I would ever talk about this . . . to anyone, especially to a Gap, well, you really don't know me at all."

"There's a lot at stake. I . . . we . . . can't afford to trust anyone who isn't totally locked-in . . . who isn't a part of this."

"Pffht, Seriously? And what *is* this about? The *Takebacks*? A gang of little boys, all pretending to mount an uprising someday? Yeah, the Shredder is impressive. Maybe you'll even get it working someday. Maybe you'll even learn how to fly it, but what then? Take on the whole Earupitan contingent with one craft? You three against all the invaders?" She gave a sardonic laugh. "Grow up, Captain Polk. Face reality . . . we're screwed . . . the whole world is screwed." She turned back to the alien, then to Donny. "And Donny, if you don't stop staring at my tits, I'm going to show you how a gal can take down a man twice her size."

I laughed. I missed this girl's spunk. What she didn't

know was that the little gang, coined the Takebacks, she was referring to, had since grown in size to twenty-six men and women.

"What do you think, Brian. Show her?" Matt asked.

Reluctantly, I nodded. "Sure, why not?"

Donny and Matt headed toward the middle of the barn, where it looked to be old farm equipment covered with more tarps. Karen, still looking annoyed, watched them with only mild interest. Donny pulled the first of the tarps free as Matt pulled the second one away. As they continued to pull all the tarps away, Karen stared, her mouth gaped open. There, situated in the center of the barn, were another four Earupitan Shredder Crafts. Nary a one showed the same, nearly pristine condition as the one in the workshop. But dirty, dented, and scarred as they were—each possessed wings, an intact fuselage, and a tail section.

Karen took a step forward, then kept on moving ahead. She studied the assembled spacecraft, going from one ship to the other. Only then did she turn back to me. "You have five ships," saying it as a statement, not a question. "You have the beginnings of a squadron."

"Yes," I said.

"And, um, Jhally's going to help you . . . repair them?"

"No. Well yes, but these . . . sure, they look like shit, but they're the ones we've already got working. They just need to be flight-tested."

I watched Karen contemplate that last bit of information. But upon seeing her eyes well up with tears, I was taken by surprise. I wanted to go to her. Pull her close and wrap my arms around her. But I knew I could not. *Why would things be any different now than they were a year ago?* Our relationship only lasted one month. How did one love someone who was still in love with another person? Someone who would always remain much bigger to her than life itself? Hell, she'd just said it: her husband was the love of her life.

"Hello? Did you hear me," Karen asked, staring blankly back at me.

"Sorry, what?"

"Do you have a plan? Like where you would deploy these Shredders?"

"You mean like here . . . on Earth?"

Her brow furrowed. "Of course, here on Earth."

"No. That would be suicide. Five Shredders against thousands."

"So, what then are we doing?" she asked, growing irritated. "God, it's like sucking water out of a damn rock with you, Brian."

"You said *we*?"

Karen hesitated. "Yeah, well, I guess I'm in this now too. One of your stupid Takebacks . . ."

I smiled. Strangely, I didn't mind showing my pleasure on hearing those words. "We're going to give the Gaps back a little of their own medicine."

She looked at me sideways. "Every other uprising has failed. How many have there been over the last two years? Twenty? Thirty? What makes yours any different?"

"Those were ground assaults. Attempts to retake city strongholds." I glanced over at Shredder Five. "Look, four of their colossal Situational Command Ships are still in orbit around Earth. The intel we've acquired states they're some kind of battle carrier . . . Weaponized dreadnoughts, used specifically for planet invasions."

"Yeah, so?"

"Well . . . I want one. I want a Situational Command Ship."

chapter 6

I awoke to the sound of a woman's unconstrained screams. I rose up onto an elbow and glared toward my open bedroom window. Mort, from where he was asleep next to me on the floor, rushed to the window and stared out. He gave a short growl, then turned back to me. The screams were now coming in long, ten second sets.

"Come on . . . just shut up already, Molly!" I yelled, as I threw back the covers and swung my legs over the side of the bed. "You'll eat when everyone else does!" I knew the wailing sounds were not coming from a terrified, stricken woman standing somewhere out there in the yard. Although similar sounding, the screaming actually came from an obese red fox named Molly. The fox was not a pet. In fact, I had no idea when the rotund animal first settled on my property. According to my late brother, some three years past, the obnoxious animal had already been seen hanging around this place. We figured our parents had probably fed the damn critter once or twice so she simply never had a reason to leave.

I stretched my arms high into the air to get the kinks out of my back, then did a few other rudimentary stretches that had become part of my everyday morning routine. Later, I'd find the time to head out for a five-mile run. I had the feeling I needed to stay in top physical form for what would be coming. Dropping down to the floor, I did three sets of one hundred push-ups. Then next, placing my toes beneath the small gap beneath my dresser, I did the same amount of sit-ups, all in rapid succession. I thought back to the previous night's meeting with Donny, Matt, and Karen. I was pleased by her reaction, seeing the five Shredders. She wanted to know all the details—more importantly, where and how we'd acquired them. I told her that for both her and our protection, I couldn't tell her everything—not yet, anyway. Of course, both Donny and Matt already knew since they helped orchestrate the acquisitions—but it wasn't a far stretch to consider Karen being brought-in for questioning. The Gap's interrogation technology was advanced enough to easily determine whether or not someone was lying. Sure, she told all of us yesterday she was *in*, but I'd give it a week, or two, before I openly confided anymore of our secrets. Although thoroughly vetted a year ago, that's as far as it went with her. A lot could happen in a year. As much as I cared about her, to some extent she was still an unknown entity. Plus, she had a five-year-old daughter we needed to consider. The Gaps would have no problem using that child as a bargaining chip to prompt Karen into divulging secret information.

How we managed to acquire the five Shredders ended up being fairly ingenious. On the day of the invasion, the Gaps systematically attacked each and every military base, independent of nationality, all around the globe. The Air Force Academy, located in Colorado Springs—just an hour's drive south of Castle Rock—was among those hit, even though its existence there was more university-like than functioning as an actual military base. Dormitories, Vandenberg Hall, as well as Sijan Hall, were all demolished. Over twenty-five hundred cadets, young men and women, were slaughtered in their sleep, while certain other areas of the large facility were left pretty much unscathed. Turned out, the Gaps had big plans for the expansive academy grounds that would later serve in their long-term needs. The Air Force Academy became the Earupitan's Central North American Logistical Center. In other words, it was where the Gaps kept track of all their physical assets—from Skim-Rovers and Shredders, to the mounting hardware on a gravity-pulse cannon and the rose-colored western shirts worn by those in the Earupitan Marshal Service.

The big break came when we discovered the alien empire utilized a certain lightning-fast proprietary network. This network even transmitted targeting coordinates for kill-and-destroy missions to their spacecraft, via laser signaling. And this same network was used by the logistical center, where orders were taken for everything: from Slap Wads, the alien variation of toilet paper, to ordering HovT vehicles for law enforcement, as two examples. Turned out, Earth's modern-day society had one thing the Earupitan Empire was concerned with only on an abstract level: *Hacking*. Sure, there were criminal elements associated with the Earupitans, as probably did all intelligent life elsewhere. Various forms of illegal network intrusion were nothing new across the universe. One of my close Air Force buddies, Mike Post, a computer genius and another member of my team, came up with the proverbial *All Aces*. First of all, the Gaps purposely did not destroy Earth's essential infrastructure like its roads, rail transportation, municipal water and electric utilities, or its telephone and other communication lines, which the alien invaders tied many of their own systems into. Mike discovered there were remarkable similarities between Earupitan Empire Prime Network protocols and those used by Humans for their ultra-secure networks, like that of the NSA, and even NASA. And he knew first hand this alien network was quite hackable. So under my relentless hounding, Mike spent a full year attempting to do just that. Hack the Earupitan Empire's Prime Network—specifically, tap into their Colorado Springs, Central North American Logistical Center. Once their back-and-forth-communications protocols were deciphered Mike and I were able to start testing. We needed to start small, like the transference of atmospheric cabin filters from one center's location to another. Or perform the deletion of minimal stock quantities of products, like Slap Wads. Then we would wait to discover what happened next. See if any alarm bells were triggered, or if holy hell broke out higher up the chain. But nothing happened. Soon Mike was ready to take bigger risks. For three weeks, Donny and Matt conducted nighttime reconnaissance missions at the logistical center's various outdoor storage yards. There were a number of them. Areas dedicated to newly-arrived interstellar freight. Separate areas for delivery to parts of the North America Sector and the world. Areas which became a catch-all for all the shit they didn't know what to do with—like broken stuff. Items that normally would be repaired on the alien's home planet or simply destroyed. Yet, according to the hacked logs, some things just sat around week after week, month after month. Some of the broken items included five Zion-9 Shredder spacecraft. Corresponding virtual paperwork confirmed none were operational. Thus, the decision was made they could be put to better use, by me and by my team. The real trick was in arranging how the five Shredders—one at a time, over the span of subsequent months—were to be delivered to a local Castle Rock scrapyard, where they'd be crushed and removed from circulation. But they weren't crushed. Instead, they secretly were loaded onto long-bed trailers and delivered to my front yard, where they were quickly hauled out of sight and into the barn.

Once I'd finished with my morning exercise routine, I began to make my bed. Something I made a point of doing every day, no matter where I slept. Whatever life had in store for me on any given day, this one simple act—making the bed, and doing it superbly—was empowering. A physical and mental reference point that seemed to provide me with a solid mental foundation, helping me deal with whatever life threw at me that day.

Smoothing out the last of the creases atop the bedcover, I heard a familiar distant sound. *Shit!* Only one vehicle's power-plant made that particular sound. A HovT. HovTs were the hovercraft vehicle of choice for the Earupitan Marshal Service. With a quick glance out the window, I saw the hovercraft pull up close to the barn. To my horror, I also noticed the aluminum trough still sitting right where I'd left it the night before. Yet that would be nothing compared to what they'd find inside the barn, if they decided to get nosey. *Did I remember to lock the barn doors last night? I always lock the doors . . . why would I not have locked the damn doors?* I pulled on my jeans, not bothering with shoes. Out the front door in under a minute, and hurrying toward them, I did my best to look unconcerned. Just ahead, were two armed, uniformed Gaps, one wearing a blue shirt, the other green. They were already climbing out of their HovT hover patrol vehicle.

"Hey there! Good morning!" I said, giving them a welcoming smile. "What can I do for you guys?"

At that same moment, I heard the sound of Jhally's shit bucket clanging against something within the barn.

chapter 7

The two uniformed Gaps looked toward the barn doors. Both simultaneously tilted their heads, as if listening for further noises.

"Rats," I said. "Big as house cats. Fucking things."

The Gap on the left, wearing the green shirt, said, "I am Marshal Black, this is Marshal Clark. This is a search for illegal contraband. The local sector is being scrutinized. Comply with our search requests to avoid being taken in for further questioning."

I knew this was no request. More like a directive. I stared off into the distance where I could faintly make out a vehicle just sitting there. A maroon minivan, parked off to the side of Lake Gulch Road. Coincidently, Ronald Gant drove a maroon minivan. *That son of a bitch!*

Both of the towering Gaps were now scanning the assortment of stuff in the trough. Picking up and inspecting each object: the circulating pump, the bag of baking soda, and the other items that were to be used for my new lobster cultivation project.

I noticed the two Gaps were of different genders, their features quite dissimilar from one another. And the coloring imbued in their scaly flesh was also different. This became more obvious seeing them now standing side-by-side. Not to say that either of the two were of the female gender. I figured I was more *informed* about the unique alien gender *thing* than most people were.

Over the preceding months of the Gap's captivity, Jhally had become more and more open, more forthcoming about the Gaps' home planet—pronounced *Gahl—s*haring specific details pertaining to its society along with other aspects of his fellow aliens. Late one night in the barn, as I was repairing Shredder Three. Donny had warned me, time and time again, not to turn my back on the *untrustworthy* alien, especially if I were within reach of his long, umbilical-like, chain. Jhally was instructing me on how to repair the steering mechanism within the ship's cockpit, and doing so in near-flawless English. The two of us had spent much time together over the past months, within the solitary confinement of the barn. Still sitting in the forward seat of the cockpit, I was well aware I'd broken Donny's rule allowing Jhally to stand so close behind me. Jhally positioned himself atop a tall stack of nearby hay bales so he could better observe the repairs I was making. But I was becoming more and more cognizant of the fact that the powerful alien could easily leap right onto the Shredder's fuselage, then snap my neck in the blink of an eye. Nervously glancing over my shoulder, I asked. "So . . . tell me . . . the evolution of Earupitans on Gahl . . . it is, or was once, similar to that of Humans on Earth?"

Jhally responded back, in his wet gravelly voice, “Hold on, Brian . . . that *nub-rod* you’re holding, it’s upside-down . . . flip it around the other way, and remember, the threading goes in the opposite direction. Tighten it by turning your wrench counter-clockwise.”

I did as told, before stealing another quick glance over my shoulder. “Yeah, that did it . . . thanks.”

Jhally, in answer to my previous question, said, “No. Evolution on Gahl was quite dissimilar to all species that I’m aware of on Earth. To start, we used different kinds of molecules to encode genetic information. But for convenience sake, I will still call these genetic molecules *DNA,* although you Humans have little in common with Earupitans DNA. Nonetheless, Earupitans DNA . . . let’s call it E-DNA, contains genetic information in the form of genes that is evolved to successfully pass this information from generation to generation. As you are well familiar with, all the cells of Earth’s higher animals and plants contain a double set of DNA molecules . . . a double set of chromosomes . . . yes?”

I nodded, “That’s right.”

He continued, “Each set springs from one of the parents. The idea of having the double set is simple: From an evolutionary standpoint, if one of the genes is damaged, the second copy still works. This way, an accidental damage to one of the important genes won’t result in the death of a whole cell, or of the body. In addition, genes coming from the parents—mother and father—may be slightly different and work better under different conditions. The organisms with a double set of chromosomes will have a broader range of conditions so they can better survive.”

Although I already knew such basic science, I didn’t want

to interrupt the alien since he was on a conversational roll.

"Well, Earupitans, and other similar species, possess a triple set of E-DNAs."

That did surprise me. "Three?"

"Which makes our genome extremely robust and resistant to any damage; you'd have to damage all three copies of the same gene to kill a cell. And, of course, having a triple set of E-DNAs makes us very versatile when it comes to inhabiting different environmental conditions. This partially explains our success as a race of being interstellar invaders. Successfully invading is one thing, but prospering on planets that have different environments is quite another."

"Sounds like a far superior genetic system than that of Humans," I said.

Jhally kept on speaking, as if not hearing me: "The genetic system has a weak point. Triple set of E-DNAs must come from three different parents. This makes the reproductive cycles of an Earupitan rather unusual, and a remarkable affair."

"How so?" I asked, intrigued.

Jhally smiled. I thought it creepy-looking whenever the alien did that.

"Earupitans have three sexes, and all three individuals must, um, get together, as it were, to produce offspring. Such an arrangement could be rather impractical and complicated. Evolution created a way out of this problem by designating one of the Earupitan sexes to be specifically used only for child-bearing purposes, and pretty much nothing else. We will call them female Earupitans, opposed to two male sexes. The representatives of the two male sexes on Earth today appear different enough to make people on your planet mistakenly think they are males and females. After all, the idea of sexual dimorphism, that there are two sexes and they look different, is deeply embedded in your Human consciousness, is that not so?"

Again, I nodded in assent.

"In reality, and back to an innate weakness of our race, the third sex, female, looks nothing like the *lizard-like sackdraggers*, as you refer to us. Our real female Earupitans are amorphous. No doubt, you would judge them to be disgusting, worm-like creatures. To us, though, that is not so. They are typically dedicated to child-producing activities. But not always. In ancient times, our females resided in deep dark caves, where they were kept relatively safe from the hazards of the outside world. These days, our females live comfortable lives under the full protection of the two male genders. When a female becomes ready to conceive, her body will start to produce certain types of intoxicating sex pheromones . . . ones that become airborne and inform the other two sexes that the time for reproduction has arrived. The time window for reproductive activity is quite narrow. The pheromones turn on a powerful genetic reproductive program within the brains of the other two genders; subsequently, the coupling with the female becomes all-encompassing. The strength of the response is directly related to the fact that all three sexes must come together to conceive successfully. If one of the genders is missing, reproduction will not occur . . ."

"Explain all this!" one of the EMS Gaps ordered, bringing me back to the here and now, gesturing down at the metal trough.

"Look . . . this is a working ranch. There is an assortment

of farm animals here; several sheep, a goat, two horses, seven chickens, a dog, and a fox. Some have special dietary requirements."

I couldn't tell if either Gap was buying my bullshit. Then the Gap, with the slightly more delicate features, said, "Open the barn doors."

"You sure? Those rats—"

"Open it, now!"

Reluctantly patting the front of my pants, I indeed felt the bulge of my keys in the right-side pocket. My mind raced while I maintained a bored expression. *Had we recovered the Shredders with the tarps? How many seconds would it take for Jhally to yell out for help?* Unlocking the barn doors, I let out a slow breath, readying myself for what would come next. I knew that inside was a double-barrel shotgun hidden between the studs. *Could I make it there, move four paces to the left before the two Gaps drew their weapons*? I doubted it.

I pushed through the barn doors before being told to hold up. Inside, I only flicked on a lone light switch, which did little to illuminate most of the barn. The Gap marshals followed behind me, their mistmaker pistols drawn. I smiled, then shot a casual glance over toward the left side of the barn. In the dim light stood Jhally's army cot and his metal shit bucket. Strange, there was no visible sign of Jhally. Even his long chain was nowhere in sight. Each Shredder, properly covered up under a tarp, looked like nothing more than covered-up farm equipment. I found both Gap weapons trained on my midsection as they took in the expansive space.

"What is this structure's purpose?"

"It's a barn. Barns are used for different kinds of things . . . to keep a roof overhead for animals . . . store farm equipment, that sort of thing."

Marshal Black ventured farther into the barn, while the other marshal stayed close by me. Of course, the alien was heading right for the workshop—for Shredder Five.

chapter 8

I tried to think of something to say, something to dissuade the lizard marshal from moving any closer to the covered Shredder. I glanced over at Marshal Clark, wearing a blue shirt, his mistmaker weapon still leveled center-mass at my torso. *Are these to be the last few moments of my life?* I wondered, then caught an ever-so-slight swaying of one of the overhead lights. Next, came a blur of movement, something substantial was falling from above. I ducked low to the ground, covering my head with my arms. In that instant, I waited for the mistmaker weapon to fire—removing one of my arms, or a leg, or my head.

I opened my eyes in time to see a scuffle going on behind me. Jhally, having swung down from one of the crossbeams high above with his long chain, stood behind the blue-shirted Gap—his forearm clamped hard against the alien marshal's throat. A choking sound emanated from the Gap's gaping jaws as he struggled to free himself, to keep from suffocating.

Marshal Black rushed forward, his drawn weapon pointed at the two intertwined combatants. His mistmaker pistol held in an outstretched, two handed, grip, he yelled something in Earupitan as he tried to line up a clear shot, one that wouldn't maim or kill his partner.

Clearly unconcerned about me now, the much smaller, weaker Human just five paces away from him, I slowly stepped backward. A stack of old, oddly-sized two-by-fours lay in a heap on the ground. Spotting a length of wood about four feet long, I snatched it up.

Marshal Black, moving ahead and shifting this way and that, was still trying to line up a clear shot. I swung my makeshift bat hard—as if my very life depended on it, *which it did*—giving it everything I had. The sudden motion caught the Gap's attention; he had just enough time to turn his head toward me before the four-foot length of timber struck his lower jawline with a solid *Crack!* Marshal Black's legs immediately went wobbly. There was a problem with the lower quadrant of his gaping mouth. Now no longer properly attached—his jaw seemed akin to a swinging trapdoor. Most definitely, he was having a difficult time staying upright in his boots. I followed-up with another torque-wrenching swing; a second hard-driven smack to the Gap's vulnerable, open, trapdoor-like mouth. What ligaments and muscles were still attached to the unsecured jaw were suddenly ripped apart—torn and shredded by the tremendous impact. It was a game-winning home run; a hit far up into the bleachers. As the alien's disconnected detached jaw sailed high up into the rafters, the green-shirted Gap dropped down—dead before even hitting the ground.

Jhally and I stood studying each other in the dim silence.

Marshal Black appeared to have suffered a broken neck. Both Earupitan Marshal Service aliens lay dead on the ground separating us. I considered the four-foot-length of redwood, still firmly grasped in my hands, then the deadly mistmaker pistol Jhally held in his left hand.

I dropped the two-by-four and raised my hands. “So . . . what now?”

Jhally raised an extended jaw. “You made me shit and piss in a bucket for nearly two years.”

I nodded. He was right; he'd been here since the very start of the invasion.

“You made me sleep on a cot that was a foot too short for me.”

Again, I merely nodded assent.

“And the food . . .”

“Look,” I said, interrupting him, “I'm sorry. In my own defense, you . . . your people, invaded our world. Killed millions. And today, they continue to torture, sometimes kill, even more Humans. And, probably worse . . . you've turned us against one another. So, if you're going to use that thing, best you get on with it. I won't beg for my life. I won't grovel.”

Jhally seemed to be considering my words.

What I could not understand, though, was why Jhally, my prisoner for well over a year, chose to kill one of his own kind versus killing me, his Human captor. I broke the extended silence with another question: “Your chain . . . you figured out how to unlock the shackle on your leg?”

Jhally nodded. “It took me all of one night to file through

the metal ankle band. I was never actually a prisoner here." He gestured over to the workbench, at the various tools populating the pegboard panel.

"In retrospect, I guess a shorter chain was called for," I said.

A phlegmy laugh escaped outward through the alien's snout. "You always showed me respect. You were never cruel, not even unintentionally. In a way, I have enjoyed my time here. I have learned much."

"And you could have killed me at any time?"

"Most definitely," Jhally said.

"So I suppose the million-dollar question is—"

"Why haven't I?" he asked.

I nodded.

"As I told you before, the Earupitan's home planet is Gahl. I want you to take a closer look at the two dead marshals lying before us." He gestured with the pistol's muzzle to the two dead aliens sprawled on the ground. "They are different gender males. Even you, a Human, can see their dissimilarities."

I studied them carefully, even though I'd noticed some differences before.

"Now, look at me. Really look at me," Jhally said.

I did just that. First eyeing—scanning back and forth—the two Gap carcasses, then eyeing the Gap standing upright before me. I pointed to my own nose. "The noses, um, the nostrils are wider on both dead guys. And there's something odd with their eyes, too. Perhaps they're somewhat closer together?"

"And several other traits, which are far more apparent to us *sackdraggers* than to any Human. The point is, Brian . . . I am not an Earupitan. I am Mannarian. And I am not from Gahl."

For the first time, I had a real glimmer of hope I wouldn't be joining the two dead Gaps on the ground.

"A mere one hundred-and-twenty of your years ago, a planet within a neighboring star system of Gahl's—a planet called Blahn—was struggling with an environmental mishap of catastrophic proportions. In contrast to Earth's present global warming, Blahn, and its Mannarian populace, was struggling with advanced global chilling. In just a few short years, my technically advanced planet . . . its populous evolved to the point where wars were a thing of the distant past, was coming to its end. In a desperate attempt to save the few that remained alive on Blahn, massive interstellar crafts—hundreds of them, each not so different in approach to Earth's early Noah's Ark, were sent off into the darkness of space with the hope of finding a new, suitable, home planet. I am the direct descendant of the Mannarians aboard one such ship. Two hundred thousand of my kindred miraculously found a compatible world, one called Gahl. One with a nearly identical environment to Blahn's, before the fatal global chilling set in. The planet's indigenous people, the Earupitans, were quite similar to our own species, as well. But their society was far more backward . . . a barbaric people. Less intelligent, but we assimilated with them as best we could. Still, for the most part, we were ostracized. Relegated to the slums; our females taken, used for . . . terrible things. All the while, advancement in technology on Gahl, thanks to the Mannarians, was happening at an astounding rate. A bad combination, though; new technology without the proper mindset to wield it wisely."

I said, "I've often wondered why you were so forthcoming to me. So easily provided such detailed information. Hell, without your help, we never would be able to repair those spacecraft. But you weren't a traitor; at least, not to your own kind. Not really."

"The Earupitans have taken our assimilation for granted. And, true enough; many Mannarians did become fully assimilated within the past century. But full assimilation was not for all of us. We Mannarians are a patient people."

"Yeah? So, what then is your endgame? Will we simply be exchanging one alien enemy for another?"

"That is a good question," Jhally said, tossing the mistmaker pistol across the expanse between us. I caught it in one hand.

"We need to move fast. These two will soon be missed. The location of their HovT will soon be tracked to this address. Hurry, help me get their bodies back out into their vehicle."

Remembering Ronald Gant, and the maroon minivan pulled off to the side of the road only a quarter-mile away, I said, "First, give me a second." Hurrying to the barn doors I peered out, hearing the roar above me before seeing it. Too late, another HovT was already descending down from above. *Shit!*

chapter 9

I tucked the mistmaker into the back of my jean's waistband before heading outside into the bright sunlight. My mind raced. *What the hell am I going to say to them? Oh, you're looking for your two comrades. Sure thing, they're lying dead in the barn . . . here, let me show you . . .*

I shielded my eyes against the swirling cyclone of dust being stirred up by the descending HovT, blinking away the grit from my eyes before shooting a glance toward the distant Lake Gulch road. The maroon minivan was gone.

The HovT settled onto the dirt drive, the gull-winged doors on both sides of the craft opening up. Two Gap marshals climbed out, then reached back inside the cabin to retrieve their Stetsons.

"Morning, fellas," I said, offering them a warm smile and a half-hearted wave. "Like Grand Central Station around here today."

They stared back at me blank-faced, neither of them getting my ill-attempt at humor. One of the Gaps said, "I am Marshal Grip. This is Marshal Stone. Marshals Black and Clark . . . you will take us to them now."

"They're somewhere here on the property. Not real sure where . . . exactly. You're free to take a look around . . . maybe start in the house?"

Both Gaps looked toward the half-opened doors into the barn. "No. We will look inside the barn," Marshal Grip said.

Of course you will, I thought. *I'm sure Ronald Gant gave you a full report.* Gesturing toward the barn doors, I said, "Mi casa es su casa."

Marshal Stone said, "This is a barn . . . not a house. And you will speak English in our presence." The two Gap marshals then strode forward, stopping when the barn doors before them abruptly slid all the way open. Surprisingly, Marshal Black, wearing a green cowboy shirt, seemingly emerged from the darkness behind him. But I knew Marshal Black actually lay in a heap, several paces deeper inside the barn. This Marshal Black was actually Jhally, now dressed in the dead alien's clothes.

"What are you doing here?" Jhally asked, speaking in an authoritative voice I was unaccustomed to hearing.

Marshals Grip and Stone came to attention, both wearing looks of astonishment on their reptilian faces.

"You're Jhall Doulk Hargoth!" Marshal Stone exclaimed in surprise. His eyes looked close to popping out of his head.

Poised to draw my weapon, I didn't expect the two marshals to recognize Jhally—not after more than a year's absence.

"I asked you a question: "What are you doing here?" Jhally asked.

"Commander . . . there was a . . . citizen's report, taken this morning. Suspicious behavior. And Marshals Black and Clark are not responding to our communication hails."

"Of course, they aren't. This is a covert operation. Blackout conditions for comms here."

"You . . . sir, were reported dead. It has been over a year."

"Do I look dead to you? Do you think two lowly-ranked marshals are privy to all the clandestine goings-on within the EMS?"

Both marshals shook their heads, speechless.

"Your presence here has compromised this important operation. I will have to report your intrusion to the Assembly of Five."

"No . . . I assure you, sir, that will not be necessary. I . . . we . . . will say nothing of what we saw—"

Jhally raised a clawed palm to silence him. "What you *saw*? What did you see?"

"Nothing! We saw nothing?"

"And my presence here?"

"We were never here . . . we saw no one."

Jhally eyed Marshal Grip. "You, Marshal Grip, your actual name is Mahl Prothan Dron, yes?"

The Gap nodded enthusiastically.

"You were a subordinate of mine . . . aboard the Situational Command Ship, Tasthmal 8. Yes, I definitely remember you. What was your position?"

"I was a Soft Code Calibration Technician, sir . . . prior to being drafted into the EMS . . . as were most of us, after arriving here."

"Primarily involved with Prime Network coding?"

"Yes, sir."

Jhally shot a quick glance toward me, then toward the other Gap marshal, who wore a brass, engraved with the word STONE, nameplate over his breast pocket. "I have heard good things about both of you. You're fine marshals, loyal and smart. So, I am enlisting both of you into the CAG."

"CAG, sir?" Stone asked.

"Covert Actions Group, a very secret organization. An elite team with only the best-of-the-best within the EMS. You will report directly to me; to me only. Understand, breaking the code of silence will not only usher forth your deaths, but also those of your families, back on Gahl. Do you understand the gravity of your new directives?"

The two Gap marshals stared momentarily at each other, then nodded their heads in unison.

Jhally walked over to the two dead marshals' HovT then waved a hand over a hidden sensor device situated above the passenger-side door. After a series of soft *clicks*, the gull wing door began lifting up and Jhally leaned inside. A few moments later he straightened up, holding a small black device in one hand. I knew exactly what it was—a Task Beam Geo Locater Unit. All Gap crafts had them, including the five Shredders inside the barn, although those were disabled long ago. Similar to a car's GPS unit, TBGLUs pretty much provided tracking coordinates for anywhere in the known Galaxy, and did so within mere millimeters.

"Listen carefully. Marshal Stone, you will pilot your HovT vehicle, but first remove its TBGLU. You will be following behind Marshal Grip, who will be piloting Marshals Clark and Black's HovT vehicle."

"Where will we be going, sir?" Stone asked.

"To a location no less than twenty miles distance from here . . . you can decide where. Only then will you will reinstall the TBGLU. Make it look like Marshals Black and Clark were en route back to the Center when they crashed into a large tree. Or maybe a brick wall . . . you can decide. Use your best judgment."

Grip said, "But sir, where should I say Clark and Black actually are?"

Jhally made an exasperated expression. "They're gone . . . must I explain everything to you? Can you not think for yourself? Maybe they deserted. It won't be the first time something like that has happened."

"Yes sir, um . . ."

"What is it, Stone?" Jhally asked, feigning increased annoyance.

"Well . . . where are they? Actually? What has become of the two marshals?"

"Do you know what happens to Earupitan traitors? What the judgment would be by the Assembly of Five?" Jhally asked.

"An Endless Death, sir?" Stone replied.

"That is exactly right, An Endless Death . . . ten years of confinement . . . and the most horrific pain imaginable. As if every nerve ending within your body is on fire. The eyes feel it the worst. That's why a prisoner's arms and legs are secured . . . to keep them from clawing out their own eyeballs."

The two marshals looked as if they were going to be sick.

Jhally, stepping closer to Marshal Stone, brought his long snout within inches of the other's. He stared into his eyes for several long moments. Jhally next moved over to Grip and stared long into his eyes also. "Are both of you loyal to the cause? Or are you traitors, like Clark and Black?"

"No sir!" they both exclaimed in unison.

I could see they meant it. Both feared for their lives, and the lives of their families. Even knowing that everything Jhally said was total bullshit; I, too, was nearly convinced by his words. What was most apparent to me was the difference between the two species, Gahl and Blahn. I also knew I would need to keep a close eye on the far more intelligent Jhally. *Sure, our objectives may be in alignment today, but what would happen when they weren't?*

"Marshal Grip. You will have the most important job of your career . . . of your life. But I'm not convinced you are up for the task."

"I am . . . I assure you, Commander, I am!"

Jhally slowly nodded. "As a Soft Code Calibration Technician, you still have full access rights to the Prime Network?"

"No . . . those rights were removed—"

"Then I have no use for you. For either of you." Jhally turned to me. "Human . . . you may terminate these two."

Pulling the mistmaker weapon free from the small of my back, I pointed it at Marshal Grip.

"Wait . . . I will get access. It will not be a problem for me to do so. I promise," Grip said.

"Good. That is the kind of dedication I am looking for; an agent within the Covert Actions Group. You have three directives. First, you will alter the TBGLU tracking records from both HovT vehicles. Neither was ever here. Second, you will remove the citizen complaint record that prompted the original dispatch. It never existed. And third, and this is the most important . . . you will designate this property . . ." Jhally turned to me . . . "How many acres?"

"Um, close to six thousand acres, most of it south of the barn."

Jhally refocused his attention back on Grip. "You will designate this entire property as Code 5 . . . off-limits to all aerial geo-scans. In fact, Earupitan crafts will have to detour around this plot of land henceforth."

"Six thousand acres?" Grip asked, unable to hide the trepidation in his voice.

"I didn't say this would be easy. A true CAG agent lives for this kind of challenge. In the future, I expect nothing less from either of you. Only then will you be rewarded. Only then will you achieve rapid promotions, and all that comes with the positions of high command."

"Sir . . . ," I said, interrupting Jhally.

"What is it, human?"

"There is one more directive . . . for your Covert Actions Group agents. The leader of the Friends For Friends, Ronald Gant, is the citizen that prompted the original report. He'll need to be dealt with."

chapter 10

Two days had elapsed since Gauz Za Chiv, Commander Level 2 of the Earupitan Landing Forces, first arrived at his latest post assignment in North America. The sector was in the township of Armonk, New York. He maneuvered his HovBB several feet higher so his troops could get a better view of him, their superior, as they marched down the gangway of the lander ship. Coined a *Crusher,* these boxy ships came in two models, the smaller *Mini Crusher* and the much larger with superior armaments, *XL5 Crusher*. Neither was streamlined in the least—but did their respective jobs well enough, providing rapid deployment of his troops from Situational Command Ship, Alcon, now above them orbiting Earth.

This morning he would be dispatching his troops to begin a round-up of all local Human inhabitants. He also would be supervising the unloading of various atomizer dome sub-components, those previously disassembled from the now-totally deserted township of Valle d'Aosta, Italy. Already, he and his subordinates were becoming accustomed to handling the operation, an ingenious, multi-phase process developed years earlier by Earupitan tacticians far smarter than himself. Now in the early test aspect of Phase II, various small townships around the globe were transitioning. Selected townships, where Earupitans and Humans shared the same, physical, earthly landscape under the strict control of satellite OECs, and their Earupitan Marshal Service personnel.

Down the ramp they exited, his small army of well-armed, green-skinned killers. Dressed in red and black uniforms, each soldier wore a shoulder crest patch with his unit attached, what translated to Hammer Fists—the symbol of a clawed fist, with a blazing comet streaking through space behind it. Slung over every shoulder was a lightweight, yet deadly, Scatter weapon. Chiv, puffing out his chest, goosed the small one-person HovBB craft to rise up higher. Old, clearly in need of a tune up, the rebelling hovercraft made an assortment of odd gurgles and farting sounds. Heads turned, curious expressions on the soldiers' faces, as they continued down the ramp and appraised what surely seemed to be their leader's gastrointestinal issues.

Chiv, raising a hand, gave them a half-hearted wave. He then scooted off in the direction of the recently designated construction site, now cleared of trees and large rocks. He arrived amidst three assembly bots hard at work. They resembled huge mechanical bipedal creatures—albeit headless ones—towering four times the height of those in his troops. Pleased to see that the atomizer dome sub-components were already partially assembled, Chiv figured the dome was about one-third of the way completed. He glanced over at one of the larger curved segments nearby, at its blackened interior façade. Only soot and grit still remained of the Humans who'd once lived within the township of Valle d'Aosta.

Chiv smiled to himself. Though he was quite certain the actual atomizing was painless, being rounded up at the muzzle of a Scatter weapon—then marched to what surely led to their deaths—was not so painless.

He first heard, then saw, a black aerodynamic craft descending down fast from above. Chiv recognized it as one of the High Order's personal StarCatchers as it noiselessly swooped and circled above. Chiv narrowed his eyes. This would not be good. Since it was not a military ship, it must hold dignitaries, of some sort, coming to assess his progress. He quickly sent out a message, via his ear puck, to his junior officers: *Look sharp! Visitors en route!*

Chiv quickly landed his HovBB. No way would he be seen riding around in the *thing*. Fortunately, the sleek slip-craft had set down close by. He hurried across the rough terrain, mindful of the stomping assembly-bots. He wouldn't be the first to unintentionally get crushed by one of them.

Waiting for the StarCatcher's hatch to open, Chiv pulled and tugged his uniform into place. He then proceeded to flick away any lint, or tiny errant fragments of Earth's grimy soil, aware that in order to impress whoever was inside the craft he must look his very best.

The forward hatch of the glossy black ship slid open without even a whisper of sound. With one following the other, three shimmering gold-and-silver-robed Earupitan dignitaries descended down the narrow ramp. Chiv's breath caught in his chest as a sudden realization took hold. Between the two lesser cohorts was none other than his Eminence, Overlord Skith, himself. There was no higher dignitary within the whole Earupitan Empire than his Eminence.

Chiv, lowering down to one knee, settled his gaze near the ground. He warily watched as the three pairs of approaching legs came to a stop before him.

"Rise, and be quick about it!"

Chiv did as told, offering a welcoming greeting to the three dignitaries. "Welcome . . . I am honored by your presence," he said, his mind reeling. *Why are they here*? *Had he committed mistakes already*? Perhaps his deployment had been too slow, or this location not to their liking? He heard Overlord Skith speak for the first time.

"What is your name and rank?"

"I am Gauz Za Chiv, Commander, Level 2 of the Earupitan Landing Forces." Chiv met the overlord's gaze. Smaller of the three before him, he looked to be in his mid-seventies, which was middle-aged for an Earupitan. His face held an unpleasant expression, as though smelling something foul.

"What is wrong with your eyes? Do you purposely insult me . . . mock me?"

Before Chiv could answer, explain his dreaded sleepy-eye condition, one of the overlord's cohorts leaned in and whispered something in his Eminence's ear. The overlord, waving his underling away, gave Chiv another irritated expression.

"We are implementing an alteration to our Phase II processes . . . an alteration that will be implemented immediately, worldwide. Starting here, with this first of the North American Sector undertakings."

Chiv nodded. "I am honored to be of service, your Eminence."

"Immediately following the *hygenicide* of each and every

Human inhabitant of this local township, you will then invade the local Oversight and Enforcement Center. Your troops will take control of the center and secure the center's Quantum Manifold System."

Chiv, not understanding the reasoning behind this directive, said, "OECs have always come under the purview of the local marshals. Sir, they will not take kindly to our intrusion—"

"Are you refusing the assignment, Commander?" Overlord Skith asked, his tone menacing.

"No, no, of course not, Eminence. My troops will take control of the local OEC."

Overlord Skith nodded his approval. "Good. You will ensure all the marshals have assembled and are accounted for."

"Yes, your Eminence."

"At that point, they will share in the same fate as the local Humans. They will be shot dead, their bodies atomized within the same dome. You will instruct your troops to never speak of this . . . not to anyone. Word of this cannot be spread to other townships, or to other OECs. To do so will result in ten years of confinement, with the most horrific pain imaginable."

"You speak of An Endless Death," Chiv murmured.

"Not just for the blabber mouth, but for each one of you."

"No one will ever speak of this, I assure you, your Eminence. But . . . may I enquire why? The removal of the marshals?"

"It is not your place to question the directives of our leader," one of his cohorts said.

"It is fine, I will answer this soldier's query. Phase I for the most part has been successful. Human uprisings are now a thing of the past. The marshals, and others of their kind, have done an admirable job maintaining civility while effectively assisting with the immunization process for those here on the ground, as well as for those waiting patiently up in high orbit."

The overlord stared out at the wooded landscape. "Unfortunately, there have been those within local OEC stations who have bonded with Humans, forgetting our purpose here. Where their loyalties belong. No, for this planet to truly become *our* home, we must take every precaution. I want the marshals dead. I also want each of the sector chancellors of communications dead. Kill the Humans first, then the others." With that, the three Earupitan dignitaries headed back to their vessel. Moments later, the craft elevated far above the ground and sped away. For the next hour he watched the steady progress as the assembly bots completed the atomizer dome.

In the distance, the first of the captive Humans were now being ushered through the wooded forest, where they would be barricaded into an awaiting holding pen. Chiv tried to ignore their screams, their pleas for help. But today, their voices sounded even more irritating. Chiv climbed into his HovBB and weaved his way through the trees until he reached them. He guesstimated there were close to two hundred Humans, most still dressed in their bedclothes. *What was their funny word for it?* Ah, yes, *pajamas.*

Chiv signaled for a nearby foot soldier to come close. Leaning out, he spoke quietly, "I want them all shot . . . now! Their incessant noise is intolerable."

"Yes, sir, consider it done," the foot soldier said.

chapter 11

Marshals Grip and Stone were now gone, off piloting the two HovT vehicles to an unspecified location. Supposedly, they were en route to crash one vehicle into a tree, or maybe a wall. Next, they would report the other two marshals missing, most likely being deserters. We'd find out soon enough if Stone and Grip fully embraced their becoming new Covert Actions Group agents. Hopefully, within twenty-four hours, Marshal Grip would find a way to soft code the necessary changes to the aliens' Prime Network.

We needed to get rid of both bodies before other visitors dropped by unannounced. Standing above Marshal Black, sprawled on the ground in front of me, I was mildly intrigued by the prospect of trying out the mistmaker weapon now. I'd never fired one before. Jhally quietly stood off to the side. I pointed the muzzle of the weapon at Marshal Black's inert body and, on pulling the trigger, a bright-blue bolt of plasma energy shot into the dead marshal's top right shoulder. The effect was not what I expected. I leaned over and assessed the damage. Sure enough, a hole was there—right where I'd pointed the muzzle. But I expected his entire shoulder to be taken off, turned into mist. But the damage was no more than a small through-and-through hole, no larger than what a .45 caliber slug would have inflicted. I looked up to Jhally. "Is there another setting on this weapon that I'm not aware of?"

Jhally shook his head. "What exactly are you trying to do by shooting a dead carcass?"

"Get rid of the bodies."

"With that plasma gun?"

"Yeah . . . it's a mistmaker. Turns organic material to . . . well, into nothing."

"It doesn't work that way, Brian," Jhally said. "The plasma charge diameter is 11.45 millimeters, which is close to a .45 caliber bullet. With that said, contact with organic flesh and bone material within the limited bore of such an energy strike will indeed create . . . a mist of sorts."

"I guess we could just bury them," I said, giving a shrug then standing up. "I'll take care of it. But first, I have a few more questions for you."

Jhally returned my stare.

"What have you been doing when I'm not around? After you've removed the chain from your leg each night?"

"I have found more . . . comfortable accommodations."

"Where?"

"The structure on the adjacent property to the west. It is abandoned. It is a fine residence, with a kitchen, bathroom, and a bedroom with a large enough bed."

When I glanced over at the shit bucket, sitting on the ground by the empty cot, Jhally produced one of his creepy grins, "Your two horses have ample bowel movements. In truth, I never once used that shit bucket."

"So I've been emptying that bucket, disgusted at needing to do so, for over a year now. While you've been lounging over at the Anderson's old place?"

"That is correct."

"Why wait till now to tell me all this?"

"You never would have believed me. You had no reason to believe my intentions. Now, after forced confinement, seeing that I could have left here long ago, could have reported your actions, the theft of the five Shredders, and your subversive Takebacks team . . . you now must know I am not a threat."

"So what do you want then? To return home to Gahl, or maybe to Blahn?"

"No, I want to . . . what is the phrase . . . join up?"

I shook my head, not getting his meaning.

"The Takebacks, I want to join the team."

A good distance into Polk property pasture land, I used my Skid Steer Bobcat, with its dirt bucket attachment, to excavate a deep-enough trench that Marshals Black's and Clark's bodies would probably never be found—at least, not within my lifetime. I was just finishing up with the final touches, flattening out the mound of dirt over the gravesite, when I noticed Jhally making his way across the pasture toward me.

He was having a difficult time walking, wearing his far-too short prosthesis. I supposed it was now time we get him something that actually fitted his seven-foot tall frame. If my friend Mike Post found a way to order delivery of broken Shredders, he should be able to order one damn leg.

I shut-off the Bobcat's motor upon Jhally's arrival. He seemed a bit short of breath.

"What's up?" I asked.

"I heard back from Marshal Grip."

"Really? How was that possible?"

"He called . . . I answered the telephone attached to the wall in the kitchen."

For some reason, I'd never thought of that. That the aliens would use such a primitive means for outside communication. But then, what else could they use? Cell phones were one of the first means of communications taken away from Humans. Same with email and texting. landlines had returned to being our primary means of communications with one another.

"What did he say?" I asked.

"He was intelligent, at least for an Earupitan. Aware that Human means of communication are monitored, so he spoke to me in a kind of code."

I had assumed some of our phone lines were sporadically eavesdropped upon, but not all of them. "What did he say?"

"Basically, that the TBGLU tracking records from both HovT vehicles have been amended. Now, neither vehicle was ever here. Grip also removed the citizen complaint record that prompted the original dispatch. It never existed."

"What about the third directive?" I asked. "The designation of my property to Code 5?"

"Grip had the most trouble doing that. Multiple sign-offs, so going farther up the chain of command was necessary."

"And?"

"And he got it done. Grip is anxious for fresh orders. It seems our *new* Covert Actions Group agent is more than willing to prove himself as a valuable asset."

Climbing down from the Bobcat, I assessed my handiwork. It would take a few months' time for pasture grasses to regrow over the dirt. I looked up at Jhally. "I think it's time we bring the entire group together for a meeting. I can't make the decision to have you become a member of the Takebacks alone. There are twenty-six of us. I'm sure some will resist the idea." I thought about what I was proposing for later on tonight. Up to this point strict security measures had been adhered to by all of us to avoid compromising the entire team. So I'd kept the Takebacks isolated—separated into four smaller, individual cells. Members in one cell knew only the people in their own cell by name. Although they were peripherally aware there were other cells, they certainly didn't know any names or what others' duties or responsibilities would be. And no one's actual name was used during meetings, which were always secret. Everyone used a pseudonym, preferably the name of some historical personality. Great lengths were taken to ensure they were conducted only when Gaps, or the Friends For Friends creeps, couldn't possibly be around to eavesdrop. There was one exception to all that: Since the Takebacks were my brainchild, I, its leader, did know who everyone was. My pseudonym was Polybius, a Greek historian of the Hellenistic period, most known for his work, *The*

Histories, a period between 264 and 146 BC. As a history teacher, I couldn't resist using a pseudonym that held special meaning for me. Vetting of new inductees came under the responsibility of Polybius—*me*. Each vetting took a full six months. Truth was, there was no shortage of people wanting to fight back. But the price was high. Within that half-year time frame a new member was required to commit a serious crime against the Earupitans order—and they needed to get away with it. A crime the inductee had to videotape, showing him, or her, committing that crime. Most assuredly, it would bring them up on charges, probably execution, if caught by the EMS. Everyone needed to put *real skin* in the game.

"Meanwhile, is there anything I can do to make myself more . . . palatable?" Jhally asked.

"For the Takebacks?

He nodded.

Yeah, there is. You can get that fifth Shredder operational before midnight tonight."

"And what will you be doing? I could use your help," Jhally said.

"I need to make a brief appearance. Show my face in town." I checked my watch. Almost 1:30 p.m., the parade had already started. "It's Friends Unite Day. I have to be in town for that. Also, it will give me the opportunity to speak with Matt and Donny."

chapter 12

Not participating—not going through the motions that one was in lockstep with the new order of things—would, sooner or later, be noticed. Noticed by the alien invaders. Even more likely, noticed by the scrutinizing eyes in the Friends For Friends society. The populous of Castle Rock was here en masse. Certainly not as a gesture of patriotism to the new order, but rather from fear of reprisal.

I had to park several streets over from Wilcox, where the Friends Unite Day parade would be taking place. I found a parking spot behind Tami's Antiques. After locking up the truck, I hurried past a few other stragglers heading in the same direction. When I arrived two blocks north of the B&B, the tail end of a high school marching band was just moving past. The music sounded off-key and lackluster. The kids were simply going through the motions as they passed beneath the orange, purple, and brown banners, with emboldened Earupitans Crests at their centers. Not ten feet to my left stood an armed EMS Gap. Farther off to my left, close to twenty feet away, stood another. Interspersed up and down the long sidewalk, the reptiles, garbed in cowboy hats, towered a foot or more above us shorter Humans. I saw one of them smile and wave at a passerby.

Next, behind the marching band, were three side-by-side shiny new HovT vehicles, hovering two feet or so above the ground. Modified—their roofs now removed—they were like convertibles out for a midday summer joy ride. Six Gaps, garbed in their finest cowboy outfits, rode inside them. All six, in pairs, waved and smiled their creepy toothy grins. They were the Douglas County chieftains. Non-elected alien officials, they dictated how those living around here had to live their lives. Lining both sides of the street, the crowds of onlookers waved back with fixed smiles of their own. Their eyes held a kind of sadness, reserved for remembrance of how things used to be. How life in Castle Rock, and in similar small towns across the country, and around the world, was once real— once true. A life worth living because it was, with all its daily faults and messiness, theirs to live out with some kind of integrity and decency. I paid little attention to the parade. Instead, I continued to focus on the faces of my fellow man, blinking away the moisture in my eyes. Swallowing hard, I inhaled a deep breath then slowly let it out. *I want to love my country again . . . I want to believe in my fellow man, in Humans.* But there was only one way that would be possible. The alien invaders had to go. Leave Earth, or die . . . I didn't particularly care which. One way or another, I would dedicate my life to that end. Those who got in my way, Gap or Human, would suffer the consequences.

I spotted Matt and Donny across the street, weaving their way through the hordes of pedestrians. I waited for an equestrian ensemble of eight Human riders—twirling ropes over their heads, and then from side-to-side—to move past me before crossing the street. Catching up to them, I said, "Hey!"

Matt looked back over his shoulder. "Hey Brian . . . we were looking for you."

Walking just ahead of Matt, Donny shot back a smile. "You heading to the fair?"

"Yeah, sure . . . I guess."

The crowd now was dissipating, to the point we could walk together side-by-side. I spoke quietly, "There's been a few new developments."

Both Matt and Donny looked at me, concern in their eyes.

Developments?" Matt asked. "What the hell does that mean?"

"It means I had some unexpected visitors show up at the farm . . . then spent the latter part of the morning digging a deep trench with my Bobcat."

Donny, leaning closer, asked, "Like a . . . grave?"

I nodded. "But it's not all bad news. In fact, some of our bigger obstacles have been dealt with."

Donny glanced around, then grabbed me by the arm and pulled me into a narrow alleyway between two small businesses. Matt followed close behind. Donny looked as serious as I'd ever seen him. Kidnapping a badly wounded alien a year ago was one thing. Stealing junk Shredders was another. But killing one or more Gaps, well, that could change everything. Change our subversive gang's behavior from more or less villainous to that of a bona fide threat. We'd become a legitimate force that would, undoubtedly, bring a lot more attention to the Takebacks than we were ready for.

"Start from the beginning. Don't leave anything out," Donny said.

I looked intently at my friends, matching their stares eye to eye. "It started when I heard a HovT coming down my driveway early this morning . . ."

We stayed in that narrow alleyway for close to an hour, while I went through the course of earlier events. Afterward, Matt's biggest concern was trusting Marshals Stone and Grip to keep their reptilian traps shut. Donny was far more leery of Jhally taking on a bigger role in our affairs. "He may not be an Earupitan, but is being a Mannarian any better? Gaps are Gaps . . . ," he said.

The walk to the fairgrounds took us about thirty minutes. We didn't discuss what occurred earlier that morning any further. For the most part, we remained quiet, mentally working through the various complications in our own minds.

Up ahead were tall twin pillars that supported arched timber beams. 'City of Castle Rock Fairgrounds' was stenciled upon them. The Gaps had added their own engraved line of text underneath, *Friends United Across the Galaxy*, but it didn't quite mesh since the Gaps used a completely different font than that on the rest of the sign.

Matt, Donny, and I fell in with the maelstrom of pedestrians—mothers and fathers escorting small children, and teenage boys and girls enjoying their first date—who were now all funneling into the fairgrounds. The carnival atmosphere here evoked a somewhat better mindset than the parade had.

People were actually smiling, or at least pretending to be having a good time. The same attractions one typically found at a summertime carnival in the last century were all set up. There were the rides: The Zipper, the Tilt-A-Wheel, and the Carousel Horses for the little ones. Also a lot of booths: The Bottle Stand, and Balloon and Darts were popular. And there were games: Knock Over The Milk Bottles, and the Ring Toss. The aromas of cotton candy, popcorn, and hot dogs and mustard wafted up in the air around us. All the booths, the various game tables, even overseeing the numerous rides, had been strictly relegated to Gap marshals' care. They looked friendly, even jovial. Combating melodies, coming from the different ride sites, only added to the surreal atmosphere.

Donny tapped my arm. "Take a look at that."

Following Donny's line of sight sat a towering red-and-white striped tent. A wooden plaque hung over the door:

The Herculean Gap!

"At least they're not above a little self-effacement," Matt said.

A line of ten or twelve people waited to get in for the first show. Two Gap marshals stood playing bouncer at the tent's entrance. I watched as a couple was allowed in, but the next group, a family of four, was turned away. Apparently, the children were too young. Then, I noticed the sign: 12 Years Old and Up.

"What do you say . . . want to check it out?" Donny asked.

I was reluctant. Felt I'd shown my face around here long enough so I was ready to leave. There was still quite a lot I needed to do back at the barn in preparation for the meeting tonight. Within five minutes, we moved up to the front of the line. The marshals, after giving us a quick once-over, let us inside. Dark within the tent, it took a few moments for our eyes to adjust. We made our way over to a six-level-high bleacher. Climbing all the way to the top, we took our seats. I sat between Matt and Donny. Across from us was a raised platform, like a stage. A solitary spotlight illuminated a hanging ten-by-ten mural—a picture of a bare-chested reptile wearing only a loincloth. The muscular alien held up a wide wooden plank above his head. Standing atop the plank were no less than ten Humans, all smiling. They appeared to be thoroughly enjoying themselves. Although the feat of lifting ten people, weighing in excess of fifteen hundred pounds, was certainly impressive, the scale proportion intrigued me most. The Humans were about half the size of the big Gap, standing beneath them.

I glanced over at Matt. He shook his head and rolled his eyes.

"The damn aliens just don't get it . . . they go to great lengths to be like us. But like we were fifty years ago . . . like wearing those mid-century TV cowboy outfits. And this carnival Tarzan sideshow bit—"

"Hercules," Donny corrected.

"Whatever. It's weird. Like their research on us was from a half century ago," Matt said.

"Yeah, like TV broadcasts from the sixties," I interjected.

As soon as the stands were filled, the last spectators in their seats, a pudgy man dressed in a ridiculous costume walked onto the platform. Something like you'd expect to see in *The Wizard of Oz* movie. Dressed in little green shorts, striped knee-high socks, and clog shoes, he also wore a white button-down shirt, with a red glittery bow tie. A green top hat sat perched atop his head.

Donny, leaning closer, whispered, "No . . . just fucking shoot me. No way would I make such an ass of myself."

"Welcome to all!" the big munchkin-like man shouted dramatically from the center of the stage. "I am your master of ceremonies today. I am Leo. You will observe something that no Human, and only a few others across the universe, has ever witnessed before. A feat of strength beyond comprehension." The costumed man then turned serious. "But I warn you . . . this demonstration is not for the meek; not for the faint of heart. You have been warned . . . Now please . . . be very still. When the show starts, be very, very quiet." Leo looked across the audience, scanning our faces one by one.

I wasn't sure if this was part of his act, or if he was trying to warn us of something. "I present to you now . . . Dalm Mor Stroph, the strongest being in all the galaxy!"

Everyone clapped as Leo left the stage and the overhead spotlight went out. We all sat silently in the dark for a full minute. When the light came back on, Dalm Mor Stroph stood before us. I recognized the Gap—the same ginormous reptile I'd seen just the previous day. The same giant who'd lifted poor struggling Barry Larson up by the top of his head in the middle of Wilcox Avenue. Dalm Mor Stroph, a marshal, was with the EMS. Like the alien in the painted mural hung behind him, Stroph, too, was bare-chested, wearing only a loincloth that covered-up his bulging privates. His musculature was like nothing I'd ever seen before. Pectorals the size of watermelons, cut in half. Quads the size of couch cushions, and those soccer ball-size biceps. When he began speaking—a low baritone gurgling sound—the audience leaned back as people instinctively do when confronted with something repulsive or disgusting. The sound of Stroph's voice was both. "For my first feat of amazing strength I will need audience participation. A strong man in the audience."

I exchanged a fast glance with Matt and Donny. The huge reptile did not speak with the same level of finesse that the other Gaps around here did. He sounded, well . . . like he had a speech impediment. It made him sound as dumb as a tree stump.

When no one volunteered to be Stroph's stage prop, Leo came back on stage. He didn't seem thrilled about the prospect for whatever would be coming next.

Stroph lowered himself down, first onto his knees, then onto all fours. He gestured with a clawed finger toward a hand crank, affixed to a metal framework on the side of, and over the top of, the stage. Then we noticed a suspended wooden plank high overhead, hanging by four cables. It was about twice the size of a typical household door. Leo began to turn the hand crank. Around and around the crank turned. The overhead plank slowly descended. It took several moments before it became level with Stroph's back. Only then did the big alien lower his entire body flat onto the stage. The crank continued to turn. Once the plank was down as far as it could go, supported fully atop the alien's broad back, Leo stopped cranking. He next unhooked the four supporting cables from the plank.

Partial daylight streamed forth somewhere behind the stage and the hanging mural. Then came the heavy sounds of clopping hoofs, also out of view. A teenage girl appeared around the mural. Holding a rope in one hand, she led an animal farther into the tent—an elderly-looking Hereford bull, the big steer was a reddish-brown, with a white face. Having spent much of my life around livestock of every sort, I could tell the bull easily weighed 1,900 pounds, and that he was old. There was no fight left in the old boy. The teenager coaxed the bull forward, loudly clicking her tongue. "Come on, boy . . . come on up," she urged. With Leo's help, they prompted the bull to come onto the stage.

"Do we really want to watch this?" Donny asked, a little too loudly.

The answer was no. It was disrespectful to the old bull, as well as to the rest of us who'd spent our lives tending such livestock. I was sure I wasn't alone in suddenly feeling sick to my stomach.

"Maybe we can just sneak out," Matt said, under his breath.

Leo and the teenage girl somehow managed to coax the colossal animal all the way onto the wide wooden plank, which wobbled just a little, supported primarily on the alien's back.

Leo bent over and murmured something unintelligible to the alien, then stood straight and faced the audience. The teenager looked nervous, holding on tight to the rope. The bull looked equally nervous, as did Leo.

"Whose damn idea was this?" Donny asked.

I, too, was now getting angry.

Leo then announced, "Meet Charles . . . nineteen hundred and twenty pounds of fine Hereford beef. Dalm Mor Stroph . . . are you ready?"

I could see the Gap's oblong head and broad shoulders sticking out beneath the plank. The huge alien nodded, expelling a grunting sound. Slowly the alien, the wooden plank across his back, and the ancient bull all began to rise. Inch by inch, nearly two thousand pounds of livestock was rising from the Gap's prone position. It seemed impossible; the strength required unfathomable. It took a full minute before the Gap rose up to a kneeling position, the plank still perfectly flat and unwavering. The bull's eyeballs loomed large, unaccustomed to rising into the air atop an alien's back. But the steer stayed put, going along with the spectacle. Perhaps this was all a well-practiced trick. Maybe Dalm Mor Stroph, and Charles, the old bull, had spent days rehearsing this very same act.

I glanced over at Donny, and we both shrugged. "Have to admit, it is impressive," I said.

The Gap giant raised his body up into a low crouch, all the while keeping the plank perfectly level.

"He's going to do it!" Matt said, sounding a bit more enthusiastic now. "He's going to raise that *son of a bitch* bull right up over his head!"

The small crowd seemed equally stirred by the alien's amazing feat of strength. The Gap, poised to stand upright, had nearly done it. One final lift and thrust of his arms overhead was all that was needed.

Right then the teenage girl, by mistake or on purpose, let go of Charles's rope. I watched in horror, witnessing the bull's reaction: his only connection to what was familiar was gone. *Why isn't someone holding my rope?* The bull had suddenly lost his connected anchor upon an unsteady sea. Everything in that moment changed for Charles. As the bull leapt from the plank everyone in the audience screamed. All hell was breaking loose.

chapter 13

As Charles the bull leapt into the air, frantic and terrified, he flailed. His head, along with his magnificent horns—a six-foot span of hardened dermal bone, with tips as sharp as spears—swung back and forth in a wild blur of motion. Instinctively, the bull's two powerful rear legs thrust out backward. Both hoofs kicked Dalm Mor Stroph hard in the face, making an audible *THWACK!*

I watched transfixed at the unraveling mayhem. A slow-motion train wreck no one could do anything about but watch in horror.

But the worst was yet to come. Probably in a knee jerk-like reaction, the giant Gap flung out a clawed hand and seized one of the bull's raised hind legs. Held tightly, the steer's nineteen hundred-pound body mass came crashing down in front of the stage. His hindquarters twisted and elevated. Bones snapped as muscles and ligaments were torn and ripped apart. The seized leg separated, tearing away from the hip socket, yet remained in the staggering Gap's still-raised grip, looking like an early caveman's club.

A horrendous screeching wail emanated from the bull's widely gaping mouth. Blood pumped and spurted high in the air from the animal's ragged leg wound. The shocked and paralyzed audience began to yell and scream as *fight or flight* instincts kicked in. The teenage girl, along with Leo, the master of ceremonies, fled out through the rear of the tent, somewhere behind the hanging mural. Others, rushing from the stands, ran for the exit. *Flight.* Only three onlookers rushed forward—Matt, Donny, and me. *Fight.*

My priority was tending to the wounded bull. His suffering had to stop. First to reach the bottom step of the bleachers, I took three running strides and leapt over the still-thrashing bull. My forward momentum carried me straight into Dalm Mor Stroph's legs, knocking them out from under him. The big alien came thundering down on top of me, with the force of a collapsing high-rise building. As the alien rolled onto his back and kicked outward, Donny, rushing forward, was smacked squarely in the balls. Falling down, he curled into a fetal position. He was down for the count.

The bull's fountaining spurts of blood had everything drenched within a ten-foot parameter. As hard as I tried to get purchase on one of the alien's wrists, everything was too slick, too slippery to hold onto. Matt, nearby, threw a punch at the alien's head and it connected. The Gap, in return, swung the bull's leg, clubbing Matt from his feet and up and off the stage.

Still trying to grab a hold of something in the wet, gooey, bloody mess—anything—my fingers found the butt-end of the Gap's mistmaker pistol. My body on autopilot, I was reacting not thinking. What soldiers are trained to do. Pulling the weapon free from its holster, I aimed it at a point beneath the alien's jutting chin and pulled the trigger. The Gap marshal went limp. I then turned the weapon's muzzle toward the still-wailing bull and once again pulled the trigger. The bull lay inert before me. My heart was pounding—a kettledrum beating in my chest.

Then Matt was next to me, his face half-covered in dripping blood. "Give me that!" he yelled. Prying the mistmaker weapon from my fingers, he placed it back in Dalm Mor Stroph's hip holster, just as Donny struggled to rise to his feet.

"Listen to me," Matt said, in a hushed voice. "We were only trying to save the alien. Got that?"

Donny, his words clipped, his voice sounding a tad higher pitched than normal, said, "But he was shot; anyone can see the fucking wound, right there under his chin."

Matt used his finger to swipe some blood from his own face then smeared it into the dead Gap's wound. He then repeated the motion, now swiping the Gap's blood onto the tip of one of the bull's horns. "No, the big dumb Gap got nailed by a horn. We all witnessed it."

At that moment five Gap marshals, their weapons drawn, came running into the tent. This was going to be a long night.

An hour later, we each had given brief statements of the preceding events to the supervising marshal.

From ten feet away, I stared into the big brown eyes, the pupils fixed and dilated, of Charles, the dead bull. Up on the raised platform, Dalm Mor Stroph lay on his back where he'd dropped lifeless.

The teen-aged girl, Colleen, was brought back in for questioning, as was the oddly-dressed Master of Ceremonies, Leo. Four steps away from them, sitting in the bleachers, Matt, Donny, and I sat huddled together, still in our blood-drenched clothing.

"I'm so sorry . . . this is all my fault, isn't it?" I heard Colleen say to Leo.

I turned to look at her. "You did nothing wrong. Plain and simple, that was a ridiculous, ill-conceived, stunt. It just as easily could have been you who was hurt, maybe even killed."

Colleen nodded, then sniffed as she wiped tears from her cheeks. "Charles was so sweet," she said.

"The bull was yours?" I asked.

"Yeah, well, my family's . . ."

We all watched as an investigative team of Gap marshals from the Oversight and Enforcement Center in town worked the scene of the *supposed* accident. Pictures and vids were shot from every angle. Measurements and other readings were taken, using an assortment of hand-held Gap devices. Apparently, we were waiting for Sleept Vogthner, the Gap's chancellor of communications, to arrive from Boulder. He'd be taking our statements. Nothing had been touched, nothing moved.

Matt, Donny, and I spoke together in low whispers. "We need to get our stories straight," Matt said, one leg nervously gyrating up and down.

Donny placed a restraining hand on Matt's knee. "Relax.

It's simple . . . we rushed over to the stage to save the girl and Leo, and the idiot giant. Colleen and Leo escaped out the back. Everything happened exactly as it appears . . . The Gap got nailed in the chin by one of Charles's horns and Matt shot the suffering bull with the Gap's gun. End of story."

I gave Matt a reassuring nod. "Hey, everyone saw the bull freak out before Leo, the girl, and the audience hightailed it out of here. I think all will be fine, but it's going to be a PR nightmare for the Gaps. That's why Sleept Vogthner's been sent for. Stick to the story and they'll soon let us out of here."

But right then a guttural moan escaped out the mouth of Dalm Mor Stroph's *undead* body. His head turned, his eyes opening wide, blinking repeatedly.

"Shit," I murmured.

We watched in horror as the five marshals rushed to the platform. Stroph tried to sit up, but strong hands kept him down in a prone position. I heard one of the marshals speak to him in Earupitan. I assumed he was asking questions—like, *"Can you understand me? Where are your injuries . . ."*

The three of us exchanged glances, unable to keep sudden trepidation from showing on our faces.

Unintelligible mumblings came from Stroph. I didn't understand much of the Earupitan language, but I knew what he said was nonsensical gibberish. Suddenly, the big alien sat up and gazed around him. I heard a siren in the distance—a fast-approaching ambulance.

"I think you obliterated his tongue, too," Donny said.

"Shhh," Matt shushed. "Keep your voice down!"

With all five marshals crouched around Stroph, I had to tilt my head sideways to get a peek at the seemingly *resurrected* alien's face. Though he was alive, no one was home. With a goofy grin, and dazed unfocused eyes, Stroph looked about his surroundings."

"Could be his brain stem took a hit too," Donny said.

"Let's just hope he stays this way. If he recovers, starts to remember . . . we're toast."

Within five minutes the Gap's equivalent of EMTs were hoisting Dalm Mor Stroph's body onto a gurney. His long legs dangled way past the end of the stretcher, but he'd returned to an unconscious state.

One of the Gap marshals approached us, his heads up display activated—evidenced by a projected translucent menu system encircling the Gap's head. Gaps sometimes used a claw to input information instead of just eye movements. The marshal made a few taps on the virtual display his clawed finger, and then looked over at us.

"The chancellor of communications has just been rerouted to the medical facilities at the OEC. He sends his apologies for the delay. You each will be contacted by EMS personnel shortly. Individual interviews with the chancellor will be held at the OEC tomorrow. You can leave now."

By the time we exited the tent, it was dark outside. I half expected the carnival to have been shut down, but the Zipper was still zipping and the Tilt-A-Wheel still twirling. The crowds had doubled in size.

"We still on for midnight?" Donny asked.

"Sure," I said, as we moved toward the carnival's exit. I had more than enough of the Friends Unite Day festivities. "I'm getting everyone together . . . I think we're all in agreement that we need to accelerate the timetable."

"By the group, you mean all of us? Multiple cells?" Donny asked, adding, "Isn't that dangerous?"

"Have to chance it . . . just be there at midnight," I said.

The three of us split up as we left the carnival. The sidewalk seemed pretty much deserted as I headed for Tami's Antiques, where I'd left my truck. Then I spotted Karen, leaning up against her Bronco, her arms crossed over her chest. A man stood before her, his hand resting lightly on her shoulder. He leaned forward and she laughed at something he said. I felt a tightening in my chest. But what did I expect? That she'd never meet someone else? That, given enough time, she wouldn't find room in her heart for someone to replace her dead husband? But I'd still hoped that just maybe that person might be me. I debated about crossing the street, avoid being seen, but decided to stride forth ahead. I had just as much right to be here as anyone else.

Noticing my approach, Karen looked my way, her eyes widening. I saw the shock on her face. She glanced over my still blood-soaked clothes. Then, when the man turned to look, it was my turn to be shocked. It was none other than the leader of the Friends For Friends society, Ronald Gant.

chapter 14

I picked up a tail on the way home that wasn't just another EMS HovT out on patrol. *Shit!* Third time this month. I already knew I was a person of interest, which could lead to my being brought in for questioning. But I've been so careful—extremely careful. Did one of my Takebacks have loose lips? Although that was possible, I had a hard time believing it.

Unless you knew what to look for, especially at night, aerial distortion wakes are damn hard to see. But by angling my side-view mirror upward, I spotted the telltale blur of the twinkling starlight above and slightly behind me. *Heat exhausts.* It was a Skim-Rover—a Gap military vehicle, specifically used for surveillance. The dark, triangular-shaped crafts are exceptionally quiet; capable of slow, meandering progressions within low to medium altitudes. Although Skim-Rovers are equipped with energy-pulse weaponry, they definitely are not in the same league as a Shredder. But then a

Shredder was neither built, nor intended to be a clandestine craft.

My headlights flashed brightly on *something* crossing the road mere feet in front of my truck's front bumper. I slammed on the breaks, locking-up all four tires. The pickup skidded sideways—the odor of burning rubber permeating the air. I watched as three coyotes skittered below into a gulch running parallel to the road. Letting the engine idle a moment, I sat there for a full minute before driving on. Through the windshield, my eyes could just barely make out the dark contours of the stealthy craft above. Five minutes later, I approached the turnoff to my driveway and the Polk ranch property line. As I slowed to make the turn, I thought I saw the craft suddenly angle off to the left. Was it due to the newly designated Code 5 allocation, or had they simply lost interest in me for the night?

By the time I parked in front of the barn, I was again thinking about Karen being with Ronald Gant. Just what I now needed, another reason to despise the guy. But there was a bigger issue—Karen knew all about the Takebacks. Hell, she knew about the shredders and Jhally, too. Yet I knew her loyalty to her brother, Matt was absolute. So maybe it was just a romantic thing. She wouldn't be the first person to be involved in a relationship having to keep secrets.

As I opened the truck's door and climbed out, Mort was there to greet me. Barking twice, he jumped up on his hind legs. Leaning over, I let him lick my face. "Good boy . . . okay, okay, you must be hungry." I pushed him back down giving him a few more pats on his flank. When the barn doors slid open, I caught the tall contours of Jhally standing there within the darkness.

"Any problems?" I asked.

"No. It has been quiet. I fed the animals."

"Mort, too?"

Jhally nodded. "You were gone longer than expected. Wasn't sure if something had happened."

"Yeah . . . got held up for a while in town." I noticed the trough was no longer sitting in front of the barn doors.

Jhally stood aside as I entered the barn. As I flipped on more of the overhead lights, I noticed off to the left the trough was now positioned where the cot had been. The shit bucket was gone, and the chain gone, too. Approaching the aluminum container, I could hear a soft hum coming from the recirculating pump. As I peered down, I could just make out five dark shapes moving around beneath the metal grate. "Hmm. Five, not six . . . looks like you've had dinner here by yourself."

"And it was memorable. Thank you for thinking of me. The larvae will take some time to mature, though."

"I can buy some more full-grown bugs tomorrow," I said, turning to assess the tarp-covered Shredder Five. "Progress?"

Jhally limped over to the workshop area and pulled the tarp away. "I believe it is now ready to be flight-tested. Until then, we won't know what tweaks and adjustments are still needed."

I circled the sleek craft, letting my hand slide across the smooth fuselage. Whereas various open panels, with exposed wiring and mechanical workings had showed before, the Shredder now was all buttoned-up. Looked ready to fly. I turned to face Jhally. "My plan was to test each craft, one at a time. Put them on a flatbed trailer and haul them up to Wyoming's most isolated backcountry."

Jhally said, "That will take much time. Perhaps weeks, even months."

"Time we no longer can afford," I agreed. "Things have changed. Gaps . . . Earupitans, are clearly readying their forces for something."

"You are worried about Marshal Grip's assertion that this property of yours hasn't actually been designated a Code 5. That he lied. Perhaps an Earupitan trap is in play?"

Approaching the alien I stood two paces before him. "It's time you fully leveled with me, Jhally. Explain the renewed military activity; those large-sized ships moving across the skies late at night. Did you think they wouldn't be noticed?"

Jhally seemed to choose his next words carefully. "Mass hysteria."

I shook my head. "What about it?"

"That's what would happen if the second phase of their invasion strategy was released to the general public."

"I'm not the general public."

"You aren't the only one with trust issues. Only this morning, did you not have me chained to a stake? I was your prisoner . . . at least that was your intent."

"Well, you're not my prisoner now. Hell, you still have the mistmaker weapon with you, do you not? I am trusting you with my life—all our lives!"

Jhally seemed to consider my words. "This was never only about an invasion, not a simple means to colonize Earth . . . some kind of galactic *real estate* grab."

"Then what?"

"Have you not noticed there are relatively few Gaps, as you call them, presently living here on this world?"

I nodded. "Advanced technology has its benefits."

"What you don't know is that the Earupitans have been in the throes of a great war that started a good many years ago, one that threatens the very existence of Gahl as well as other worlds within the distant star systems, including Blahn. Bombings have taken their toll."

"A war? With whom?"

"Does it matter?" Jhally asked.

I shook my head. I was in no mood for mind games, or for half-truths. "So you were at war. It's probably a common outcome throughout the universe, just as it is here on Earth. You'll need to tell me everything."

"Fine. I've already told you about the Earupitans and the Mannarians mating practices."

"Uh huh . . . the threesomes. Yeah."

"For both species . . . Earupitan and Mannarian . . . the females are our most prized possessions."

"Possessions?" I asked.

Jhally stared back at me blankly.

"Just go on . . ."

Jhally said, "The war on Gahl was short-lived, about six years. Some of our cities were bombed, but nothing compared to what the Earupitans did in reprisal to the enemy's world. Between the Earupitan fighting forces, and the Mannarians' high-tech weaponry, the enemy was defeated, their world destroyed. Then life returned to normal on Gahl. All was well."

"That's a good thing, right?" I asked.

"Yes, it was a good thing. That is until eight of your years ago when a terrible discovery was made. The bombs dropped years earlier onto our major cities had an organic component to them. An organic component nearly impossible to detect that had spread and reproduced throughout all of Gahl's atmosphere."

"What exactly did it do? You said everything was fine after the war."

"Our females were becoming infertile. Their E-DNA had been modified so radically, giving birth had become impossible."

"So what, then? Are you saying both the Earupitans and the Mannarians were . . . a dying species?" I asked.

"Yes, Brian. That is correct."

"Your scientists . . . the Mannarians, they couldn't edit out the bad E-DNA genetics? Seems that would be a fairly straightforward thing to accomplish for such an advanced race of people."

Jhally scratched the top of his head. "Think of it this way. What is the most common ailment here on your own planet?"

"I don't know . . . maybe the common cold."

"Exactly. The common cold. And the reason why it is so difficult, perhaps impossible, to cure?"

"It's constantly mutating. This year's cold or flu bug isn't the same virus that infected millions of people the year before."

Jhally raised his oversized head.

"So you're saying that's what the E-DNA altering bombs caused? An ever-mutating, adaptable virus that never allowed your females to reproduce on your home world?"

"Basically, yes," Jhally said. "So now you know why we are here."

"I do? Explain . . ."

"The search has been relentless. Very difficult. But out of the many millions of worlds assessed, Earth was selected. They love it here."

"They?" I repeated.

"Our females. Earth is where they would most like to start breeding again. Hundreds of our females are already here, although you would not know where to look for them."

"Why here? Why Earth?"

"Earth's climate is almost identical to that on Gahl. Your oceans contain a flourishing, almost unlimited, supply of shellfish."

"Your females, how is it they do not suffer the same fate as—"

Jhally cut me off. "The females, close to one million of them, have never set foot on Gahl. They were born in what you would refer to as a test tube. Bred in space, they never once breathed Gahl's corrupted air."

I let what he shared sink in. For a long time I'd wondered what the real reason was. What lay behind the aliens' invasion and occupation. Everyone had wondered the same damn thing. But Jhally's disclosure made sense. It was far too bizarre of an explanation to be anything but true. My eyes found his. "This planet is not large enough to contain Earupitans, Mannarians, as well as Humans, is it?"

Jhally didn't answer right away. "No, long term, it is not."

"What are the Gaps waiting for? Why not just obliterate the Human population and be done with it?"

"Humans still provide something necessary; at least, for the short term."

"What's that?"

"Quite simply, it's your breathing . . . more specifically, Humans breathing around us Gaps."

"I think I understand," I said. "You're describing the process whereby, in the case of Humans, we are protected against illnesses caused by infections. Like with micro-organisms, um . . . pathogens. Yes, we spread things around like the common cold, and flu, and such, but we also build-up a resistance to those diseases. Like an immunization process, is that correct?"

Jhally shrugged. "Close enough."

"And once the Gaps' resistance to illness is sufficiently built-up?"

"I believe most, if not all, of the Human race will be eliminated."

I let that sink in. "One more question . . . where are they now? These 'waiting to breed' females of yours?"

"I told you, only a select few have been brought down to Earth."

"And the rest?"

Jhally looked uneasy and didn't answer. I could see he was

experiencing a primordial conflict of sorts. The third gender of their species, female, was incredibly important to him. "The rest are protected by a dedicated Situational Command Ship. Another vessel is in orbit around the Moon, called a Solaris Habitat," he finally said.

"And you're saying a million females exist up there on that . . . Solaris Habitat craft . . . just waiting to breed with the male Gaps here on Earth?"

Jhally nodded back, although he didn't look too happy with the way I'd characterized things.

chapter 15

I'd instructed Matt and Donny to arrive at my place a half-hour early. There were some things I wanted to discuss with them prior to everyone else's arrival tonight at midnight. The bright headlights on Donny's Cherokee were now coming into view. As the SUV jostled its way along my long and winding driveway, I exited the barn and waited for him to pull up close. I signaled for him to hold up and gestured with a winding motion for him to roll down his window.

"What's up?" Donny asked.

"I'm having everyone drive around to the rear of the barn. Pull all the way inside and park."

"You got it, brother." As he throttled forward, I watched the Cherokee's taillights disappear around the corner of the barn. I knew Jhally was waiting back there, and he would direct Donny where to park.

Three minutes later, Matt's Subaru was also coming down

my drive. Once close enough to see inside, I saw Tim's dark form sitting in the passenger's seat. I was surprised to see Matt wasn't alone. Annoyed, I repeated the same instructions to Matt that I'd just given to Donny. Karen, sitting in the back seat, made eye contact with me but neither of us spoke.

I stared up overhead, scanning the black, star-filled sky. I neither heard nor saw anything, but that didn't mean a high-flying Skim-Rover wasn't lurking somewhere up there in the night sky above me.

After closing, then locking, the barn's double-doors, I hurried to join the others on the opposite side of the barn.

"Hey Brian," Matt said, fast-walking to reach me before I joined the others. "I just wanted to say I'm sorry. You know, about Karen being here . . . for this early part of the meeting."

"I did say I wanted to speak with you and Donny alone, Matt." I watched Karen and Donny speaking together, back where the cars were parked. Karen glanced over at me.

"I know, but she *kinda* insisted. And all her questions! God! Like, why do we need to take two cars? Are you telling me he still doesn't trust me? On and on it went . . ."

I raised a palm, and said, "It's fine. What's done is done. It's just that when I left the fair today, I saw Karen and Ronald Gant together. They looked pretty cozy."

"Karen and Gant? Really?"

I nodded. "If it were anyone else, I wouldn't have brought it up. But Ronald Gant could bring everything crashing down on top of us. I don't need to tell you lives are at stake." I could see both concern and guilt written all over Matt's face.

"Screw you!" Karen barked. Somehow she'd crept up on us

and overheard our private powwow without being noticed. "You know, Brian, not everything is about you. Not everything is about your Takebacks!"

Not again, I thought, forcing myself not to reply back to her. As it turned out, I didn't have to.

"Do you know what that asshole Gant does just for kicks?" Matt asked her, already yelling. "Don't you know that because of his involvement with them that our good friends and neighbors are hauled into the Oversight and Enforcement Center? That a good number of them are never seen again? It's the work of a traitor . . . to his own kind, his own race of people! That is the choice he's made . . . and by associating with him, well, it's the choice you've made, too. You need to leave, Karen! Now!" Matt pointed to the parked Subaru. "Take it, I'll get a ride back with Donny."

Karen stood up straight, her arms crossed, and her head tilted to one side. She forced a fake smile and blinked her eyes. "Are you done yet, Matt?"

"Yeah . . . I'm done."

Karen then focused her eyes back on me. "Cozy? You think I'm cozy with Ronald Gant?"

I shrugged. "Tell me . . . what would you call it ?"

"Normally, I would call it none of your damn business. But if you have to know, I was being your James *friggin'* Bond."

It didn't help any that tonight she was nothing short of stunning, wearing a short yellow sundress that emphasized her long, tan legs. Her black cowboy boots had stenciled characters of Mickey Mouse on one, and Minnie Mouse on the other.

"I don't understand," I said.

"Look, having his hand on my bare shoulder made my skin crawl. Was he hitting on me? Of course, he was! I've got news for you. That happens. A lot! But what he was sharing with me was important. Maybe could save lives. So I smiled and just acted coy. I gazed up at him with stars in my eyes, while learning new details I was pretty sure you'd want to hear about!"

"Okay. So what did he say?"

Eyes narrowing some, she tightly pursed her lips. She was as mad as I'd ever seen her, yet she was holding it together.

"He said he was being offered a prominent position within the oversight side of things, at the Oversight and Enforcement Center. You know, where the Assembly of Five decides who lives and who dies."

The Assembly of Five was the closest thing we had to a judicial system around these parts. A panel of Gap uppity-ups, who, as far as I knew, had never once sided with Humans. Probably figured it was best to err only on the side of their own species, if there was even the slightest chance someone, namely a Human, might—even remotely—be guilty of something or other.

"So, what will he be doing there?" I asked.

"That's the thing. Apparently, he will become one of them . . . the Assembly of Five will become the Assembly of Six. Did you know that Ronald was a lawyer before everything went to shit?"

I nodded, "Yeah . . . he's mentioned that to me more than once over the years."

"I asked him directly, you know," Karen said, "where his true loyalties lie. He said something interesting . . . that people shouldn't make assumptions about his patriotism."

"So how's any of this supposed to help us?" Matt asked.

"Really, you're asking me that? How knowing someone who sits on the *new* Assembly of Six can help us? How being privy to insider information won't be of use to us?" She glared at her brother as though he were an idiot.

"So you're going to keep on seeing him, then?" I asked.

She thought about that. "Why don't I leave that up to you, since you're the big cheese here."

"Okay, 007, but be careful. Gant's a slippery one."

I heard the sound of multiple car engines approaching in the distance. Catching Donny's eye, I asked, "Can you go out there right now? Direct everyone to pull around to the back and park inside?"

The four Takebacks cells would soon be together for the very first time. Something, though, kept nagging at me—this still might be one big mistake.

chapter 16

Yet to be noticed, I lazily sat up on my perch, which, to most, looked like just some tarp-covered piece of tall farm equipment. Judging by the simple fact so many cars and trucks were able to fit into a small section at the rear of the barn only emphasized how large a structure the barn really was. Several fellow cell members drove here together, but even so, there were eighteen vehicles parked in three rows of six. I watched as the crowd of mostly men, along with several women, eyed people belonging to other cells. A few already knew each other outside of being Takebacks. Perhaps they were neighbors, or attended the same church services on Sundays. I paid special attention to each new arrival. Looked for clandestine signaling between members; for the tiniest off-guard facial expression—perhaps just catching another cell member's eye, or for telltale indications secret associations were going on. But I witnessed nothing of the sort. I didn't expect to and felt something akin to pride while watching them now. Each Takeback present, with the exception of Karen, and Jhally, who was kept out of sight for now, had committed a serious crime against the new order. True subversives, they all were anxious and ready to take things to the next level. Starting tonight, that wish would be granted.

I stood and raised a hand up high. "Listen up everyone, can I get your attention?"

Heads turned both this way and that—eyes scanned their surroundings until they eventually found me. Everyone then moved closer in. "Tonight we should continue to use our pseudonyms. So, I am Polybius, your leader of the Takebacks. Most of you are probably wondering about the additional members present here. I can tell you now, there are twenty-six Takebacks here from four separate cells. Soon, I'm hopeful, that number will grow to twenty-eight."

I let their cross-talk murmurs subside before continuing on. I scanned the crowd looking for Karen but didn't find her. I continued, "None of you were individually selected to become a member simply because you wanted to be a part of some kind of revolutionary group. You needed to have certain essential skillsets; one that would make you a crucial asset to the Takebacks. Most of you are ex-military. We have four pilots among us. Orville Wright, and yes, that is his historical pseudonym, is a commercial airline pilot. One is a software engineer; another, a hardware engineer. We even have an MMA fighter among us, an instructor of Krav Maga."

"That's all well and good, but why weren't we told there were other cells in the group? We didn't know you were a part of other cells. I don't like the smell of this situation . . ."

The fellow who interrupted my little speech was none other than Thomas Edwards. He went by the pseudonym of

Titus Quinctius Flamininus, or just Titus, a historical Roman General—one who lived some two hundred years B.C., and was instrumental in the conquest of Greece. I try to get along with just about everyone, but I've never really liked Titus. The guy's bossy and abrupt. Now in his fifties, he was short and muscular—built like a fireplug. His salt-and-pepper gray hair was worn high and tight. A former sergeant first class in the Army, I should have expected his outburst. Some people needed to be in charge, be the 'big boss' in the room. Titus was one of them. Finding out now that he was part of a larger organization, that decisions were made without his knowing, probably came as a personal affront. Still, he was a necessary cog in the machine I'd been piecing together for close to two years. He was also a former M1 tank commander. He knew armored, ground-based vehicles better than just about anyone. Plus, he possessed a highly illegal, full-sized operational M1 tank. Built in secret over the course of a decade, it was made of spare parts and pieces he'd acquired from here and there from all over the world.

"That's a fair question, Titus . . . but as I've told you before for obvious security reasons, members needed to be kept in the dark about certain aspects of the group and about the Takebacks specific agenda. It was for your own protection as well as everyone else's." I could see his face start to redden. His fingers closed into fists. Here it comes, he was digging in for a fight.

"I don't know most of these people here. Am I supposed to take your word for it that they've each been properly vetted? I have a family to protect."

"The short answer is yes," I said. "Everyone that's here tonight I have personally vetted, can personally vouch for. It's taken years. And, just like you, Titus, they, too, have skin in the game." I caught sight of Karen then, hanging out by the horses. In truth, not everyone here did have skin in the game. Something that would soon need to be remedied.

Titus still seemed angry, but then he always looked angry. One of those 'glass half-empty' kinds.

"Any other surprises we should know about?" he asked in a snarky tone.

I heard others in the crowd now quietly parroting Titus's remarks.

"Look, it's taken a lot of time and effort to arrive at this moment. The moment when I finally can be completely transparent regarding the full scope of the Takeback's charter." I stared down at some growingly perplexed faces. "And before you start objecting, yes, of course each Takeback cell has been fully dedicated to one, all-important goal . . . to disrupt the Gaps in their invasion of Earth. To make life for the aliens not worth living, at least not here in Castle Rock. What you were not aware of was the much bigger picture. And to be honest, newer revelations of late have forced me to think *much* bigger. Bigger than Castle Rock, or Colorado . . . or even what used to be the United States of America."

"What the hell are you talking about, Polybius?" a black man standing near the back of the group yelled out. He was none other than Shawn McGee. I knew him more as Spartacus, who, historically, was a Thracian soldier. Captured by the Romans, sold as a slave, he later became the most famed gladiator fighter of all time. This Spartacus was also our MMA fighter—the instructor of Krav Maga.

"Tonight, I'm here to set out a far bigger picture of things to come. How you, both individually and as a group, will henceforth be the instigators of real change. *Real* revolution. I know each and every one of you personally. I know you are willing to fight, even die if necessary, for the return of freedom and liberty to the Human race. Your commitment to the Takebacks is not in question. But now you need to get your minds wrapped around something new. Something I like to refer to it as . . . *our counterstrike*."

Titus raised his hands to quiet the group. It took a full minute. He then pointed a stubby finger up at me. "There have been more homegrown military uprisings around the world than we probably know about," he argued. "Not a one has been successful. The Gaps have technology we can never match. I'm not sure what this new charter bullshit is that you're talking about. Staying small and nimble has always been our mode of operation. So, Polybius, you're going to tell us what the hell's going on here. I don't like this. Not one bit. How can you somehow imagine we could go big against these alien assholes?"

I let more of the cross talk subside before continuing. There was no way I was going to let Titus pirate this meeting. "All valid points, Titus." I jumped down from my higher-up perch. I knew Matt and Donny were ready to assist me. "Ready boys?" I yelled out.

One by one, Matt, Donny, and I uncovered the five Shredders. The silence in the barn was such I could hear my two mares chomping on hay, some one hundred fifty feet away.

"You have . . . Shredders!" Orville Wright, the commercial pilot, exclaimed, as he approached the closest of the alien craft. His eyes widened and an expression of pure astonishment lit up his face.

We watched as the entire group now weaved around all four crafts before walking toward the more pristine-looking Shredder Five, over by the workshop.

"Most of them look pretty beat to shit," Titus said. "I hope you don't expect me to fix 'em . . . I don't know shit about alien tech."

I climbed back up, again standing on the same Shredder I'd stood on earlier. "Okay, everyone, bring yourselves back around. We still have a lot to talk about." Both Matt and Donny joined me atop the fuselage. "For those here who don't know them," I gestured to Matt, "this is Noble, and this fellow is Crazy Horse," I said, gesturing to Donny. Donny chose to name himself after a nineteenth-century warrior of the Oglala Lakota tribe, while Matt chose the moniker of Alfred Bernhard Nobel, the industrialist who invented dynamite and founded the Nobel prize award.

"First things first. Who here still has doubts that we haven't substantially elevated our game?"

Nobody raised a hand. Nobody disputed the claim.

"Of the four pilots among us, Wright, Yeager, Rickenbacker, and myself, who'd be interested in taking one of these *bad boys* up for a little spin?"

All four pilots, including me, raised a hand, real anticipation reflecting on each face. "Who here knows how to fly, maneuver, and initialize the weaponry systems for a Zion-9 Shredder spacecraft?"

No one raised a hand. I looked out upon growing expressions of apprehension. Glancing over my shoulder toward the workshop area, I twirled a finger high in the air above my head.

Shredder Five's argon boost drive suddenly spun to life. Disturbed dirt, dust, and remnants of hay swirled up and around the craft's fuselage. The noise was not all that loud, somewhat similar to the sound of a throaty big V8 engine. Definitely unique once you've heard it, especially if you've been attacked by one or more—you never forget it. Shredder Five suddenly lifted off the ground and leveled off to a height of five or six feet, spun one hundred-and-eighty-degrees on its axis, then slowly began to fly toward the opposite end of the barn. All of us watched in awe. These craft were the primary assault weapons of choice for the Gap invasion forces two years prior. Witnessing one now taking flight, I surmised, could evoke conflicting mixes of feelings: fear, anxiety, even hopelessness . . . to name only a few. But as the dangerous craft slowly made its way closer toward us, what I viewed on the Takeback members' faces was not that. Instead, I was seeing exhilaration. I was seeing the hope of some kind of vengeance.

Earlier, we'd purposely left an area open between where the cars and trucks were to be parked, and where the four Shredders were clustered together; the same area where the airborne Shredder was now descending. Once it touched town, its drive began to decelerate. The still-spinning swirling dirt devils, losing their momentum, quickly dissipated and a quiet stillness returned to the barn. An internal latching mechanism on the Shredder was then released, causing the craft's canopy to slide back into the fuselage. Only then did Jhally stand up, ready to be seen.

As if on cue, no less than ten handguns, with a variety of caliber, were drawn out—previously hidden beneath shirt-tails, under jackets, and even ankle holsters. After all, this was Colorado, where people love their second amendment rights, when such rights had still existed. The punishment for carrying a weapon today most certainly would result in death.

"Don't shoot!" I yelled. "Keep your damn fingers off those triggers!"

chapter 17

Jhally raised his clawed hands.

Maintaining his outstretched, two-handed grip on his gun, Titus took three deliberate strides toward the now-landed fifth Shredder. "Get down off that aircraft, Gap! Move real slow, and keep your hands right where we can see them."

I let out an exasperated moan. I should have expected this. "Come on, Titus, he's not with them . . . he's with us!"

"Like hell he is . . . they're all the same. Damn lizards are born killers. It's in their slimy green blood."

I was tempted to mention the Gap's blood is red, the same as Humans, but decided this was not the time.

Titus pulled back the hammer on his pistol, a big Colt Anaconda. A serious .45 caliber handgun that, at such close range, would blow a significant-sized hole through Jhally's chest. "Titus . . ." I said, in a voice just above a whisper, "I personally watched this alien snap a Gap marshal's neck yesterday. He's been living here with me for close to a year now." I didn't feel it necessary to further tell him that I thought I had Jhally securely chained up during that time. "I know it's a big leap to trust me on this . . . but you're going to have to try."

Titus shot an angry snarl in my direction. "It just keeps coming out of you, Polk . . . one lie after another."

I felt Donny tensing next to me. I said, "Keep your cool, buddy, I've got this." I jumped down from the Shredder, signaling Jhally to do the same. The last thing this crowd needed was seeing a Gap standing above them looking superior.

By the time Jhally was standing at my side, everyone had taken a step or two backward. I noted Spartacus had moved to the front of the group, looking ready to dole out a little Krav Maga whoop-ass on the limping, one-legged alien.

None yet had re-holstered their weapons. I said, "That Shredder . . . it's locked and loaded. Jhally could have taken us all out with the pull of a trigger. He could have flown right out of here then turned back around and leveled this barn in mere seconds."

I saw several Takebacks lower their guns. Titus wasn't one of them.

"I don't want any part of this bullshit," Titus said, glaring at me. "And I don't want any part of the Takebacks, either. We're out of here." Only then did he lower his pistol, tucking the gun into the back of his jeans. "Come on, guys," he said to his fellow cell members, "we'll go it alone." He began striding toward his pickup truck but slowed and then stopped completely when he saw the other three in his cell weren't following him.

"We should at least hear them out," a tall, bald man said. He went by the historical name of Hiram Berdan. Berdan was a famous sharp shooter with the Union Army during the Civil War. "I mean . . . who else is going to show us how to fly these things? You, Titus?"

"Screw you, Kyle . . ."

Typically, it takes a good while to get my ire up, but once it's up, it's best to stay out of my way. "Enough! No more using our real names here, Titus!" If you want to go, then go. If not, shut the hell up and let me speak."

He glowered at me but didn't leave the barn.

"This is Jhall Doulk Hargoth. He goes by Jhall, or Jhally. Sure, he looks like just another Earupitan Gap, from Gahl. But Jhally is from a neighboring planet, called Blahn. He is a Mannarian and feels no allegiance to the Gaps. He in no way condones the Gaps' invasion of Earth. He is a friend. Without his help we'll have no chance in hell to set in motion a true revolution."

I watched as my fellow Takebacks quietly assessed the alien standing quietly next to me.

Matt, standing at my other side, said, "Instead of pulling your guns on him, you should be thanking him. Befriending him, for God's sake."

I saw several heads nodding. One by one, everyone put their weapons away.

"Believe it or not," I said, "We do have the makings of a plan. But with that said, there's a good chance some of us could be killed. I can't lie about that. But even if we die, we'll be showing the rest of the world that a brave few have found the courage to stand up to the aliens—that confronting the Gap invaders is not impossible."

One of the pilots, a lieutenant in the Air Force, who went by the alias Yeager, said, "If you're the real deal, you'll answer the one big question that every man, woman, and child has been asking for close to two years now. Why are the Gaps here? Answer me that, here and now, and I just might believe you. Might even stay and consider you something other than my enemy."

Up to this point, Jhally hadn't spoken a word. He finally lowered his hands, confronting the Humans standing around him. Making eye contact, he even nodded to several.

Clearing his throat, Jhally began to speak: "As your leader has stated, I am a Mannarian, a species very similar to that of the Earupitans. One hundred twenty of your years ago, a planet in the neighboring star system of Gahl—a planet called Blahn—was struggling with an environmental mishap of catastrophic proportions . . ."

Jhally went on to tell the Takebacks the same story he'd told me, about the mass Mannarian exodus from Blahn. He spoke of the landing of 200,000 desperate souls on Gahl, and finding a less than warm reception there. He spoke of his technically advanced, far more intelligent species, having few life choices on that hostile world. He briefly shared the aliens' unique means of reproduction: the three versus two strands of E-DNA. He then spoke of the not-so-long ago war on Gahl and the subsequent bombings that made the female gender infertile. Finally, he spoke about the Solaris Habitat craft—protected by the fifth Situational Command Ship somewhere in high orbit above the moon. That vessel carried a million Earupitan females who were waiting to mate. Waiting to conceive and rebuild their dying race.

When Jhally finished speaking, I scanned the faces around me. They believed him. I could see it in their eyes.

"So what exactly are you telling us? That Earth's just going to be one big happy planet of Gaps and Humans running around?" Titus asked, now rejoining the conversation.

I placed a hand on Jhally's shoulder. "Let me answer this one. No, Titus . . . that's not the plan. Haven't you wondered why the Gaps will go out of their way to be near us? Act as if they are our good friends? Be amongst us every chance they get?"

"I guess . . . when they're not dragging some of us into an OEC to either torture or execute us," Titus said.

"Before they can bring their females down to Earth, the male Gaps first need to properly build up their immune systems. For two years now, they've been *breathing in* what Humans are *breathing out*. As you know, each day Humans exhale all kinds of nasty shit . . . bacteria, viruses, and fungi. That's how illnesses are spread. The most dangerous airborne bacteria include whooping cough, diphtheria, meningitis, tuberculosis, pneumonia . . ." The last thing the Gaps want to do is to bring down their remaining females, only to have them immediately die off from pneumonia just a few weeks later. They're building up their immune systems. Some of the male Gaps make regular trips to those ships. That way, the Gap females are slowly being introduced to our unique environment . . . while also building up their immune systems." I glanced around me. "That process is nearly complete. Soon, the Gaps will no longer have any need for us Humans to exist."

"And then they'll do what? Somehow *fucking* exterminate the entire Human race?" Titus asked.

All eyes went to Jhally. He said back, "That is correct."

"How long do we have? Weeks, months?"

"Weeks . . . no more than that," Jhally said.

chapter 18

Let me be perfectly clear here, about the crux of our plan. No longer are we targeting one of the Situational Command Ships orbiting Earth. Instead, we're going after the Solaris Habitat craft. I'm just waiting to receive more intel about the vessel's layout. Apparently, it is massive in size since it houses close to a million Earupitan females. How they are distributed throughout that ship, I have no idea. But taking that craft . . . will be our mission."

"I like it! And we'll kill every last one of those Gap bitches," Titus said, staring directly at Jhally.

I knew Jhally had conflicting feelings about any plan that involved harming the females of his species. *How could he not?* Tonight wouldn't be the last time someone would try to push Jhally's buttons. Great feelings of resentment, held by those in the barn toward the Gap invaders, were justified. But I wanted to see if Jhally was up to dealing with it without flipping out. He remained calm, looking to me to reply to

Titus instead.

"No," I said. "Think about it. We'll get a hell of a lot more mileage out of this plan if we use the female Gaps up there as a bargaining chip. For without those females, their entire race is doomed."

I then noticed Karen had joined the main group, studying me now with questioning, raised brows. "Intimidation is only effective if you're willing to go through with the threat. Are you willing to kill a million of these female aliens?" she asked.

"I've thought about that. Honestly, I don't know. The invaders of our planet certainly deserve every shitty thing that comes back at them. But in the end, do we want to be like them? Become despicable, ruthless, killers? Or does being Human also include being more humane?" I looked back at her, but couldn't read her expression.

"I still say we burn the lot of them. Give them no quarter . . . they don't deserve any," Titus said.

"Let's move on," I said. "These Shredders accommodate a crew of two Gaps each. Including myself and Jhally, there are five here with extensive piloting experience. I want to get each pilot behind the controls, up in the air and training in these things, starting tonight."

That surprised everyone. Again, I waited to let all the nervous crosstalk subside.

"What about the rest of us? We're not all pilots? So what . . . we get left behind?" Titus asked.

"Not at all. We're all going. Some will be sitting in the aft seats. Also, as part of our plan, we will be commandeering another, far larger, Earupitan craft."

"And what's that?" Spartacus asked.

"We're going to need a Milonge Bi-Hull transport."

I waited for the laughs and snickers to die down. "You see, we're not going to *invade* the Solaris Habitat. That would be suicide. Instead, we're going to cruise right past that protecting Situational Command Ship and head right for the Habitat ship, since we've already received full clearance to do so. We'll wait for them to open their flight bay doors, then fly right inside as if we own the place."

"Beyond the fact it sounds pretty much impossible, why the need for that bi-hull transport?" the airline pilot, Orville, asked.

"Every Tuesday evening, a Milonge Bi-Hull transport takes off from the OEC building and heads into space. A contingent of five, on up to eight, security force Shredders go right alongside it. It could be that these weekly routine treks are related to the environmental, immune-conditioning we spoke about earlier. I'm not one hundred percent certain about that, though. In any case, we need to be ready to hijack their transport ship by next Tuesday night. That gives us six days."

One of my mares whinnied, breaking the dead silence in the barn.

"Jhally will be taking those of you who are pilots up one at a time in Shredder Five, sitting right over there. Don't get too excited. Tonight we're keeping our training sessions strictly within the barn. Mostly, you'll be watching Jhally as he takes off and lands . . . makes a few low circles, that sort of thing. You'll have the opportunity to learn about the various indicators and controls. So—who wants to go first?"

All the Takeback pilots, including Karen, enthusiastically raised-up their hands.

"Okay, Orville, let's start with you."

The other pilots moaned in disappointment, sounding like a bunch of kids in middle school.

Donny said, "All non-pilots come over here. Let's talk about the rest of the plan, about who'll be responsible for what."

Mike Post, our resident software hacker, reached an arm out to stop me. Up until now, I hadn't seen him in the crowd.

"Polybius!" he said, "We need to talk. When you have a minute." Typically, nothing seemed to faze him, but he was looking more serious than I'd ever seen him.

"Can it wait? I can drop by your place in the morning."

"Earlier the better," he said.

I made my way over to Karen. "Hey, can I talk to you a quick minute?"

"Sure . . . what is it? I want to get in line to go up with Jhally."

I walked her over to the stalls, away from the others. "Look, I'm thrilled you want to be a part of this. We need you."

"But?" she asked, offering back a *sideways* glance.

"Two things—One, no one uses their real name here. The Gaps have been known to put listening devices all over the place; bugs—part of their ongoing search for subversive Humans. So come up with a historical figure's name. One you find interesting, or can relate to, and let me know as soon as possible."

"Got it. And what's the other thing?"

"Every one of these Takebacks has what I call skin in the game—"

Karen nodded. "I know all about that. Matt told me. Basically, it allows you to blackmail each of the Takebacks members with incriminating evidence. Like a video of them doing something illegal in the eyes of the EMS."

"That's right," I said.

"So you want me to do something that could get me killed? Leave my daughter with no living parent?"

"That's why you should think long and hard about what I'm asking of you. Truth is, we've put the cart before the horse in your case. You already know enough to foil our plans and get us executed. I'm trusting you."

"Earhart."

"What?"

"Amelia Earhart. That's my pseudonym choice. Will that work?"

"Yeah, I like it." I then waited for her to answer the more important question—question number two.

"I'm in. How soon do I need to get this done?"

"Tomorrow," I said. "And I know just the thing you'll be doing."

When it was my turn, which was dead last, to sit in the cockpit of Shredder Five, I was as excited as a six year old on his first trip to Disney World. The cockpit's seating arrangement had one pilot sitting behind the other. The space was tight, but since a Human is much smaller in size than the typical Gap pilot, there was ample room for me to move around. Jhally, seated in the forward seat, was positioned lower than me. Even so, I had to really sit up straight and scoot a tad forward in order to see over his shoulders to view the various controls. There was little similarity to what I was used to in the F-16 fighter jets I'd piloted in the past. In them, the side-stick controller was placed at my right, my movements interpreted by the flight control computer. On the left sat the throttle stick and the landing gear's controls. I'd also had a heads-up display projected on a clear panel in front of me.

"What we see before us, Brian," Jhally said, "is a highly intuitive spacecraft interface. This onboard computer does much more than what you were used to on your primitive, atmosphere-required crafts. The Shredder has only one tactile node the pilot needs to be concerned with." Glowing blue, he gestured a clawed finger toward the projected, three-dimensional sphere hovering several inches above his lap. "Let me show you how to manipulate it." Bringing his right hand closer to the virtual ball, it seemingly interpreted the approach and jumped into the curvature of his palm. As he moved his hand—either right or left, or up and down—the sphere followed his movements as if, somehow, it was a part of him.

"Every movement of your hand, your individual finger digits, will have an effect on the sphere. Also, there is tactile touch—by squeezing the sphere you can control certain functions of the craft. Alternately, by spreading your fingers wider, expanding the sphere other functions are controlled. I will demonstrate them. But first, let me show you how to power on the vessel's argon boost drive to make a controlled lift off."

Within minutes, Jhally had the Shredder in the air—making slow circles and figure eights within the barn's confines. At first, my attention was drawn to the timber crossbeams, sitting right above us, as I stared upward through the canopy. I quickly realized Jhally was a master at the controls, easily keeping the Shredder positioned exactly where he wanted it to be. My eyes took in the glowing indicators and virtual levers. *How on earth will I learn to fly this thing in just a few days?* I wondered.

As if reading my mind, Jhally said, "I am sure all this must look daunting to you. But it is actually quite simple. I will show you only what you need to know at first."

I nodded, even though Jhally couldn't see me seated behind him. Glancing out the side of the canopy, I could see those below gazing up at us. Waving down, they all waved back to me. I signaled to Donny.

"Do me a favor, Jhally."

"Yes, Brian?"

"As soon as Donny gets the rear barn doors open . . . fly us out and into the night . . . give me a real demonstration of what this thing can do. Just stay within my property lines."

chapter 19

It was close to four o'clock in the morning when I finally made it to bed after my first flight training inside the Shredder. I hadn't been asleep for more than an hour when something, maybe a sound, or maybe a movement, stirred me awake. I heard Mort's low growl coming from his usual spot next to me on the floor. Then I saw a dark shape, looming at the open window on the other side of the room. Without taking my eyes off the early morning visitor, I slid a hand beneath my pillow where I found the butt of the mistmaker. Since I typically left my bedroom window wide open at night, the dark figure had little trouble entering. Already partially inside—he appeared to be straddling the windowsill, one leg in and one leg out. I said, "You move an inch farther into this room and I'll send you straight to hell."

The dark figure stayed perfectly still as I fumbled for the bedside light, nearly knocking the lamp over before getting it switched on.

"Jhally? What the hell!"

The alien looked back at me through hooded eyes. I watched as he teetered on the sill, as if he were drunk, or high, or *something*. He responded with two words, "Need help . . ." then he toppled over and crashed onto the floor. I stared at his prone, unconscious body for several moments. *What the hell?* Then the stench hit me. A foul odor—one I instinctively knew was associated with decomposing flesh.

I hurried over to him, trying to assess what his illness might be. Unfortunately, I knew next to nothing about Gap physiology. Using two fingers, I pried open an eyelid and found a fixed lizard eyeball staring back, albeit one still reactive to the light. Pupils of this alien species are vertically oblong in shape and span the entire width of the iris. I next placed a hand on Jhally's scaly forehead. His skin most definitely felt warm. Truth was, I had no idea what the core body temperature of a Gap normally was supposed to be. Was their body's temperature similar to a Human's since they also were warm-blooded creatures? In the end it was the overwhelming smell of decay that led me to the crux of the problem. I saw the exposed prosthesis, between the hem of his pant leg and his shoe. Scurrying back to my bedside table, I pulled open the top drawer where I kept an old, Air Force-issue, Ontario Survival Knife. Older than me, it was in good condition since I kept it well-oiled and sharpened. Sliding it free from its sheath, I then went to work on Jhally's pant leg, slicing through the fabric from ankle to just above the knee. I gagged, smelling putrid flesh. I immediately saw the problem. There, right above the prosthesis, Jhally's stump was discolored. A dark brown in color, I watched as oozing puss dripped onto the floor.

"You'll have to remove the infected portion of my leg," Jhally said, his faint voice weak. His eyes remained closed.

"Why the hell didn't you tell me your stump was infected like this? Why wait till the damn thing's a festering mess?" I knew my incensed irritation wasn't helping him any, but for shit's sake, I wasn't a doctor. Jhally dying here on my bedroom floor would be a big problem.

He swallowed, attempting again to speak. "This time . . . do not . . . suture the . . . stump."

"What?"

"Leg . . . will grow . . . back, if not . . . sutured." Jhally's head tilted upward, his breathing slow but steady as he drifted into deep unconsciousness. I sat back and stared at the putrefied stump, Matt's old prosthesis still attached.

I was the one who'd first found Jhally over a year back, when aerial reconnaissance missions were routine over Castle Rock, and probably everywhere else in the world. Seeing distant smoke, I saddled up Patty, one of my two still-living mares, and rode out to see what had happened. The still-smoldering spacecraft was a half-buried crumpled mess. From my mount atop Patty, I could see the canopy was open. Clicking my tongue, I coaxed Patty a bit closer until I could see within the cockpit. One alien had survived, the copilot had not. Jhally, seated in the forward portion of the wrecked craft, watched me as I dismounted and slowly approached. I'd brought along my BRNO 800. It's an rare double-barreled weapon that had both a twelve gauge shotgun barrel above, and a standard rifle barrel below it—the best of both worlds. But the rifle was ridiculously heavy.

I dismounted and leveled both barrels at the alien's head. Then, peering farther into the cockpit, I could see that the alien's foot and lower leg had been mangled in the crash. I assessed what needed to be done. It involved making another round trip back to the ranch. Returning in my Bobcat, instead of on Patty, I brought an assortment of tools along with me—including a shovel, a medical kit, and a sharply honed, log-splitting ax. I figured I'd have to sever the alien's limb just below the knee. If the Gap died in the process, I really didn't care. I'd just bury the alien, along with his Shredder, right here in this pasture.

Mort, now licking Jhally's face, brought me back to the here and now. The dog liked the alien, which explained why he didn't go *batshit crazy* when the Gap attempted to crawl through the open window.

I turned my attention back to Jhally's smelly, putrefied stump. I supposed using my log-splitting ax a second time would be counter-productive. Before, I didn't care what damage I might cause the alien. Hell, at the time I found my brutal hacking away at the damaged limb even somewhat cathartic. But things were different now. Jhally was a crucial member of the Takebacks. Without his help going forward, our plans were in jeopardy. I decided I needed a hacksaw. A hacksaw and that bottle of Jack I had on a shelf in the kitchen cupboard. I'd already decided there was no way I was going to hack off a limb while sober. But first I had to try to drag this alien's near dead weight into the bathroom and get him into the tub. This was going to be messy.

Two hours later, his wound cleaned and bandaged but not sutured, Jhally was sound asleep in my brother's old bedroom. He appeared to have come through the impromptu surgery well enough. Clearly, Gaps were a hearty species. Perhaps it was due to having the three, versus two, chromosomes I mused. In the end, I played it safe and removed a good portion of his leg, including his knee joint. Since doctor's prescriptions were a thing of the past, and drugs now unregulated, I already had a good stock of both antibiotics and pain meds on hand. I had to guess what dosage to use on a typical Gap, Throwing the proverbial dice; I simply doubled whatever dosage was recommended on the bottles. I wondered if Jhally's leg really would grow back. I knew if typical lizards' tails were cut off they would, in fact, grow back. Perhaps the alien Gap invaders really were related somehow to our domestic, lowly, home-spun reptilian critters.

Bleary-eyed from lack of sleep, I was in my truck, racing toward town. An earlier phone call, from Gap Marshal Steel, let me know my presence was required at the OEC building. I was to be interviewed by none other than Sleept Vogthner himself, the Gap's North American Sector Chancellor of Communications. I'd given little thought to the whole Dalm Mor Stroph and Charles the bull fiasco since yesterday.

I pulled into the OEC building's parking lot, maneuvering my oversized F-250 into a space better suited to hold an economy car than a big truck. Before climbing out, I watched nearby comings and goings of both Humans and Gaps. It occurred to me that upon entering this facility, I might not be exiting it any time soon—if ever. Getting out, I headed for the entrance. I felt, then heard, a familiar rumbling vibration penetrating down from above, as a Milonge Bi-Hull transport descended and landed atop the building's rooftop. Dollars to donuts it was Sleept Vogthner, Chancellor of

Communications, arriving to interview Matt, Donny, and me. *Shit!*

chapter 20

I entered the OEC building so deep in thought I didn't notice the three Gap marshals. Standing side by side in the corridor, they presented an impenetrable blockade in front of me.

"Hold up, citizen," said the Gap on the left. His name tag read, CROSS. "State your full name . . . what your business is here today." Marshal Cross accessed his ear puck's virtual HUD screen. Using a long, curled nail, he readied to enter the information, his eyes met mine.

"Brian Polk, and I have an appointment. You fellas called me this morning."

Hearing my name, the three Gaps stared at me with renewed interest. Marshal Cross began tapping on his ear puck HUD with a little more gusto.

"Stand to the side. Let these people through."

I did as asked. Four Humans moved past me, each giving

me a quick glance in the process. Their darting eyes revealed their internal thoughts: *What did he do to get himself in such hot water? Better him than me.*

"Ah . . . Captain Brian Polk!" A Gap was halfway down the staircase to my left—descending with uncommon agility for someone so large. His voice was an octave higher than most Earupitans, his diction one a Harvard English professor would envy. None of the typical southern twang to this guy's voice. It was Sleept Vogthner, the Gap's Chancellor of Communications. Today, instead of wearing the customary blue jeans and snap-button cowboy shirt, he wore a tailored dark-gray business suit, with a striped red and blue silk tie. Stepping onto the waxed linoleum floor, I noticed his dress shoes were polished to a mirror-like shine.

Gesturing at the three marshals with an irritated wave of his hand, he said, "Don't you have something to do? Go!"

His smile returned as he approached me. Tilting his head, he held out a clawed hand for me to shake. *That's a new one,* I thought. I couldn't remember a time when any Gap purposely had physical contact with a Human, other than with a clenched fist or the toe of a boot.

"So very good to meet you. May I call you Brian . . . or do you prefer Captain Polk?"

"Um, Brian is fine. I've been out of the service for well over three years now," I said, though I had little doubt the Chancellor already knew everything about me, including my military background.

"I so appreciate you coming in today for this little visit," presenting his outstretched palm before me. "Shall we?"

We climbed the stairs together in silence. Halfway up to

the top landing he hesitated. "Brian, I would like you and me to be friends. Do you think that is possible? Earth Human . . . friends, with an alien, Earupitan dignitary? Is that even remotely possible?"

Fuck no! I thought, though I tried to look as if I were pondering the question. "Sure, anything is possible, I guess," I lied.

The chancellor's expression turned pensive. "Truth be known, Brian, I don't have many friends on this planet." Smiling, he added, "Of either species."

We reached the top of the stairs on the second floor. "This way. Familiar with this building, Brian?" he asked.

"A little. Though I think all my business before took place on the first floor."

Sleept nodded. "Yes, down on the first floor is where most Human services are located. On this floor you'll find our Technology and Health Services departments." He gestured toward a series of large, floor-to-ceiling tinted windows on our left. Behind them, I could just barely make out a series of eight, glowing, three-dimensional rectangles—each one the approximate size of an old-fashioned phone booth. All were spinning round and round on their axis in perfect unison with one another.

"This is our Quantum Manifold System. It's comprised of those eight spinning Causal Intelligence Nodes. Think of Causal Intelligence as, well, as the great-great-great-grandfather of what you may remember as AI, or Artificial Intelligence, here on Earth. Needless to say, this system is incredibly robust. Computing power your Human scientists would ascribe to being nothing short of Godlike. With its sheer number-crunching capabilities, its ability to decipher mathematical probabilities, is . . . what is the Human term for it? Oh yes, mind- blowing!"

I already knew much of what Chancellor Sleept Vogthner was telling me. What he failed to mention was the Quantum Manifold System was also the computing power behind the Gap's Prime Network system. The same system my new covert agent, Marshal Grip, had successfully hacked into just two days prior. We stood silently together for a few more moments, watching the glowing phone-like booths flip round and round.

"Let's keep going, Brian. Next, we have our Health Services Department. Services utilized by us . . . aliens to you. Of course, Humans still have their own physicians and medical facilities elsewhere."

We were now walking past one open door after another. Like individual hospital rooms, Gap patients were curled up on beds. Medical devices that looked highly advanced populated the back walls of each room. I thought of Jhally. How he would have benefited from such cool technology on his festering leg. We slowed as we approached another room. Here, too, the door was open. Inside were two Gap medical personnel conversing with a patient sitting up in bed; a very large patient—probably eight-feet-tall in height. What I found most surprising was that Dalm Mor Stroph, the carnival-show freak who'd tried to lift poor Charles the bull over his head, was now doing his best to converse with two Gap doctors.

"This is an interesting case. Dalm, here, was apparently struck in the neck by a cow's horn."

I almost corrected the chancellor. Charles was a bull, not a cow. But I kept my mouth shut.

"His tongue was lacerated, and his brain stem pierced. Both will be as good as new in a matter of days. And with the help of that Quantum Manifold System we passed down the hall, we will be able to virtually reconstitute all his disrupted synapses. His memories will return showing far more detail even more vivid than ever before."

"You can do that? Repair one's brain? Bring back lost memories?" I asked.

"Most certainly. Take the big lug on the bed in there," the chancellor said, with a smile. "Not only will he be back to work in a matter of days, better than ever, but our EMS investigative team will have a viewable reconstructed memory file to work with . . . one which will be used to reconstitute the detailed course of events that occurred within the carnival tent during the Friends Unite Day festivities. I believe you were there . . . witnessed the dreadful ordeal?"

I nodded. "Yeah, I shot Charlie, the bull," I said, making a grim face.

"Yes, yes . . . I know. We're going to get into all that in just a bit. Have ourselves a good talk."

I glanced back at the oversized patient and realized the giant Gap was looking at me. I thought I saw recognition in his eyes, but it could have been my imagination.

We climbed the stairs to the third floor in silence. The chancellor was letting the whole Dalm Mor Stroph situation sink in. I was well-aware he was toying with me, letting me see for myself that the Gaps suspected foul play.

"And here we have the Enforcement Department . . . which pretty much takes up the whole third floor."

I saw armed marshals milling around, along with a goodly number of Humans. Five men and one woman were seated, their chairs placed against a wall, each handcuffed to the chair. Ignored by the chancellor, we strode past them and turned left at a narrow hallway. We passed three empty, brightly-lit, windowed interview rooms. We came to a stop at the fourth room, occupied by two individuals. On one side of the metal table was an irritated-looking Gap marshal, while across from him was none other than Donny Kuruk. His face was badly bruised, his swollen right eye partially closed. His bottom lip was bloodied, split in several places.

"You are friends with the Indian boy in here . . . am I correct about that?"

I continued to stare into the interview room. My heart rate was already elevated so I needed to control my breathing. I pictured myself pummeling *mister fancy-pants* next to me, the sanctimonious asshole. The only reason I managed to hold it together was because I knew I was going to kill this piece of shit someday soon. Without looking at him, I said, "He's a Native American . . . and yes, we're friends." I then turned to stare up at the chancellor. "Why do you ask?"

"Why?" he asked back incredulously.

"Well, you've pummeled the living shit out of my friend in there. Something I wouldn't have recommended doing. Donny's not one you want to piss off."

"Is that a threat, Brian? Are you threatening me?"

I merely shrugged as I turned back to watch the interview going on inside the room. "No, not a threat at all," I lied. "What is it you want from him? From me?"

"You know we are watching you. Your movements . . . your

associations. Listening to your telephone conversations. You have become what we call 'a person of interest'."

I shrugged. "That's fine. I think you'll discover, or continue to discover, that my life is as boring as hell. I'm a history teacher and a rancher. But hey, knock yourself out."

"Remember me telling you about the Quantum Manifold System on the second floor?"

I nodded.

"About its number-crunching capabilities, its keen ability to decipher mathematical probabilities?"

Instead of replying, startled, I stared into the interrogation room right before us. I watched the marshal stand up then backhand Donny with a hard blow across the face. One that normally would have knocked Donny across the room, if he weren't fastened down by handcuffs to his chair. Donny spit blood onto the floor then smiled back at his abuser. I couldn't hear what was being said inside the room, but I watched Donny being Donny. My friend's behavior could be incredibly annoying. If I were to guess, Donny had said something insulting. Maybe called the Gap marshal, a bumbling *shit shot*—one of his favorites.

The Chancellor continued. ". . . so when a typically quiet small town, such as Castle Rock . . . with its near-zero crime rate, all of a sudden has a flurry of issues, this computer is going to notice. It's going to inform us that the probabilities of such things occurring are way out of whack. Imagine, then, two alien marshals going missing on the same day. Their HovT smashed up after colliding into a tall oak tree. And you witnessed what happened to poor Dalm Mor Stroph . . . the very next day. Add onto those occurrences a series of strange comings and goings by certain individuals, ones we were already quite interested in. Well, the truth is, we didn't need the Quantum Manifold System to tell us something nefarious was afoot."

Actually, I was relieved to hear the EMS didn't have even more data. With all the stuff the Takebacks were up to these days, things could have been a lot worse. It didn't seem that our session today was any more than a rousting, an attempt to get more information out of me. I figured I'd probably be the next one handcuffed in that room. Matt, too, would have his turn. No *big* deal.

The Chancellor placed a heavy claw upon my shoulder. "But Brian, when a prominent, outstanding citizen is so brutally murdered in his own home, clearly, our quiet little town of Castle Rock has become something else. Something has changed here for the worse."

I turned to stare up at the Chancellor. "Murdered? Who's been murdered?"

I realized he'd been watching me. Watching my reactions.

"One of the few dear friends I had in your community. In fact, he was to be one of the first Humans to work alongside Earupitans in this same building. Ronald Gant. I believe you know him. Although the word is you haven't always seen eye to eye with the man. Maybe we should start right there. Let's have ourselves a little powwow on the matter. There's an empty room right next door."

chapter 21

I tasted blood as it streamed down inside my nose and into my mouth. As far as beatings go, I'd received far worse than this one. And, surprisingly, it was not at the hand of a Gap, like the green alien sitting across from me now. It occurred about seven years ago. I was in my mid-twenties, halfway through flight school at Randolph Air Force Base, in San Antonio, Texas. A cocky, smart-mouthed junior pilot, I thought my shit didn't stink. One night, off the military base at a local redneck bar with fellow U.S. Air Force pilots, four of us became just a little too boisterous. With too many brews consumed, and not enough food in our bellies, one of our cohorts kicked the proverbial hornet's nest. He gave one of the pretty ladies in our midst an affectionate slap on her backside. As it turned out, she was the girlfriend of one of the local cowboys. An honest to god bar fight broke out next. Suddenly, the four of us were up against no less than ten *redneck* good ol' boys. In my own defense, I wasn't the guy who'd slapped the beautiful girl's derrière. But, being a good team player, I sided with the squad of drunken flyboys. By the time the two local sheriffs rolled into the establishment, we'd battered seven locals onto the floor.

We were all standing, our fists raised, but what came at us next was the biggest surprise of all. To our dismay, both sheriffs pulled their batons and joined the group opposing us—the local shit-kickers—in the fight. It ended quickly. To this day, I believe the two sheriffs continued to beat us with their sticks even after they knocked us out. It took weeks for me to look in the mirror without wincing, seeing my splotchy red reflection.

So, yeah, though I'd just received a few backhanded slaps, a couple of punches to the face from an interrogating Gap lizard, I honestly wasn't worried about it. Not yet, anyway. For one thing, the questions—repeated over and over—were strictly about the course of events that took place in the carnival tent. It was more about them wanting to ensure no funny business had gone on, than having any real evidence we'd done something wrong. As long as the giant Gap's memory stayed fuzzy, we'd be fine. Apparently, my EMS interrogator did not suspect me of having anything to do with Ronald Gant's murder, nor suspect me of having five Gap Shredders in my barn back home.

"Tell me again . . . why would you grab a marshal's service weapon? That alone is a capital offense; one that demands quick justice. Namely, your execution!"

I didn't buy it. I figured if I were to be executed, that course of action would already have taken place. Nope, I was pretty sure they were only fishing at this point.

"My concern was for poor Dalm Mor Stroph," I said. "

He'd taken a mighty blow, either to his head or his neck, and that damn bull was still thrashing about. Truth is, I believe my actions saved the marshal from further injury. Frankly, I'm surprised you're not thanking me. Hell, pinning a medal to my chest."

The Gap instead leered back at me. I was fairly certain another backhand slap was in the works when a large shape stepped close to the room's observation window. Outside, in the hallway, stood Sleept Vogthner, Chancellor of Communications. I wondered if he'd been watching the long interview in its two-hour entirety, or if he was just now checking in on us. Seeing him there, expressionless, something else occurred to me. His eyes were set a bit farther apart than other Gaps, and his coloring was off. Like Jhally, this Gap was not an Earupitan, he was a Mannarian, which certainly explained his higher level of intelligence, but not his allegiance to the Earupitans. The way Jhally had explained it to me, the Mannarians despised the Earupitans, although they kept their feelings a secret.

The Chancellor gave a nod to the marshal, now standing before me. I wasn't sure what that meant. *Was I wrong? Was the marshal just given a subtle order to execute me right here and now? Shit!* The truth was, I never did see Donny get escorted out past the window. I wondered if Donny was already dead.

"You can go," the interrogator said, rising to his feet. He came around the table and unlocked the shackles on my wrists. I heard them clank to the floor.

"Just like that? And we were just getting to know each other."

The alien gave me a disapproving glance before opening the door and heading away. I used the back of my hand to wipe the blood off my upper lip. The chancellor stepped into the room then stared down his reptile snout at me.

"My friend, Donny . . . who was next door?" I asked.

"He was released an hour ago," he said.

"Okay . . . I hope you've got everything you need from me . . . from us."

"Your stories don't perfectly match. There were a number of discrepancies."

I didn't react to that, only wondered which one of us had screwed up, gone off script. "Well, I'm not sure what to say about that."

"No need to say anything. It would be far more suspicious if all three of you had given us the exact same accounting of events. No, for now anyway, I am content none of you possessed criminal intentions. So only one of you will be facing charges."

"Charges?" I asked.

"You did fire an unlawful weapon in the presence of an EMS officer, did you not, Brian?"

"Against a thrashing, two thousand pound bull!"

The Chancellor held his stern gaze for a full ten seconds before smiling. "Got you . . ." he said, pointing a long clawed finger toward my abdomen. *Had this alien just pranked me?* It took a moment for me to redirect my facial muscles, provide back with some semblance of a smile.

"You certainly did, chancellor . . . you certainly did."

Placing a hand on my back, he gestured for me to now exit. "I hope there are no hard feelings, Brian. Sometimes my job requires a bit of nastiness. You understand, don't you?"

"Well, I know you have a difficult job. I sure wouldn't want it," I replied.

He proceeded to walk me out of the Enforcement Department then back down the main corridor. A nervous-looking, fast-moving young Gap marshal approached us. "Sir?"

The Chancellor turned to listen to the underling. Speaking in low tones, I did hear the words *Prime Network,* as well as *intrusions,* mentioned. The Chancellor nodded several times, looking concerned, then sent the young marshal away.

"I'm sorry, Brian, but I must attend to urgent business. About to move away, he abruptly turned back to face me. "I was wondering, would you be . . . interested in having lunch with me sometime this week? Here in town?"

The question nearly floored me. Why in hell would he want to have lunch with me? Wasn't this the same sack dragger that had just me interrogated and slapped around? "Sure, that would be fine," I said, hoping he wasn't too proficient reading Human expressions.

By the time I was halfway home, I was in a relatively good mood. Sure, there was the chance I could be dragged back to the OEC again. But this time, the charges would stick and I'd be executed. I had growing concerns, too, about the idiot giant's memory coming back. But I only needed a few days more to finalize our plans. After that, it was time for a payback. A payback I doubted I'd survive.

All of a sudden, the sun above became momentarily blocked, and the road ahead fell into deep shadow. Peering through the windshield, I watched a kind of Gap Troop Carrier vessel make its way south. As the flatbed open aircraft flew past me overhead, I could see two thousand, or so, armed Gap soldiers packed together within the big flying *Frisbee.* I'd witnessed two similar craft earlier this morning, also headed in the same direction. It looked like the infantry troops on board were readying for battle. The only problem was—no one was left to go to battle against, the Gaps had already won the war on Earth.

chapter 22

Gauz Za Chiv proudly wore his uniform's new additions; he took every opportunity to parade around in front of his troops to show them off. Still the same black and red colors of the Earupitan Landing Forces, but he now wore ornate shoulder epaulets and several new colorful ribbons upon his chest. The Hammer Fist patch, worn upon his upper arm, was now a bright, reflective gold. No longer the uniform of a Commander, Level 2, but that of a General, Level 8. Apparently, all due to his two highly successful land campaigns—first, for European Sector's Valle d'Aosta, Italy and then, North American Sector's, Armonk, New York. Surprisingly, the two successful eradications had made an impression upon his Eminence, Overlord Skith. And he'd recently learned that the campaign covering this small township would be the final one of their Phase II tests. Next, would come worldwide deployment and mass extinction of the entire Human race—all based on Chiv's recent small townships campaigns. Only then would the hundreds of thousands of armed Earupitan ground forces, and many hundreds of the far larger atomizer domes, be deployed in a unilateral, worldwide, onslaught.

Chiv barked off orders to his junior officers. The assembly bots were to be unloaded off the nearby XL5 Crusher lander vessel. It would be hours yet before the Human roundups would commence.

Chiv noticed the approach of the HovT craft. He'd reached out to the local Chancellor of Communications, Sleept Vogthner, just an hour earlier, requesting his prompt presence here on site. The confinement pens and the atomizer dome weren't assembled yet, so—as far as anyone else was concerned—the site looked just like any other military encampment.

Chiv raised a scaly, green hand high in the air, signaling the HovT where to land. He turned away as debris swirled underneath the lowering craft, and only turned back once the craft had settled on the ground and one of the gull-wing doors lifted up. General Chiv approached the surprisingly well-dressed, albeit garbed in a ridiculous Human business suit, Chancellor. "Thank you for coming here on such short notice, Chancellor Vogthner. Please open up the other door for me. We're going for a short ride." Sleept Vogthner did as asked, then waited for the military leader to take his seat.

Lifting off, Chancellor of Communications Sleept Vogthner appraised the small military leader with a quick sideways glance. Gazing out through the side window, he noticed more ground forces now hurrying down the gangway of the oversized Crusher lander ship. Already aware of the newly arrived ground forces in Castle Rock, he, too, had witnessed the disk-like, open-air transports whisking from one indeterminate location to another. Word had it, some kind of military exercise was going on. But, then again, there was evidence to the contrary.

"Chancellor, I am General Gauz Za Chiv. Chiv pointed a clawed finger toward the distant horizon. "Let's take a little flying jump to that large rock over there."

Vogthner nodded and adjusted their new course setting appropriately. "I was surprised to receive your summons this morning. It sounded important, so I rearranged my schedule for you." Vogthner wanted to make it clear to Chiv he wasn't part of his military hierarchy. In fact, as far as he was concerned, they held approximately equal levels of authority.

"Let's set down right on top of that rock. Would that be possible, Chancellor Vogthner?" the general asked.

"Of course!" High above the massive block of solid granite, Vogthner began his descent—the HovT's landing thrusters fully engaged. General Chiv had his door swinging upward, began climbing out, even before the craft had fully set down. Vogthner, after powering down the small craft, also climbed out. Seeing the general standing close to the edge of the rock, Vogthner went over and joined him. He never much liked heights but tried not to let show his present discomfort.

"We're four hundred feet above the supporting plateau. Did you know the township, Castle Rock, was named after this castle-shaped natural rock monument?" Vogthner asked, standing at General Chiv's side. Before their eyes, the quaint little town nestled a thousand feet below. In the distance were several upscale neighborhoods, although mostly sprawling ranchlands encompassed the hilly landscape. Vogthner continued, "I understand that native Human tribes once inhabited this land. The Arapaho and Cheyenne people."

"Like the Humans living on this world today, all are primitive savages," General Chiv said in disgust, turning toward Vogthner.

Easily a head shorter, Vogthner was taken aback by the general's two misaligned eyes. Not wanting to offend the officer, he chose the right eye to sustain his visual contact with. Vogthner said, "Some Humans are more tolerable to be around than others, I suppose."

"No, Chancellor, that is a fallacy," Chiv said. "And there lies the crux of the problem. There are some of you who have lived amongst these barbaric alien Humans far too long. You have become overly indoctrinated in accepting their primitive society. Look at you. All dressed up, wearing that absurd humankind costume."

Only then did Vogthner notice the small energy pistol gripped within one of the general's claws.

"His Eminence Overlord Skith has personally spoken to me of this issue," the general continued. "How Phase I deployments here, many thousands of you, have, over the past two years, become contaminated. Coming into such close contact with these fetid Humans . . . well, we should have expected as much. But I must be honest with you. The killing of so many of our brethren Earupitans, mostly marshals, in the township of Armonk . . . well, it was quite difficult."

Vogthner had heard bits and pieces, rumors mostly, of what recently occurred in two far-away townships—some kind of mass killing spree. But he had never believed it. He had not been informed by his superiors that any such thing had occurred. *Since when did Earupitans scheme to kill off more Humans, and even their own kind?* It was unheard of. But studying General Chiv, now standing before him, he realized it was all true and a deep sadness gripped his heart. In truth, he liked this place. He even liked several of the Humans who lived here and had been looking forward to this maybe being his forever home. "So all the Phase I personnel across the globe are to be eliminated?"

General Chiv shrugged, then nodded in assent. "But I wanted to handle this one aspect . . . you and me . . . personally. As one of the few Mannarians living among us, I thought you should know . . . soon all of your kind, along with Humans, will be stricken from this world. The mere thought of *off-worlders* like you breeding with our kind, our females . . . well, it sickens me." He raised the pistol and pointed it at Vogthner's chest. "Any last words, Chancellor?"

It was clear to Vogthner this truly was the end. The only real decision to be made was how he would go. "Yes, just one thing . . . a Human phrase I learned just recently: Fuck you and the horse you rode in on." With that, Chancellor of Communications Sleept Vogthner took a step backward into the empty void behind him. Before falling, he had enough time to catch the utter look of surprise in General Chiv's wide open, cockeyed stare.

chapter 23

The kitchen wall phone began to ring. I answered, "Hello?"

"Hey."

"Good to hear you're still among the living!" I said.

Donny chuckled. "That rousting was total bullshit. But whatever . . . all's well that ends well."

"You hear from Matt?" I asked.

"Yeah, he's here with me. Think he got the worst of it. Looks like he has a broken nose. But hey, are we still on . . . um . . . for bowling tonight?" Donny asked.

Bowling was our code word for holding another late-night meeting. "Yeah, but not all of us will be able to make it. Our out of town expert player has been held up with an injury. Could take a few days to recover. But I'll call around, make sure the rest of the bowling team's here to practice anyway."

"Got it. Hey, you hear about Ronald—"

I cut him off, knowing the line was probably tapped. "Let's talk later about that." I glanced over at Karen, now walking into the kitchen. "You up for bowling later tonight?"

Furrowing her brow, she shook her head. Then, as if changing her mind, she nodded. "Yeah. I think that might be good for me. I'm in."

Once I'd hung up the phone, I felt we needed to finish our talk about Ronald Gant. "So, as you can see, Jhally wasn't in any condition to go about killing anyone. It may end up being one of those things we never quite figure out. But I'm sorry for your loss, Karen."

She stood at the threshold into the kitchen, both arms wrapped about her. I had the feeling she just wanted to leave. Be anywhere but here with me. "Hey, I've got a bunch of monotonous chores to do around here. You don't need to stick around."

"You want me to leave?" she asked, her voice soft.

"No, of course not." I said, surprised by her answer. "Um, you want to help?"

She nodded, "What do you want me to do?"

"I need to feed Jhally soon. Could you head on over to the barn? Pluck one of those lobsters out of the trough. Just be careful, don't let its pinchers grab a hold of you."

She smiled and said, "I'll be careful," then left through the front door.

I headed back to my brother's bedroom. Jhally awoke midway through my changing of his bandages. Through half-open eyelids, I saw him fighting to stay awake. I'd given him another dose of painkillers and he was fading fast.

"Your flight training must continue, Brian," he murmured, his words slurred.

"I agree, but that little stunt of yours put the kibosh on that."

Once his momentary confusion passed, I continued, "Did you think I wouldn't figure it out? That you'd killed Gant?" Jhally closed his eyes, but I could tell he was still conscious. "Six miles there and six miles back on foot, no wonder your stump got so jammed up."

"He had proof . . . of your Takebacks. Photographs, documents, in his home." I wasn't surprised. "You . . ."

"Destroyed . . . everything," he said

"That's all well and good, but I believe our time is running out, Jhally. And you're in no condition to play flight instructor."

He swallowed and said, "You will have to take my place."

"That would be like the blind leading the blind."

"I anticipated this setback. Go to Shredder Five. I preprogrammed a virtual mentor for you . . . just sit in the forward seat."

I had no idea what he was talking about. I shook his shoulder. "Hey . . . still with me? You want to try to eat something?"

Jhally's faint breaths had turned into soft snoring. He'd fallen into a deep sleep state.

I left the house to look for Karen in the barn. Tell her to forget about the lobster for now, but she was nowhere to be found. I checked over by the stables and even went up into the hayloft. Halfway down the ladder, I wondered if she had decided to go home after all. Then my eyes caught a flickering of light on the other side of the barn, shining within Shredder Five's cockpit.

By the time I climbed up onto the craft's wing, the canopy had been retracted and Karen was waving me closer. "Get over here!"

Seated in the forward seat, she said, "I just wanted to steal a moment in this ship. God, I miss flying. Then suddenly things started to come alive in here. I heard Jhally's voice . . . and then he was here, like right in front of me. Well, not really him, but a projected virtual version of him. He was giving me instructions." She looked up at me, her excitement contagious.

I smiled back at her. "Jhally told me about that. He wanted to make sure we'd still continue with our training until he was back on his feet."

"You mean foot," she corrected.

"Ha, ha," I said, smirking.

"Can we go through the training? Together?" she asked.

I looked at the virtual projection of Jhally. His image had either frozen, or maybe paused when Karen opened the canopy. "I think it's meant for a solo pilot seated in the front seat."

She pursed her lips, then suddenly leaned forward. "Get in! Step in behind me. I'll sit on your lap. We can both watch it, learn together."

About to protest I realized it just might work. Since Gaps

were far larger than Humans in size, there probably was room enough for two. "Hold on." Climbing down from the craft, I sprinted toward the far end of the barn and slid the two rear barn doors open. By the time I returned to the Shredder, I was out of breath, huffing and puffing away.

Standing below Karen, she waved me up to come sit behind her, then leaned forward, giving me a bit more room in which to maneuver. Settling myself down in the seat, she looked back over her shoulder, catching me looking at her perfect rear end. She rolled her eyes then sat down on my lap. Tapping a button, the canopy began to slide forward, soon enveloping us within its tinted enclosure.

We listened as Jhally started up again, going through much of the same information he'd conveyed to me the previous night in person. It was a good review, though mostly I was distracted. Karen's hair tickled my nose and I could smell her fragrant strawberry-scented shampoo. She turned her head back and asked, "Are you even paying attention to this?"

"Of course. "He's going over the flight's various controls."

I felt the warmth of her trim body perched snugly atop my lap and had to really struggle to concentrate on Jhally's voice.

Then his voice stopped. I peered over Karen's shoulder and saw the projection had again been halted. She'd figured out how to pause the virtual training lesson.

I took that to mean she wanted to talk. Karen often was an introspective girl: Her mind always spinning—working overtime.

"I think we should talk about us," she said, not turning her head around this time.

"Us? Karen, there hasn't been an 'us' for a long time. Ever

since you broke things off—"

Nearly turning around in my lap, she exclaimed, "Me?!"

"You told me *this* wasn't working. You said you didn't see our relationship moving forward," I said.

She looked back at me as if I were speaking a foreign language.

"I never did feel I could compete with your husband. That you'd ever want to make room in your heart for someone else."

"So, let me get this straight . . . you thought I was breaking up with you?"

"You *were* breaking up with me," I said back, defiantly. "Weren't you?"

Karen slowly shook her head side to side. "No, I was not. It wasn't me who wasn't ready for a relationship, it was you. You'd lost both your parents and your brother in a matter of months. You were so saddled with guilt and heartache you just closed yourself off and became a rock emotionally."

I listened to her, wanting to protest, to tell her it was she who'd been closed off, not me. But now I wasn't sure. I looked up and our eyes met.

"Do you know how shattered my life was . . . after you left me that night? How long it took for my heart to stop missing a beat just hearing your name? Damn it, Brian, I was in love with you!"

I let that sink in. I thought about everything she'd said. "I don't know what to say. Maybe it *was* me? I do know one thing . . ."

"What's that?"

"I never stopped loving you. I haven't dated anyone else. I spend every night with the various Takebacks groups, vetting the new applicants, and overseeing their individual crimes against the Gaps. Making sure they have skin in the game. I've had no life since we—"

Karen suddenly leaned forward to get up off my lap. *Shit!* I'd said something wrong. But if she were going to leave, storm off, she needed to open the damn canopy first. Resigned to the fact our conversation was a total clusterfuck, I reached for the button. Karen slapped my hand away. She wasn't trying to leave; instead, she had turned completely around atop my lap. We were now face to face. Placing a finger over my swollen, split lips, she gave me a mischievous smile then kissed me. Gently and tender at first, our passion grew ever hotter from there. We made love seated together in Shredder Five's cockpit. All the while, the paused virtual projection of Jhally looked on. Once it was over, both of us sweating and out of breath, Karen leaned close and whispered in my ear, "Can we still fly this thing . . . together?"

"I think that can be arranged."

She reached into her back pocket for her cell phone, then held it out at arm's length.

"You do know cell phones don't work anymore . . ."

Karen rolled her eyes and I heard the telltale click of a photo being taken.

"Do you think making love in a Gap Shredder constitutes us having skin in the game?" she asked, showing me the selfie she took of the two of us. The image left no doubt we were seated together within a Shredder cockpit.

"But how are you going to forward that picture to me

without cell service?"

She shrugged, "Hmm, good question."

chapter 24

Now airborne, we took turns at the controls, listening to, and watching Jhally give virtual flight instructions. The Shredder was surprisingly easy to fly. Intuitive and forgiving, its maneuverability was remarkable. With my right arm wrapped around Karen's waist, my hand snugly grasped the center control sphere. I eased the ball to the right—turning it ten degrees in the process. Immediately, the Shredder responded—the fuselage angled on its centerline axis and we banked into a slow turn, three hundred feet midway across the Polk property. I let my hand drift lower and the craft, in turn, descended so fast my stomach lurched.

"You have to employ a subtle hand with this vessel," Karen said. "Give it to me. It's my turn, so stop hogging the controls." She tapped my hand away from the center control sphere. And so it went in the air for close to five hours. We followed Jhally's virtual mini-training instructions several times until there was nothing more to learn. The rest of the time we explored what the lightning-fast ship was capable of. What we hadn't learned, would need Jhally's help with, was how to use the onboard navigation AI. Also, how to initialize the various weapons systems.

"We should head back to the barn," I whispered into Karen's ear.

"I'm having too much fun to go back," she said, "but I do have to pee even more so . . . so I think you're right. Mind if I take her in?"

"Not at all," I said, as I kissed the nape of her neck.

Karen headed home once we'd landed the Shredder back inside the barn. Mort and I then made a quick trip into town for groceries, plus a few other odds and ends. When I arrived back at the house, I was surprised to find Jhally sitting up in bed. I could see he had taken it upon himself to clean his bloodied stump and change the bandage. He was working an ear puck device—his upper body partially obscured by the bluish HUD display. We'd retrieved two pucks from Marshals Black and Clark after they were killed in my barn. Jhally kept one of them, and the other went to my hacker buddy, Mike Post. Mike had ingeniously hacked the devices' code so not only Gaps could operate the devices, but Humans too. The update to the code had gone out all across the Prime Network making all ear pucks universally compatible across the globe—maybe even the universe. Jhally had disabled both the identification and TBGLU functionality, so the two units couldn't be tracked. It made me a little nervous to see Jhally using the device, but at this point, if he was going to screw us, there wasn't much I could do about it.

"Feeling better?" I asked, looking in on him.

"Yes, thank you. My fever has subsided. Pain is manageable."

"I got you a present." I held up an adjustable aluminum crutch I'd just purchased at a medical supply store in town. "You'll have to configure the size to fit your own height."

Jhally eyed the crutch. "I could have used that a year ago."

I shrugged. "Didn't know you were tromping around the property at night back then. But if you don't want it, I can take it back."

"No, I will be able to utilize this item until my leg grows back."

I looked at his stump. "How long do you think that will take?"

"About three weeks."

"That's incredible!" I then cringed. "I guess I really blew it, suturing up your leg in past months like I did."

Jhally asked, "Did you enjoy your time in the Shredder?"

"I did," I said, wondering if he somehow knew about Karen's and my impromptu lovemaking. "It's an amazing craft. Thank you for the virtual instructions. I'm getting the hang of it, I think."

"That is good."

"But there are a few things you left out of your instructions . . . like the use of the navigational AI and initializing the weaponry."

Jhally seemed to ponder on that. "That last functionality will best be demonstrated in person. One mistake could be catastrophic. Deadly."

"Well, whenever you're up to it. So you ready now to slurp down a bug or two?"

That suggestion seemed to brighten Jhally's mood. "Yes, I think two would be good. I seem to have regained my appetite."

After feeding Jhally, I began making phone calls to my Takebacks—letting each of them know that tonight would be another late-night training session get-together, under the guise of team bowling. There were more than a few moans and complaints about my last minute notice. Halfway through my call list, I had an incoming call.

"Brian!"

I recognized the voice but didn't say anything.

"Okay . . . fine, Polybius."

"That you, Titus?"

"Have you seen them?"

"What are you talking about? Seen who?" I asked.

"All the Gap troops at the outskirts of town . . . thousands of them. An obvious deployment, how could you not know what's going on there?"

My mind flashed back to the open-air troop carriers I'd been seeing of late. "They're probably only performing military exercises. I wouldn't give it too much—"

"Then why have they constructed a compound? And that big ginormous igloo-thing being assembled?"

"Igloo? Titus, I honestly don't know what the hell you're rambling on about. In any event, we're getting together for a bowling meeting later—"

But Titus wasn't finished. "It's a damn dome of some sort. And there are cordoned-off areas that look like holding pens. Fuck, man, you're not getting it! This is it! You don't have to be a genius to put all the pieces together."

Neither of us spoke for several seconds. *Was it really possible?* "So you're thinking that dome is for . . . what?"

"Don't be a moron, Polk . . . it's got to be some kind of death chamber. They're going to round everyone up and gas us, or something. Why else have all those armed troops? Why the holding pens?"

"Just hold on. Let's not do anything rash, okay, Titus? Remember, we have a plan. Sure, it's early and we don't have all the details set in place yet, but we just need a few more days."

"You're not getting it. Either you're in denial or just plain stupid, I don't know which, but time's up, man. We either mobilize now, or we accept their leading the lambs to slaughter scenario."

I thought hard about what he was saying. I had to admit he could be right.

"It's time I bring Betty out of mothballs," he said.

I knew he was referring to his pieced-together M1 Abrams tank. I was about to tell him to just wait. That we'd meet later tonight and come up with a new, more expedited plan that would put that tank of his to good use. But deep down I suspected we might not have much time. "Titus . . . I can't tell you what to do, but I do think you're right, for what it's worth. I guess it's now or never to put whatever assets we have to good use. Even if it's a lost cause at this point."

"I'm glad we're finally on the same page. Too bad it's taken us until now, the end of days," he said.

"Could you at least hold off 'till dark? Say, nine o'clock tonight?"

"I guess. Yeah, it'll probably take me that long to get everything up and running by then. FYI, I've called my other cell members . . . looks like I'll have a full crew . . . be locked and loaded for bear."

"Good. So your plan then is take out that dome?" I asked.

"That and kill as many of their Gap troops as humanly possible. Bring our own form of whoop-ass to them before we're turned into hamburger meat. Hopefully, give you a diversion. Let you get those birds of yours airborne so you can do your thing too."

As soon as we hung up, I called my hacker friend Mike Post. By this time I'd pretty much given up using our pseudonyms. Even if my phone line was being tapped, someone listening in, I suspected it would take the EMS hours, if not days, to take any action over our conversations.

"Mike!"

"Polybius . . . what's—"

"Listen up, it's going down now, tonight."

Mike hesitated. "Um, okay . . . not sure what that means exactly."

"It means it's *go time*, time we make our stand. It's now or never. So if you have any last minute intel . . ."

"Some," he said sounding nervous. "Marshal Grip still believes he's one of Jhally's Covert Actions Group agents. I've gone back and forth with him using that Gap ear puck device you gave me. Although he's super nervous talking to me—"

"Mike, just get to the point!"

"Oh, yeah, sorry. It seems there's been a change in the frequency of Gap trips flying up and back to those mother ships in high orbit. That Milonge Bi-Hull transport lands and takes off from the OEC building on most nights now."

"Tonight? Will it be making a trip tonight?"

"I don't know. We have no way of knowing that," Mike said defensively.

"We're going to need that clearance . . . to enter the Solaris Habitat."

Mike laughed sarcastically. "Sure, coming right up. There's no way for that to happen. Remember, I thought we still had days, even weeks, to pull everything together. I only have limited access to the Prim Network via this ear puck thingy."

"Get a hold of Marshal Grip and tell him he'll have to hack the Prime Network . . . Tell him something, *anything*, to motivate him. Tell him he'll be first in line to get one of those female worm bitches up in space . . . just try, Mike."

"All right, I'll do my best."

chapter 25

The Takebacks started arriving around eight o'clock in the evening, some four hours earlier than expected. But by now, of course, word was out all across Castle Rock, and its neighboring communities. Clearly, the Gap invaders were up to something with the arrival of so many ground forces—perhaps preparing to mount another, maybe final, military offensive. Everyone was scared, fearing the worst. To be honest, I'd expected most of my Takeback comrades to remain with their families—even going so far as to barricade themselves within their own homes—readying themselves to make a last stand against whatever the next Gap onslaught entailed.

I was encouraged when our four pilots started to trickle into the barn; first, Orville Wright, the commercial airline pilot; then Chuck Yeager, a USAF Lieutenant; then Baron Von Rickenbacker, a seventy-year-old Vietnam airman; and finally Karen, a.k.a. Amelia Earhart, our Apache helicopter pilot. But perhaps the most surprising arrival of all was the contentious old Titus, the M1 tank commander, along with his team. The fact that everyone showed up tonight spoke volumes. It would be now or never. Without some kind of last-ditch effort on our part—even as futile as that effort might end up being—I suspected we would have no home, no families left to protect.

I assumed my customary perch atop one of the Shredders. Sitting next to me was Jhally, who'd been up, stumbling about, since early this afternoon learning to use his new crutch. It wasn't lost on me that at any moment my barn could be infiltrated by EMS marshals, or even the Earupitan military personnel we'd spotted lately around these parts. But if so, there was nothing I could do about it.

One after another, more and more cars and trucks drove inside through the barn's rear doors. I caught Donny's eye. As he shepherded numerous vehicles within, I gave him a questioning gesture—*what the hell? Why so many cars, so many strangers,* far beyond our regular number of men and women, members of the Takebacks? I noticed most everyone was armed with either a pistol or a rifle. But I really shouldn't have been surprised to see that word had spread beyond our fledgling group, now readying to strike back. At this point, it didn't matter. We had more pressing concerns than maintaining secrecy this night. But the same questions and thoughts kept running through my mind, *Is this really happening? Could this really be the end of days for Earth's humanity?*

I watched as more arriving newcomers first took sight of our small squadron of Shredder craft, and then the alien, Jhally—seated next to me. Their startled expressions turned to curiosity, then something akin to hopefulness.

Matt approached. Climbing up onto the Shredder's wing, he leaned in. "Hey, too many cars to fit inside here. I don't know who half these fucking people are. They're parking on the driveway . . . and even beyond, out in the pasture."

"It's fine," I said. "We can't worry about it. After tonight, all bets will be off, anyway. Do me a favor, gather-up our pilots and co-pilots. We'll make time to provide them with one more training session later on tonight."

"You think that'll be enough?" Matt asked, looking skeptical.

I glanced over to Jhally and we both shook our heads in response. "No, but it'll have to do."

I looked down to see Karen, below me amidst the crowd, gazing up at me. She was wearing her badass outfit with the sleeves of her T-shirt torn free at the shoulders. She said, "Maybe you should say something to them. They're scared and need direction."

"I guess you're probably right." I stood and waited for the crowd of at least three hundred men and women to take notice of me. Moments later, their voices had completely hushed within the old barn structure. "Some of you know me, some of you don't. You can call me Polybius. For a good bit of time now, I've run a small contingent of dissident Human rebels. A few Humans willing to face the consequences of torture and inevitable death, all for the opportunity to strike back any way we can at our Earupitan invaders. Over time, we've acquired these five Shredder craft. With the help of Jhally, here . . . yes, an alien, but a sympathizer and friend to our cause, we've repaired them and are able to pilot these vessels."

More men and women were funneling their way into the barn, some even had children in tow. An elderly couple, who had to be in their eighties, joined the fray.

"Look, it's no secret the Gaps are mounting a major offensive of some kind. It could be several days off, but hell, it could happen tonight. So we're going to strike back as best we can . . . mostly in space, where the Gaps have their command ships and other vessels. But I have to be honest with you, other than causing a small diversion, a planned ground offensive was never part of . . . part of our plans. Mostly because it wasn't something I gave much credence to as being all that effective. But maybe that was my mistake."

"Damn straight it was a mistake," Titus yelled. "We're not taking the Gap's shit lying down . . . not again . . . not this time. We're going to fight back, or die trying."

A chorus of loud cheers followed as the mass of people stood around below. How our secret group and meetings had gotten disclosed, I had my suspicions. Titus had broken the covenant of secrecy—both near and far. He'd spread the word. I again made eye contact with Karen and nodded.

"Listen up. There will never, ever, be a better time than now to make a difference—to tip the scales, as slight as they may be, and strike back against Earth's invaders. So I extend to all here a warm welcome into my barn. Personally, I believe with all my heart and soul, and the fire of payback I now breathe, that this isn't the end of humankind." I spoke the words passionately, with strong conviction, and almost believed them myself. "Simply put, I am offering each one of you the opportunity to perform like a true warrior; to do what is humanly right and decent. This call to arms comes only once, so please . . . don't wait too long to answer it."

"What in god's name do you expect us to do, other than defend our homes? Most of us here aren't soldiers!"

I was flabbergasted to note the person asking the question was none other than Randy, the big, bearded lobster farmer from Elizabeth. I shouldn't have been so surprised, seeing his mother, the Ma Kettle look-a-like, standing right next to him. A drooping cigarette hung from her mouth, a shotgun in one hand.

"Maybe we should just hide. Try to escape . . . maybe up in the mountains," Randy said. Several around him agreed, while most others vehemently shook their heads. More than a few said no.

"Randy, we're not running, and we're not hiding any more. It's too late for that. Let me tell you about a relatively small historical battle, a series of engagements known as the Hussite Wars. The crusade, launched against the Hussites, in Bohemia, by Pope 'Oddo' Martin V, was in July, in the year 1420. The pope's crusading forces, four thousand knights, upon reaching the walls of Prague, mounted their attack at a key strategic location, called Vitkov Hill. No more than sixty local soldiers, with the help of a few lowly peasants, defended their position there . . . defended their homeland. They fought with unexpected, and extremely violent, resolve, driving the surprised knights back time after time. They eventually pushed the pope's attacking knight forces off a steep cliff. Eventually, the few knights that survived panicked and fled. The most remarkable part of the Hussite victory was that a rebel army of sixty, plus a few peasants, secured their independence from the Church in Rome and its professional crusader army. As a history professor, I can tell you scores more of such stories. Of how the righteous and brave, though few in number, succeeded in victory in spite of the incredible odds against them. We should have fought harder two years ago. We can't make that mistake again."

I found Titus in the crowd. "Titus . . . I'm glad you decided to attend this meeting. Before climbing into that big tank of yours, would you be willing to lead your own ground offensive . . . with the people here? Since it was you who invited most of them here, anyway?"

Titus gave back a sheepish, half-smile. "I wasn't about to stand around and watch my friends and neighbors get massacred. You've got something good happening here. It's time we capitalize on that."

"So then the answer is yes?" I asked.

"Yeah. We'll coordinate our actions with yours whenever they start," he said.

I rallied my pilots and co-pilots together—including Matt and Donny, along with several who were part of the original Takebacks group. People were already gathering at the far end of the barn where Titus was organizing his ground forces offensive. Jhally, Karen, and I were ready to take the other pilots up in three of the Shredders—give a crash-course in flight training, although each pilot had already learned the basics. Over the next few hours they would get all the necessary hands-on experience needed in order to implement our still mostly undefined plan. I suddenly remembered I needed to speak with Mike Post. I was due an update on his and Marshal Grip's latest hacking endeavors. I knew a Milonge Bi-Hull transport landing at the Oversight and Enforcement Center was scheduled sometime tomorrow before sunrise, but we still didn't have the specifics. If Mike Post couldn't get me that information, we were already in trouble.

The three Shredders revving up made it hard to hear anything anyone was saying. Paired now with the commercial pilot, Wright, to continue his flight training in Shredder Five, I waited below by the wing for him to slowly get situated in the forward seat. I thought back to earlier that afternoon, when Jhally and I took a short flight around the Polk property. I was sitting in the forward pilot's seat and Jhally sat in the seat behind me.

Under his guidance, I continued to improve my flying techniques—getting pointers on what I was doing wrong, but also getting tips and tricks on how to better hone my flying capabilities within this amazing, but deadly, craft. Most importantly, Jhally showed me how to interact with the onboard AI, the primary interface to the navigations system, and also to the onboard weapons system. A good bit of time was learning to use the ear puck and virtual HUD. Mike Post had done a good job making the device compatible for Humans, but I wasn't convinced all of the Earupitan to English translations were right on the money. I then realized why Jhally had waited so long before providing the weapon's systems training. Even one mistake could be catastrophic. The gravity-disruptor cannons, one mounted aft on the bottom of the fuselage, and the other mounted forward, were deployed from hidden compartments once the AI system was verbally activated. While I practiced fast starboard turns, and port banking turns, and backward overhead barrel rolls, and so forth, Jhally was tweaking the onboard AI with Mike Post's ear puck updates so that I, and the other pilots, could implement all necessary Shredder AI commands. From behind me, I heard Jhally say, "There, on your heads-up display we're now seeing, via three dimensional telemetry, the landscape of your property below us."

Having been a fighter pilot for many years, I had no problem multitasking, both piloting the craft while diverting a segment of my mental focus to the HUD system. But the detail now showing was amazing—took every bit of willpower not to get too caught up in the distracting visuals.

"That small wooden structure at the tree line, is that of importance to you?" Jhally asked.

I saw on the HUD that the weapons system had already placed a tracking box onto the small log house that had its roof caved in. "No, it's just an old hunter's—"

Before I could finish the sentence, Jhally orally issued a series of commands. Within moments, I watched through the canopy the old structure become completely decimated. No bright flashes of light—no ensuing fireballs—it was as if an invisible giant's foot suddenly stomped down on the old timber structure and hammered it into the ground—leaving behind a ten-foot-deep crater.

"Brian, the gravity-disruptor system was configured at its least destructive power setting. And only one of the two cannons was utilized. A very powerful weapons system, as you can see." Jhally then said, "Now I will demonstrate how to evoke the twin, wing-mounted plasma guns. Do you have another such structure on your property?"

I felt a hard tug on my arm bringing me back to the present moment. I turned and found Donny standing next to me.

"What is it? I yelled above the noise.

Donny said, "It's Karen . . . she left in a hurry. Said she'd be back as soon as she could."

"What? Why? She knows how important this is!"

"Someone told her that on their way here they noticed a raging fire at her place. Her house was already ablaze."

"Oh, no . . ."

"One more thing, Brian . . . gun shots can be heard all over Castle Rock. I guess it's started."

chapter 26

It was after midnight when Jhally finally finished up with the other pilots, giving each one a scaled-down version of the same flight training I'd received over the last few days. But Karen's absence was becoming more and more of a concern to me by the minute. Could we still implement our plan with four Shredders instead of five? Probably. But it was her welfare that concerned me, less that we'd have a piloted ship.

Matt and Donny, having gone up multiple times as my rear seat co-pilots, had begun learning some of the more rudimentary aspects of flying a Shredder. The truth was, these vessels were incredibly intuitive and easy to fly. Given time, I was certain both would be able to pilot these alien crafts on their own. Taking a break from our multiple flight trainings, the three of us wandered over to the ground assault team's location in the barn. Considering three to four hundred people were still gathered around, I was interested in learning what they had in the works, what was being planned.

Pushing and weaving our way through the crowd, we found Titus holding court within a large open area. Standing, holding onto a long stick, he was using it as a pointer. A rough diagram had been drawn in the dirt. Rocks, along with various tools from my workshop, depicted primary geographic locations, and the major structures within Castle Rock and the surrounding area. I recognized some of the main thoroughfares, such as Lake Gulch Road and Plum Creek Road and Wilcox Avenue. I saw that the OEC building was appropriately depicted by Jhally's old shit bucket. Titus was in the process of dividing the large group into smaller teams, assigning them to hold certain points. From what I could discern, after arriving late to the party, Titus was outlining classic guerrilla warfare tactics, using natural terrain and man-made structures as examples to instigate fast attacks and just as speedy withdrawals only to regroup again at new alternate locations. I was impressed. Beginning to feel somewhat guilty that I'd ignored the utilization of ground forces in our plans merely because of what had happened two years prior.

As Titus continued speaking, my eyes locked onto an area he'd drawn in the dirt with his stick. It was located several miles away on the outskirts of the town proper. He'd placed a half-deflated basketball there to symbolize something. I couldn't recall there ever being much of anything out that way, having traveled the whole county extensively since childhood. I raised a hand, interrupting Titus mid-sentence.

"What is it, Polybius, I still have a lot yet to get through," Titus said.

"What's that?" I asked, pointing toward my deflated basketball.

Before Titus could answer, a woman across from me spoke

up: "That's the dome *thing* the Gaps started erecting a day or so ago. Lots of alien troops there too."

"Dome?" Donny repeated. "What kind of dome?"

Titus said, "The kind that, after much discussion tonight, we can only surmise isn't intended for anything good. And, added to that fact, they've set up what appears to be fenced-in pens. The dome may be a kind of death chamber for the masses . . . for us Humans."

"Best you get up to speed on things, Mr. Polybius," Randy's mother said. "That there's a Human concentration camp nearby with only one purpose: our extermination!"

"Who here has seen this place?" I asked.

Several people in the crowd raised a hand. Then I noticed Matt's face. His brow was furrowed and his eyes fixed. He said, "I didn't realize it before." His eyes then shifted over to me. "Brian, my parents' property is right there . . . less than half a click away from that dome."

I nodded back, then suddenly got it. Karen lived over there too, along with their parents. And she'd run out of here about a half-hour ago due to some kind of fire on their property. *Running right into the lion's den.*

"I've got to get over there," I said. "She may already be captured. Or worse."

"I'm coming with you," Matt said.

"Count me in, too," Donny added.

Together, we hurried toward the barn doors. "Keep on doing what you're doing, Titus . . . we'll be back soon," I said.

"And if you're not? Titus replied.

I stopped and looked around for Jhally and found him above the crowd. High up, he was standing on Shredder Three's wing top, observing us from afar.

"Jhally knows what to do. But I have every intention of making it back here before it's our planned *go* time." With that, I unlatched the front barn doors just wide enough for Matt, Donny, and me to slip through. Mort ran out before I slid the door closed. Pulling the keys from my pocket, we ran in the direction of my truck, which I'd parked closer to the house. Halfway there, I saw three sets of lights fast approaching down the long driveway.

"Shit! Those are HovTs . . . we have marshals inbound!" Donny exclaimed.

Immediately, the three of us slowed our pace to a walk. Glancing behind me, I knew it would be obvious to the inbound marshals that something big was going on inside the barn. Out front there had to be thirty parked cars, and that many vehicles again parked along the side yard. Many more cars were parked farther out in the pasture. A large gathering like this was just another thing frowned upon, punishable by the EMS.

I smiled and waved toward the hovering, now descending, vehicles. "I take it you two are packing?"

"Yup," Donny said.

"Uh, huh," Matt said. "You?"

"Mistmaker," I said.

The three HovTs landed on the drive, their gull-wing doors opening.

"You do know we're totally fucked, right?" Donny asked,

smiling and waving too.

"Let's just see what they want. God, I can't believe their timing. Just be ready. You see them make any attempt to call this in, if they pull their thumb pads, shoot them."

I heard a deep growl coming from Mort.

chapter 27

Every second I was kept waylaid here by these damn lizards was stealing time I needed to rush to Karen's aid. Try to save her life. I couldn't keep the dread, fear of what might be happening to her, from my mind.

Silhouetted behind the three sets of bright headlights, I watched as four figures climbed out of each one of the HovTs. *Terrific*! We had twelve armed Gaps to deal with—making the odds of our surviving the next few minutes that much worse.

Tense, and ready to make our move, Donny, Matt, and I stood shoulder to shoulder. We smiled, as if welcoming friends to a summer birthday party.

"I can't see a damn thing," Donny whispered, squinting into the light.

"We're so screwed . . ." Matt said.

Mort's growls were louder now.

Things only got worse when I caught the dark outline of a figure rising out of one of the HovTs to a height of eight feet. I knew only one Gap who would fit that description, since I was the one who shot a mistmaker energy bolt smack into his chin just days earlier.

"Isn't that your good buddy from the carnival tent?" Donny asked.

Matt nervously laughed at that. "Payback's a bitch, Brian . . . hope you have your affairs in order. Maybe a last will and testament."

Mort barked several times. I could feel him pressed up against my legs. He was trembling. I gave him a couple of pats to his flank.

"Shut up, Donny, this isn't funny," I whispered back, inwardly acknowledging—in a pathetic kind of way—that it sort of was.

Matt leaned in closer: "I think one of those guys is . . . a Human."

I nodded, already knowing exactly who he was. "Hey, you okay, Mike? They hurt you?"

"Hey, Brian," Mike replied, ". . . that you, Matt? Donny?"

Matt said, "Yeah, man. Um . . . so what are you doing with these Gaps . . . I mean, with these marshals?"

Mike Post, hacker extraordinaire, didn't answer. At least, this sort of explained why I had not heard from him of late. My eyes leveled onto the tallest Gap in the group. *Damn, the Gaps must possess even more amazing medical capabilities than I'd thought possible.*

Two dark figures shuffled forward. One seemed to be

assisting the other—as if helping him to stand upright. When he spoke, I immediately recognized his voice.

"Captain Polk . . . please excuse our uninvited intrusion here."

"Chancellor? That you, sir?" I asked, lifting up a palm to block out some of the glare from the blinding headlights.

"In the flesh. Well, what's left of me, anyway." He looked back over his shoulder and said, "You can cut the lights . . . we're among friends here."

It took a few moments to adjust to the sudden darkness as three sets of HovT headlights switched off, one after another. The only illumination now came from the barn's outdoor lights in the distance. Still, there was more than enough light to see that Sleept Vogthner, the Gap's chancellor of communications, was in pretty bad shape. A bandage encircled the top of his head. Much of the scaly skin on one side of his face was a bloody mess. One arm was in a sling. Judging by the way he was being propped up, supported, I surmised he'd either suffered from a broken leg, or a badly sprained one.

"What happened to you? Were you in some kind of accident?" My eyes went to Mike Post, wondering if he, too, was involved somehow. Their joint appearance was becoming more and more confusing to me.

"Slid down the side of a cliff earlier today . . . Listen to me carefully, Brian, we don't have much time," Vogthner said. "First of all, we are not here to arrest you, or to accost you in any way. We simply are here to help, if you'll accept it."

"What?" Matt asked.

"Help how, sir?" I asked. "Um, as you can see, we're having a little barn party here. Probably should have cleared it with the EMS—"

"Drop the dumb act, Brian," Vogthner said, becoming more serious. "I've known about your Takeback group for months now. Our Quantum Manifold System searches specifically for the kind of activities you and your friends exhibit. I know about the two marshals you killed, and I know about the five Shredders you have hidden in that barn of yours."

"Oh, shit," Donny exclaimed under his breath.

"I also know about your ill-conceived plan to invade the Solaris Habitat in your moon's high orbit. Seriously? You were going to hold one million female Earupitans hostage?"

Slowly I inched my right hand behind my back to where the mistmaker was tucked into my jeans.

"Don't be stupid," Vogthner said. "If we wanted you dead, you'd already be lying on the ground in a broken heap."

Mike Post said, "Listen to him, Brian. I think we're on the same side here. Hacking into the Prime Network, with Marshal Grip's help . . . we uncovered a sub-level communications stream. One specifically used by the military's upper echelon. We tapped into real time communiqués between a ground forces general and none other than his Eminence, Overlord Skith. But I didn't know Chancellor Vogthner had eyes on my network activities."

"So you know what's happening locally? The military ground forces that showed up this week?" I asked.

"I already suspected something was brewing," Vogthner said. "Suspected there had to be some kind of Phase II in the works . . . that humankind would always be in jeopardy. Sorry, but it was only a matter of time."

"And what, you were just going to let it happen?" Donny asked.

Vogthner ignored the question. "Turns out, we, too, will soon be at the mercy of the military."

"We . . . who is we?" I asked.

"All the EMS stations around the world: the marshals . . . and the chancellors, such as myself. Turns out, we've been 'overly corrupted' by our close contact with Humans. Mixed loyalties have blossomed. Which, in my case, may be true. Look, any of the Oversight and Enforcement Centers around the world, their Quantum Manifold Systems and their eight spinning Causal Intelligence Nodes, could have preemptively forecasted the kind of problems currently being exhibited. Overlord Skith, with even more powerful computing resources at his disposal, will have determined as much, too. He will not let anything get in the way of having a smooth transition in bringing a million awaiting females down to Earth. Any further need for a marshal's service is gone. The need for a local chancellor of communications will be gone."

"Why do you need me . . . need us?" I asked. "There are plenty of EMS personnel around the world, many thousands of you, right? Start your own damn rebellion."

"I considered that," Vogthner said. "But the military has taken control of all Prime Networks and sub-level township networks. They've been locked down. Sure, we may convince a few local centers to move against the military, but there's simply no time to do that on any significant scale. No. Our only hope is banding together with you Humans. I fully understand any reluctance your species will have . . . trusting us. Hopefully, you'll see we are in a similar predicament.

Only by working together, can we all survive."

I nodded, considering all that he'd said. But something still didn't make sense. "How'd you find out about the Shredders?"

"From me," came a deep gravely voice.

I didn't need to turn around to know it was none other than Jhally, now standing behind us.

He moved past us, leaning on his crutch to hobble by, placing himself directly in front of Chancellor Vogthner. Neither spoke for close to a minute. Matt, Donny, and I exchanged perplexed glances.

Then Vogthner raised his good arm higher and the two aliens embraced.

"This shit show keeps getting crazier and crazier," Donny whispered.

Eventually, they stepped apart from one another. Deeply felt emotions were evident on both their faces.

"So, I take it you two know each other?" I needlessly asked.

"We are brothers," Jhally said. "Do you not see the similarities in our Mannarian features?"

"Um, sure, I do," Donny said. "Now that you bring it up."

Matt and I both scowled at Donny, shutting him up.

Jhally said, "I have been using a telephone at the abandoned Anderson's home to speak with Vogthner most every night." Jhally tore his gaze away from his brother and looked directly at me. "It would not have been safe to let you know you always had a friend in high places, Brian. I apologize for the dishonesty."

"So what now?" I asked. "There are between three and

four hundred Humans back there in the barn behind us, preparing to make an attack on the Gaps. You're not going to be welcomed with open arms in there."

"More likely drawn and quartered," Matt said.

"And yet, we must try," the chancellor said. "Perhaps with your help . . . your introduction—"

"Maybe later. Right now, someone I truly care about is in trouble. There's a dome of sorts . . . a place where they will be holding prisoners."

"We know all about that place," Mike said. "It's crawling with soldiers. You'll be shot on sight getting anywhere near there."

"Not to mention, you have a certain raid upon a Solaris Habitat to head up," the chancellor added.

"I thought you weren't a big fan of that idea," I said.

"I'm not. But honestly, it's the only plan that could even remotely work if our intention is to make a difference worldwide."

"Lend me one of your HovT vehicles, Chancellor. Give us an hour to bring back my other pilot, then we'll do this thing together," I said.

Jhally said, "I shall attempt to convince the Humans inside the barn to accept my brother's help. It may be . . . difficult."

"Yeah, good luck with that," Donny said.

"One more thing," the chancellor added, "you will take Dalm Mor Stroph with you. He is brave and an unparalleled fighter."

"Um, not so sure that's a good idea."

"Please," Vogthner said.

I leaned closer to the chancellor, and asked, "Does he remember . . . exactly what happened to him . . . in that carnival tent?"

chapter 28

It was determined that Stroph, the Earupitan giant, should drive us since neither Donny, Matt, nor I had ever driven one of their HovT crafts before. I occupied the passenger seat, next to Stroph, while Matt and Donny sat in the back. Leery of the alien's ability to drive due to his all too recent head injury, I watched him carefully in my peripheral vision as he navigated between double stands of large oaks, flanking both sides of my driveway.

"You need not concern yourself, Human, with my piloting abilities. I have adequately recovered from my recent injuries," Stroph said.

Before I could answer, his massive, clawed right hand shot out sideways, and tightly wrapped around my throat. My airway cut-off, I couldn't so much as squeal. Using both hands, I desperately tried to free myself from his iron grip but was having zero success. Both Donny and Matt yelled at the giant to let me go. Donny, his Glock pistol pressed hard into the giant's temple, shouted, "Let him go, asshole, or I swear to God, I'll end you right here and now!"

My legs kicked and flailed about—the mistmaker pistol wedged into my jeans, came loose and fell to the floor. As I began to experience narrowing, tunnel-like, vision from the lack of oxygen to my brain, I still could see Stroph, casually sitting beside me, his left hand on the controls. He looked relaxed, a creepy satisfied smile on his oversized green face.

"Don't shoot him, Donny!" Matt yelled behind me. "We're too fucking high above the ground now . . . you'd kill us all!"

At this point, I had no more fight left me. I weakly pawed at Stroph's strangling hand, but my useless arms felt like heavy lead weights. As they dropped to my side, I was resigned to the fact I was dying. I thought about Mort, back at the barn. How long would my loyal dog wait for me to come home? Then I thought of Karen—was she still alive? I could barely hear Donny and Matt's yelling now, my auditory receptors fast shutting down. *Blind, deaf, and soon dead.*

I suddenly felt a release from the giant's clawed hand around my throat. I gasped and gagged, struggling to fill my burning lungs with air. My airway still felt constricted—swollen from the alien monster's impossibly tight grip. But I slowly managed to take in several full breaths of air even though I was hacking like a five-pack-a-day chain smoker. In reverse order, my senses began to return, first back was hearing, then seeing. Slumped down in my seat, staring out through tear-streaming eyes, I found Stroph still at the controls. Thanks to Donny, his face was a mess. Several deep red gashes highlighted his right cheek. His long snout of a nose was bleeding profusely and his creepy Gap smile was gone.

My words croaked out, "So I take it . . . your

memory . . . returned?"

Stroph, shooting an unfriendly glance in my direction, nodded once.

"So are we good now, or do I need to teach you another lesson?" I asked, attempting to smile.

Again, after another quick glance toward me, he offered a single nod back. "We are good."

I retrieved the mistmaker from the floor by my feet and tucked it back into my waistband. "How much do the other marshals know about what's going on here . . . with the military ground forces, and all?" I asked Stroph.

"Word has spread of his High Eminence's backstabbing deceit. He has dishonored those within all EMS stations. There is much uncertainty amongst all of us." Stroph said, gesturing toward his ear puck device levitating over his right ear. "But we communicate with each other . . . all around your Human world we speak of our uncertain fate. We speak of two Earth EMS stations that no longer respond to our queries."

"Sounds to me like you're maybe in the same boat as Humans," Matt said.

"I know not of any boat," Stroph replied.

"It's just an expression meaning your marshals may be facing the same fate now as Humans, unless you join with us," I said.

"I am here, am I not? That does not mean I have to like it. The chancellor has chosen to trust you. He is honorable."

"Good to know," I said. "You know where we're going . . . our intended destination?"

"No. You must further direct me," he said.

The sound of distant gunshots crackled in the distant night. I was pretty sure the Gap ground forces would find Colorado's Humans far better armed than they expected. Only a few of us turned in our weapons as required, and few here would go down without a fight.

Stroph was piloting the HovT a hundred feet above the ground at this point. Out the side windows, we could see flashes from energy weapons as well as from human-fired pistols and rifles. I recognized the sound of automatic gunfire, maybe from an M16, or a newer version of that, like the M4A1 carbine—issued to the U.S. Army before the alien invasion.

"You need to change your heading a bit," Matt said, from the rear seat. His hand slid between Stroph and me, pointing toward where his and Karen's parents' ranch was situated, several miles to the northeast.

Stroph's ear puck made a noise. The Gap initiated the HUD and looked to be reading what looked to be some kind of alien text message. He turned to me: "It is from the chancellor. The Human you call Titus, along with his Human cohorts, are not far behind us . . . in another of the HovTs."

"Why's that?" I asked.

Stroph, glancing at his HUD, asked, "I do not understand . . . what is an M1?"

Donny grasped my shoulder, then said, "Titus and his crew are getting a ride back to his place. Time to get *old Betty* up and running."

The alien still looked mystified.

"An M1 is a tank . . . an armored ground assault vehicle," Donny said. "And let me tell you, you wouldn't want to be targeted by that old bitch."

Matt tapped Stroph's shoulder, but only getting a sneer in response, said, "You'll want to descend. We're getting close."

Right then we all spotted the dome structure. Ominous, it loomed high over anything in the vicinity. I figured it was roughly the size of a small athletic stadium. It seemed to be glowing from within.

"Find a place where we can hide this vehicle, Stroph. There's a dense wooded area off to the right," I said, pointing into the near-total darkness ahead.

By the time we landed, just inside the tree line of tall pines, sounds of gunfire could be heard from all directions now. I listened to the all too familiar sound of war.

We swiftly exited the vehicle then waited as Stroph moved to the rear of the HovT and opened a recessed hatch panel. He retrieved a rifle, but not like any rifle I'd ever seen before. One by one, he handed each of us one, keeping one for himself. Studying the weapon, I found it somewhat similar to the handheld, mistmaker weapon.

"Um, is there a trick to firing one of these things?" Matt asked.

"Point it and pull the damn trigger, Matt . . ." Donny said.

Stroph nodded, keeping to his typical economy of voicelessness.

Suddenly, a large spacecraft appeared overhead, barely missing the tops of the trees. Stroph said, "That is an XL5 . . . the largest of the Crusher lander vessels . . . used for deployment of large ground forces."

We watched as the long XL5 moved past overhead, headed in the direction of the dome. "Let's go! We'll check out Matt's parents' place first. It's less than a click from here," I said.

"Or what's left of it." Matt said, running fingers through his thinning hair. He looked nervous and defeated.

"Keep the faith, brother," Donny said.

I led the four of us deeper into the trees. Before long, acrid smoke stifled the air around us. Using the crook of my elbow, I covered my nose and mouth. When we eventually broke out through the trees, Matt rushed ahead.

"Oh God . . . the place is gone. They *fucking* torched everything!"

Matt was right. The main house, once a pristine white, two-story colonial, with dark green shutters on the windows and a bright red door, was gone. A beautiful home—built at the turn of the previous century—was now little more than blackened fallen timbers and glowing embers. Two chimneys loomed up out of the charred mess looking *lonely* in a way at suddenly being untethered to anything substantial.

I approached Matt, who was bent over, his hands on his knees. Placing a hand on his back, I felt him weeping. "At least your parents and Gwen weren't here," I said, knowing Karen had sent her parents and Gwen out of state—off somewhere in Utah. "But we still have to find Karen. We need to keep it together, we have to go." I looked off toward what used to be the barn. The horses and other livestock were all surely dead.

Matt sniffed and wiped his eyes with his sleeve. "There'll be a payback for this, Brian. I swear to you . . . I'm going to kill every last one of them. And keep that fucking Gap giant away from me."

Together, we headed toward the distant glow of the large dome.

chapter 29

I took another glance at the burnt-out structures before heading out with the others of our team. *Why torch this old ranch?* I wondered. It certainly wasn't a common practice for Gap invaders to do something like that. At least, it hadn't been up until now.

Another three of the shorter Mini Crusher vessels flew right above us—seeming close enough to reach up and touch. I wondered if it was due to a higher level of Human resistance that caused the Gaps to engage additional troops. But maybe that was just wishful thinking on my part.

We were little more than four darkened shapes, out traversing the hilly landscape in the dead of night. I noted Stroph, the largest of us, moved with surprising agility, even grace, as he melded within our little group. I wondered if he really was onboard with our mission, one of us, or, in the end, if he would choose to stay loyal to his own kind. Even knowing he'd been betrayed—by the Earupitan leadership—in any case I knew I'd have to keep an eye on him. I wouldn't hesitate to shoot him *again*, if necessary.

It was close to a mile-and-a-half hike before we reached the outskirts of what was the invading ground forces encampment. Staying low, we were on a rise that overlooked the entire Earupitan garrison. With the immense dome in the distance, there were four Crusher vessels and no less than ten of those open-air disk transports below us. Armed troops were assembling into companies, one hundred and fifty Gap soldiers in each. One of the companies was funneling onto one of the flying disks—readying to head off into the night.

"Get down!" Donny whispered.

A flying disk, no less than thirty yards away, descended down just to our right. This transport wasn't filled with Gap soldiers, but instead was tightly packed with humans—*captives*. I heard their heart-wrenching moans of despair—pleading by both men and women, and the cries of their children. In the darkness, I could barely make out that some wore an assortment of pajama, underwear, or nothing at all.

We watched as the flying disk continued past the encampment and then the dome, setting down somewhere on the other side. I squinted into the darkness and realized that what I assumed were only more of the same rolling hills beyond, like those we were standing upon, were not. Hills don't move and fluctuate. There were people moving around out there, perhaps hundreds of them.

"Let's go . . . stay down. Keep to the tree line," I said. But before we could take a single step, the dome came alive, brightened by a factor of five. A throbbing, humming sound emanated from its core. Vibrations disrupted the ground beneath our feet. The encampment below then became illuminated—soldiers, too many to count, became stationary in their tracks. Every head turned toward the not-so-distant vaulted structure. I watched, stunned, unable to breath. *How many of my Human neighbors had just been killed? Annihilated, nary a trace left behind?* I felt sick, swallowing the reality of what I had just witnessed.

The dome again stilled and darkness returned. It was Stroph who spoke first. "I am sorry. This is not right"

His words were of no comfort. "Hurry," I said. "Who knows how often they'll get that dome thing turned on."

We all ran full out. I tried not to let my imagination get the best of me. Tried not to think of Karen, if she were amongst the group that had just been exterminated.

Skirting around the other side of the dome, we found multiple containment pens set up. Fifty yards out, crouching now behind a thicket of scrub oak, we took in the ominous sight.

"Fuck . . . there must be hundreds of people over there!" Donny said.

"Yeah . . . with no fewer than fifty armed sentinels," Matt added.

It was hard to think around the noise, the cries of anguish and desperation. But I knew only by maintaining a certain level of detachment would I be able to come up with a plan. One that had eluded me thus far. I took in the huddled-together groups. They were being isolated into electrified, energy field pens. Every so often, a flurry of sparks would brightly flash along the outskirts, quickly followed by someone's pain-stricken screams.

"Oh, no . . . another group is being ushered into the

dome," Matt said, pointing to an arched opening on one side of the domed structure. Gap soldiers were jabbing the muzzles of their rifles into anyone moving too slowly—or physically dragging other prisoners forward into the death chamber. They, of course, would know they were being led to an inevitable death.

"We must act," Stroph said.

"You think?" Donny snapped back.

"Shush! Let me think . . ." I said. In irritated desperation, my eyes tracked the ever-watchful sentries constantly patrolling the outer perimeter of the pens. Already, half of the next hostage group had been shoved and manhandled into the dome. *Shit!* My eyes scanned the darkened faces—the hordes of panicky people—I was both hoping, yet not hoping, to see Karen. I was thankful it was too dark to see any one person's features. And then my eyes spied something, scanning the crowd one more time—not someone's specific facial features, or a unique profile, but a T-shirt with its sleeves ripped off at the shoulders. And long dark hair, bunched together and tied down her back in a scrunchie. I knew it was Karen. Relieved she was still alive, but that her group would be next. If the Gaps were keeping to a rigid schedule, she maybe had fifteen minutes before her group would forcibly be ushered inside the dome.

"What we need is some kind of a diversion . . . ," I said.

Before anyone could answer me back, I heard a familiar noise. It was Stroph's ear puck. The giant lizard looked at me.

"Answer the damn thing," I said in a hushed voice.

He did so, bringing up the HUD as he read the message. Stroph then looked at me. "It is Marshal Drake. He is with the one called Titus . . . he says they are close now to approaching the dome."

Leaning over, I tried to make out the faint HUD display. It was reversed, since I was reading it from a reversed viewing angle, but even so, it only contained a gibberish stream of weird icons and symbols. I shook my head in frustration. How could he be here so soon—and what happened to his plan getting that tank of his fired up? "Well, if he's arriving here in a HovT, with just rifles and pistols—"

"Shhh!" Matt said. "Listen . . . do you hear that?"

I shook my head. I didn't hear anything but a baby crying in the distance. And then I *did* hear something. I remembered Titus's ranch was no more than a half click from here. I listened and smiled; there was nothing alien about that sound. It was the low rumbling of a Honeywell AGT1500 powerplant. Fifteen hundred pounds of raw horsepower, with close to four thousand pounds of peak-level torque, the Abrams M1 tank has a very unique sound profile. And in that moment, the loud rumbling noise it made was most welcome to my ears. But with Titus's team soon to arrive, who was left in charge back at my barn? I thought about Titus's ground assault diagram, scribbled into the dirt. Had he deployed those various teams he'd organized for guerrilla warfare tactics? I had far more questions than I had answers for. I knew Jhally would still be readying the other pilots with Shredder training. Did that leave Chancellor Sleept Vogthner in charge? Hell, for two years he'd been considered the enemy—maybe the worst of the worst of the Gaps. There was the strong possibility I would find him swinging by his ankles back in my barn when I returned.

"Tell him to be careful of the area directly north of the

dome where the Human prisoners are being held. And tell him to have that big gun of his start making some damn noise," I said.

As Stroph tap-tapped away on his device, an open-air troop carrier set down with another batch of terrified-looking Humans onboard.

chapter 30

Sorry to disturb you, sir . . . we have an emergency situation taking place."

General Gauz Za Chiv did not appreciate being awakened in the dead of night. Wasn't that why senior officers had subordinates, to handle this kind of minutia?

"Fine. Give me a minute . . . and this better be important, Corporal," Chiv said to the indeterminate speaker over his comms, hidden somewhere within his cabin. Swallowing, he grimaced—from dry throat and cottonmouth.

Three minutes later, still securing the collar fastener on his uniform, he entered the XL5's elevator and waited for the AI to hurry up and acknowledge his presence within the confines of the enclosed lift.

Finally, the AI asked, "Desired destination level, General?"

"One . . . and let's move it along."

"Destination level one acknowledged."

Chiv rolled his eyes, stifling a yawn, as the elevator began its rapid descent. Then, somewhere off in the distance, he heard: *Boom! Boom! Boom!*

By the time Chiv scurried down the gangway, it seemed as if all hell had broken loose. He ducked, cowering, as exploding ordinances rained down within the fortification and on top of his garrison. Troops were now breaking loose from their ranks and firing off into the trees. He spotted a nearby sergeant, yelling commands into his comms unit: "Bring back that troop carrier, we're under attack!"

Chiv grabbed him by the arm. "What the hell is happening? Who is attacking us?!"

"General, sir . . . it's the Humans . . . an armored vehicle is firing upon us. And there's sporadic plasma fire coming from those trees surrounding us!"

"Attack . . . that's not possible! What kind of vehicle did you say—"

Just then, a behemoth armored tank—with squealing treads and a thundering motor—broke free of the nearby tree line and headed directly toward them. Chiv could see a gray-haired man, partially exposed, sitting within the turret. Projectile gunfire suddenly erupted out—mowing down seven of the nearest Earupitan soldiers. Chiv dove, crawled for cover behind the inactive, forty-foot-tall assembly bot's left foot. On seeing the sergeant join him in his hiding place, Chiv yelled, "Get me an open channel with command!"

Chiv continued to watch as the clunky armored vehicle performed wide circles within the encampment, firing a mounted machine gun at will, and running over anything—and anyone—in its way. Now, holding the sergeant's comms unit to his own ear, Chiv said, "Yes . . . we're under attack! No, I don't know how this could happen but we need air support! We need Shredders, and we need them now!"

Hunkering down lower as projectile rounds dinged and pinged nearby, Chiv listened to the far too drawn out explanation. He wanted to argue with his superior above—there in Earth's upper orbit, in the Situational Command Ship Alcon, that things below were now out of control. But he held his tongue and instead said, "I understand, sir. Yes, of course, we will triumph." Signing off, he shoved the comms unit back into the sergeant's chest.

"No Shredders, sir?"

"No . . . no more damage can be made to Earth's infrastructure. Apparently, the evacuation of Gahl has been expedited. Deteriorating atmosphere, or some other *fucking* thing. The whole population is heading here en masse. Dwellings . . . all structures, are to be preserved at any cost. With that said, we're to eradicate all Humans here immediately, without fail."

Chiv found the ground troops, having recovered somewhat from the surprise attack, had begun to reassemble again into an organized force. Two of the smaller nearby Mini Crusher landers directed plasma fire down onto the tank. Glowing red pockmarks cratered the vehicle's surface. As soon as more of the Lander's big guns came online, Chiv had little doubt this skirmish would soon be over.

An inbound open-air troop carrier came into view and hovered, then began to descend. *Good, more troops to fortify my ranks,* Chiv thought, rising to his feet and brushing himself off. But no sooner had he done that, gunfire from the open air carrier began to pepper down from above.

Somehow, armed Humans had managed to abscond with his Earupitan vessel. And that archaic armored tread vehicle was still causing havoc around him.

"Sergeant, get this assembly bot activated . . . turn it loose on that tank!"

But then, doing a double-take, General Gauz Za Chiv witnessed the impossible. He'd personally seen the chancellor die. *Or did I?* he wondered. As the troop carrier settled onto the ground, and hordes of Humans disembarked—firing their primitive weapons—there, in the midst of them was none other than Sleept Vogthner, the local chancellor of communications. The two made eye contact. Chiv abruptly shoved two of his nearby ground troop soldiers toward the now approaching, determined-looking chancellor. "Get out there . . . protect your superior," he ordered.

Startled by the sudden movement behind him, he saw the forty-foot-tall assembly bot come alive. Letting out a relieved breath, he nodded to his sergeant, who was inputting control commands into his ear puck's HUD. "Good job, now put it to work!"

The big, headless robot moved directly into the path of the M1 Abrams tank. The tank's main gun began to rise—the torso of the bot coming into firing range. Lifting up one of its colossal feet, like someone preparing to step on a bug, the bot stomped down with all of its considerable weight, right on top of the tank—bending the main gun up skyward and crushing the turret like an empty soda can.

chapter 31

Five minutes earlier . . .

The four of us—Donny, Matt, Stroph, and me—spread out, finding cover amongst the surrounding trees or behind several of the larger boulders. Firing into the melee of Gap ground troops, we caught the garrison off-guard—immediately causing confusion and mayhem within their ranks. Was it enough to halt further progressions of the dome exterminations? I could only hope. I'd lost track of Karen's position within the hordes of captive Humans, forcibly being ushered closer and closer to the dome's entrance. *Had she already been forced inside?* Our diversionary tactics had not made much of an impact so far. I was tempted to charge forward, gun blazing—attempt some kind of rescue. But too many Gap sentries were on duty. A suicidal outcome would do nothing to help Karen, if she was still alive.

Unfortunately, I kept missing my intended targets. The energy rifle was so lightweight—had so little recoil—I was having trouble mastering effective marksmanship. Stroph, some twenty yards off to my left, was having far better results, having already killed no fewer than ten Gaps. Any doubts I had regarding his residual loyalties to his fellow Earupitans, were now dismissed.

He glanced my way, sheer annoyance on his face. "Pull the stock firmly into your shoulder, Human . . . aim high."

I did as suggested. Unsurprisingly, I had far better results—killing my first Gap soldier. But there were hundreds of them about, and our initial surprise confrontation would not be effective for long. *Damn it, Titus, you need to get your ass over here soon!*

As if on cue, the M1 tank broke out through the trees on the opposite side of the compound. With no hesitation, it ran over a tightly clustered group of Gap soldiers. Soldiers who didn't move quickly enough to avoid being trapped under the big, churning tank treads. Resulting screams of agony were obscured by the sound of the tank's fully engaged fifty-caliber machine gun. As dark out as it was, I still was able to see Titus, partially visible, seated within the tank's turret. He wore a broad, toothy grin as scores of lizard combatants were literally shredded into pieces right where they stood. *Payback's a bitch.*

My heart sank as I watched a flying-disk troop carrier suddenly drop down from above, then land. "Seriously? More of them!" I yelled out in frustration, before realizing they had Human faces, not lizardy ones. Over a hundred armed men and women. Among them were Randy and his mother, and others, who also had recently assembled back within my barn. Standing a foot taller than the rest was Sleept Vogthner. How that troop transport had been commandeered, I had no idea. In any case, they were a very welcome sight indeed.

The M1 tank circled first one way, then another, tearing up the terrain while Titus's trigger finger continued to spread mayhem. All in all, we clearly were making a difference. I even dared to hope we just might succeed. But my eyes kept flashing over to the dome, at the captives being propelled forward.

A seemingly inanimate object suddenly sprang to life. It was an immense headless robot. Forty to fifty feet tall, the bipedal mechanical albatross strode forward, massive hydraulic pistons powering each of its four limbs. It moved with a kind of animus force that was both impressive and unnerving at the same time. The ground shook under its deliberate forward strides. Gunfire quelled, as warring Humans and alien lizards refocused their attention toward an apparent robot versus tank confrontation. I, too, was held spellbound by the ultimate face-off between the two deadly machines. Titus was yelling commands to his crew, his smile long gone. The tank's big gun began angling upward. The long cannon could shoot 120mm ammunition; capable of making a direct hit at a range of 2,500 meters. This headless robot was about to experience a whole lot of *hurt*. But the robot didn't just idly stand there, waiting to be annihilated. Instead, lifting one of its huge leg appendages high, it drove its heavy foot down hard on top of Titus's head—crushing the man, the turret, and disabling the tank.

As a result, a momentary stillness prevailed. Then gunfire resumed, from both sides. I began firing, trying hard not to think about Titus, and the others now lying dead within the ruined tank. Some Human combatants had taken cover, while others—ridiculously standing out in the open—were easy targets. Clearly, they were untrained, unprepared. One by one my compatriots fell. I continued to send plasma bolts into the alien forces, even though my weapon was becoming so hot I could barely hold onto the thing. It crossed my mind that it might actually explode in my hands.

I noticed that the chancellor, his head still wrapped in a bloodied bandage, seemed to have a single preoccupation—a lone Gap officer, trying to escape, was running, tripping, attempting to flee—to find anywhere to hide.

The ground began to vibrate again as a familiar, dreaded, humming sound filled the air. Then the dome brightened for an extended brief few moments. Afterwards, I could smell the ozone. *How many more Humans had just lost their lives? I'm so sorry, Karen . . .*

Disheartened, I fought on and fired my plasma weapon until it finally seized up, a steady stream of hot steam spewing outward from the barrel. Only a few of us appeared to be alive at this point. I wondered how Donny and Matt were faring? Had Titus's fate befallen them, too? Would I be next . . . probably soon?

I ducked low as incoming plasma fire came in from my right. The alien garrison had outflanked us. Of course they had—and there were so many of them.

Again, the ground began to vibrate and a loud humming filled the air. *Fuck—again from the dome?* No, it wasn't the dome this time. In the early dawn light, I caught sight of a newly arriving sleek vessel. Two additional crafts were slowly circling higher in the sky—like birds of prey—waiting for the opportunity to pounce. By now, I was quite familiar with the craft's unique visual contours. The first to arrive Shredder was moving fast, on a straight vector—*lightning fast.* It abruptly banked left, then descended a thousand feet. Firing, bright flashing bolts of plasma shot from its wing-mounted guns.

Pandemonium erupted all around. Humans and Earupitans alike ran and dove for cover.

When I realized those of us here on the ground were not the primary target of their attack—that the targets were the four landing crafts—I knew just who was up there in the cockpit—*Jhally.*

chapter 32

Six Gap soldiers made a mad rush toward my hiding place behind the boulder. A series of plasma bolts exploded near me, sending chunks of rock so close that shrapnel-like shards shredded my shirt and inflicted tiny cuts along my back and left side. Ignoring the pain, I discarded the useless rifle and pulled out my mistmaker. I attempted to return the Gap's rapid fire, but had to keep ducking down behind the boulder for cover. They continued running toward me, while firing back with surprising accuracy, especially since they were moving fast. I knew within seconds I would be overrun. One Human, unfamiliar with his weapon, versus six aliens wielding far more powerful energy weapons had no chance. This had to be it. Had to be the end. Well, I wasn't about to just hide, cowering behind the boulder. Inhaling a deep breath, I prepared myself for a last stand, one out in the open. I leapt out from my position behind the rock.

But I didn't get very far. *Something* grabbed me by the nape of my neck, pulled me back behind the rock. I knew it was Stroph.

"You are brave, Human, but annoyingly stupid." Still holding onto an operational energy rifle, Stroph wasted no time using it, firing quick shots around the big rock. I moved toward the boulder's other side and, hunching low to the ground, returned fire with my mistmaker. Three Gaps fell down, while the other three continued to advance. I noticed Stroph's aim seemed nearly as bad as my own. Taking a quick glance behind me at the giant Earupitan, I realized his face was a bloody mess. Apparently, he, too, had suffered rock shrapnel hits—maybe into his eyes? By the time I refocused my attention, back on the incoming assault, one of the Gap soldiers was almost upon me. I ducked down, missed being hammered by the butt of his rifle by mere fractions of an inch. Lying prone on the ground, I rolled hard left—careening my body into his legs. The alien toppled over, landing right on top of me. We both scrambled to get our weapons into firing positions. In this one instance, holding a pistol in my hand, versus gripping a far longer rifle, ended up being an advantage. I snatched a hold of the rifle's muzzle with my left hand, forcing and angling it away from my face, while shoving my mistmaker pistol hard into the Gap's abdomen. I pulled the trigger five times before he finally slumped over, his dead weight falling on top of me.

Extricating myself from beneath the dead soldier's body, I witnessed a vicious fight ensuing several feet away. In hand-to-hand combat, Stroph was fighting the other two soldiers. All three had dropped their weapons—either accidentally, or on purpose. One thing was for sure—I didn't want to get in the middle of that battle. Stroph, taking heavy blows to his head and body, mostly missed out with his own clench-fisted strikes. So much blood was flowing down the top of his head he couldn't see. Suddenly, the glint of a knife appeared in one of the soldier's hands.

"Gap on your right . . . knife!" I yelled.

Stroph blocked the incoming strike enough to divert what undoubtedly would have been a lethal stab to his neck. His arm suffered the damage instead. Blood sprayed into the air. The other soldier seized this opportunity to retrieve his long rifle from the ground. Bringing its muzzle around, he was all set to fire, but before he could I shot him in the face.

Stroph, still infuriated, grabbed a hold of his opponent's wrist. Then the giant clasped his free hand around the other one's wrist and, without missing a beat, swung the dazed Gap soldier around—almost three hundred-and-sixty degrees—until his body struck the boulder. *Like a bug hitting a windshield at sixty miles an hour.* The Gap, dazed, probably had mere seconds to live, but Stroph wasn't done with him yet. Using his oversized boot to press the opponent's limp body further into the ground, he wrenched the soldier's arm up and away. I heard the sounds of bones snapping, of flesh ripping, as the arm was torn cleanly from the shoulder. Using the dismembered appendage as a club, Stroph proceeded to beat the Gap over and over again—even long after the battered, one-armed, soldier clearly lay dead—*thump, thump, thump*—the wet clubbing sounds continued.

Plasma strikes streaked overhead, the dome now taking direct hits. Jhally's relentless aerial attacks had somehow managed to bring the Gap ground forces to their knees. As the Shredder banked—first this way, then that—it avoided counter strikes from a lone lander craft, the only one of four still operational. Higher overhead, our other two Shredder craft were circling. The Human pilots, aliases *Wright* and *Yeager*, obviously weren't comfortable yet calling up their onboard weaponry systems.

I watched, *stunned*, as the remaining Gap forces, perhaps seventy-five or so, raised their hands high up above their heads—emerging from where, moments before, they'd taken cover. Just as many sentries standing by the dome were now doing the same. Raising their arms while moving toward the center of the compound. Chancellor Sleept Vogthner, standing within a cluster of armed Humans, was holding one Gap officer prisoner.

Behind me and off to my left, I saw Matt and Donny walking down the hillside slope toward me. I was relieved, seeing both good friends still alive.

But the toll extracted from the fierce battle was staggering. So many dead lay before us—both Gaps and Humans had lost hundreds. It was difficult to fully comprehend the carnage.

Over near the dome, tightly grouped together Human captives stood quietly—their electrified pens still energized. They stared about them transfixed, although slow realization was settling in for all of us that a favorable outcome, considered incomprehensible and impossible just hours earlier, had actually taken place; Human resistance forces had not only fought bravely here, but had won the day.

I yelled over my shoulder to Donny and Matt, "The dome . . ."

By the time I reached the towering structure, I could hear the three Shredders setting down—their landing thrusters fully engaged. A cluster of Gap sentries, their arms now raised, eyed my rapid approach. "You, there," I ordered, "get those electric pens turned off. Do it, now!"

A puzzled sentry looked over at me, then toward his nearby cohorts. Clearly, the Gaps military forces did not possess the same educational level linguistically as EMS personnel. Then, Stroph appeared at my side. I was taken aback seeing the dead soldier's arm still gripped in one of his claws. He spoke in Earupitan—angry commands that had the sentries nodding their heads in unison, looking eager to please. They quickly dispersed over to the holding pens, where, one by one, the various energy fields were shut off. A wave of Human voices full of both relief and joyful gratitude filled the air. We watched as they embraced one another. Some wept, others gazed up to heaven offering a silent prayer. Matt, Donny, and I moved through the crowd, thankful hands reached out to touch us as we passed. But we were looking for someone specific. Within minutes, it was evident Karen was not among those still living. She was nowhere to be seen.

Matt, moisture filling his eyes, gestured toward the entrance into the dome. "We should check inside."

"Yeah . . . okay." I headed toward the dark, looming archway. Inside was the death chamber. I knew there couldn't possibly be any survivors, so entering would be a futile act. One of the sentries ran forward. Now a helpful compatriot, he used one of his long clawed fingers to tap at an access panel I didn't know was there. Immediately, humans—ecstatic at being freed—began to pour forth from the dome's dark interior. Apparently, an energy field had kept everyone enclosed. Like salmon swimming upstream, we fought through the crowd toward the entrance.

I heard Matt yelling her name, "Karen? Karen?"

Then Donny and I did the same. "Karen! Karen! Karen!"

The outflow of released prisoners was soon reduced to a trickle. Still, there was no sign of her. Entering into the dome's dark gloomy atmosphere, my eyes took several moments to adjust. The dome's curved inner walls were nearly black, making it almost impossible to distinguish anything. The air was permeated with the strong odor of ozone. I scanned the cavernous space, searching for any sign of movement.

"It's just like you . . . wait till the last frigging minute to make your rescue." And there she was. I watched as Karen emerged from the dim darkness helping an elderly man, his arm was draped over her shoulder. He barely seemed able to walk. Even with her face streaked with soot, to me, she looked like an angel. I'd never been happier to see someone in my life. We ran to help her. Donny took her place, assisting the old man. I threw my arms around her and pulled her into a tight embrace. Kissing her face, I found her lips, tasted the saltiness of tears. Matt pulled her away from me and hugged her tightly.

Once he released her she grabbed a hold of both our arms. "Get me the *fuck* out of here!" she exclaimed.

chapter 33

I left Donny and Matt to organize the surviving Takebacks, and then find other Humans willing to help deal with the dead. Before very long, this place was going to become a stinking, fly-infested open gravesite. For now, I chose to have the bodies, both Human and Gap, moved to within the cooler confines of the atomizer dome. As Matt was heading away, I said, "Oh, and one more thing: collect all the ear pucks from the dead, plus all their weapons. I want us to have tight control on everything."

Karen and I approached Sleept Vogthner, who appeared to have taken charge, barking off orders to his subordinates. Eyeing our approach, he offered up a smile. Gap smiles always looked somewhat creepy to me.

"A remarkable day,' he said. "A day that will be remembered in history books—Earth's fight for independence has commenced!"

"You foolish traitor . . . you have done nothing but ensure your own excruciating death," a bound-up prisoner said.

I appraised the Gap military officer. On his knees, his hands were secured behind his back. One scaly green cheek was bloodied, as well as his lower lip. His snug uniform was torn, one of his shoulder epaulets missing. He sneered at me.

Vogthner said, "Let me introduce you to General Gauz Za Chiv. He and I recently spent some time together, but his attempt to kill me was unsuccessful. Prior to his failed attempt, I learned he was entrusted with supervising what was referred to as a test program for Phase II of the original Earupitan invasion plan—"

"Yeah . . . we already know all about that," I said, glancing around at the mayhem surrounding us. "Phase II . . . the eradication of all Human life." I glowered down at Chiv. "So I guess your trial tests here in Castle Rock haven't quite gone as you planned, eh?"

"You must be the one called Polk," Chiv said. "The instigator of this . . . this fiasco. Your demise will be that much more gratifying. A public example will be made of your execution. Perhaps his Eminence will see fit to have you skinned alive . . . we'll make it a public spectacle. You do have a town square, do you not? But then again . . . surrender to me now, and I may see fit to recommend a fast and painless death for you instead."

"Uh huh, I'll keep that in mind," I said, not hiding the sarcasm. I turned my attention back on Vogthner. "Chancellor, it's only a matter of time before new aerial reinforcements and more ground forces arrive here. Ultimately, this confrontation may have done more harm than good. The original plan was to take control of that habitat ship in space . . ."

"Please. Let me bring you up to speed, Brian," Vogthner interrupted. "All across this continent . . . this once great American country and, in fact, across the world, what was accomplished here today has already spread to every EMS station around the world. A good many of my counterparts, other chancellors of communications, have been apprised of their own upcoming fate. Humiliation . . . and death." Vogthner gestured to his ear puck comms unit. "Also, the fate of so many thousands of our township marshals. That our decreed elimination was ordered by none other than his High Eminence, Overlord Skith himself."

I nodded. "That's all well and good. I'm pleased that what happened here today helped save lives."

Karen took a step closer to the Chancellor, her face as serious as I'd ever seen it. Her eyes narrowed. I then realized the mistmaker—shoved into the waistband at the small of my back—was now firmly gripped in her right hand. She raised the weapon, leveling it toward the chancellor's face.

"There's something you need to understand, right here and now, Chancellor. Or, so help me, I'll fucking blow your head off without giving it a second thought."

Everyone went silent—the cluster of marshals, Gap captives, released Human prisoners, the Takebacks—*everyone.*

"You're a pompous ass. I never liked you, and you never had our best interests at heart. So don't start playing the concerned comrade now." Karen, taking another step forward, raised the muzzle higher, placing it against the chancellor's chin. "You will not give orders. We will not allow one alien enslaver to take the place of another. I would sooner shoot you in the head right now and accept whatever fate befalls me."

"Just shoot the motherfucker!" came the voice of an elderly woman. I turned to see it was none other than Randy's old mother. Somewhere along the line, she'd gotten a hold of a plasma rifle.

I raised a steadying palm toward the *Ma Kettle* look alike. "Hold on, ma'am . . . don't start making things any worse." I then placed the same hand on Karen's shoulder. "Shoot him if you want, I won't try to stop you. Not after what you've lived through in that dome over there. But he just might be useful. Humans, standing alone, have already proven themselves incapable of defeating these alien Gaps."

Karen raised her chin, not looking back at me. Clearly, she really wanted to pull the trigger. Her voice, though softer now, was no less threatening: "There is only one person in charge here. The one person who had the spine, tenacity, and smarts to stand up to you aliens." She then shot a quick glance toward me. "Brian Polk led this charge. So he is the one who makes any decisions. We trust him to have our best interests at heart. If he chooses to trust you, which I think is a big mistake, then we'll all go along with it . . . for now."

I appreciated Karen's faith in me as a leader, though I wasn't sure I was the right man for the job. What started in Castle Rock was only a small town rebellion, not a worldwide uprising. But I wasn't about to back out either. Not now, not ever.

"Chancellor, I want you to think hard before you reply to Karen. We will not answer to you or your kind ever again. I'm inclined to reinforce that point by suggesting she pull the trigger," I lied. I stepped closer to her side—we stared up at him, our intense gazes unfaltering.

"You can aim that weapon elsewhere, miss. I do not wish to die today."

Karen shrugged a shoulder. "You're not saying the words we need to hear."

"Brian Polk is in charge. I won't presume to make any major decision without seeking his counsel. And that I promise you," Vogthner vowed.

Karen lowered the mistmaker and took a step back. The weapon was still pointed at his torso.

"What would you have happen to my people?" the chancellor asked. "Perhaps eradicate them, like they did yours?"

"Sounds good to me," someone shouted from the crowd encircling us.

"How many more of these dome things have you built?" someone else asked. "How about we teach you by using a little of your own medicine?"

"The Gaps will have to find someplace else, another planet to call home," I said. "Simple as that."

Vogthner shook his head. "And the marshals . . . and the other chancellors? You'll be condemning the thousands living here to their deaths."

"Just like you planned to do to us!" Karen said, raising the mistmaker again.

"Look," I said, "we're a long way from any kind of victory. Castle Rock is a mere spec of a town. There should be little expectation that what we've accomplished here can be accomplished anywhere else on the planet. So we're talking hypotheticals. But one thing I can assure you of—what happened here today will spread like wildfire. The impossible shown to be possible. Humans . . . humanity, will rise up, take back what they have lost, or die trying. So my answer to you is this, Chancellor, on which side will your compatriots stand today? Because when all this is over, one way or another, we'll remember who our friends are. Perhaps there will be a place for them, too."

Karen shook her head. "Oh, you'll really need to fucking prove yourselves first . . . we're not going to forget the interrogations, the tortures you inflicted on us. Your marshals were animals. There'll be a heavy price to pay for that."

I noticed Jhally, standing on his crutches, along with the other two pilots, coming closer through the throngs of onlookers.

Chancellor Vogthner didn't answer right away. He made eye contact with his brother, Jhally, then looked down at Chiv. Next, he surveyed the crowd: Some were Earupitan, others were Human. Then he looked at Karen.

"A phrase you Humans are fond of is . . . 'I give you my word' . . . I, too, like this phrase. We shared a similar phrase on my world of Blahn: 'Without honor, Soul is adrift on a sea of conflict.' I give you my word, and my sincere commitment, to help make things right again on Earth."

"Good, I suppose we'll have to trust you to be honorable." I said.

I focused my attention back to Chiv. "Next up . . . you're going to tell me who's hiding inside these lander crafts of yours."

Chiv snickered, "I will never assist you. In fact, I would rather die than turn my back on His Eminence, Overlord Skith. Do what you will with me."

"So be it," I said. "I'd like you to meet a friend of mine, Dalm Mor Stroph. Don't mind his unique size. He's a real pussycat once you get to know him."

Chiv's contemptuous expression quickly changed to that of fear when he noted the sheer size of the approaching Earupitan giant. His eyes then locked onto the bloodied appendage that Stroph still clasped in one clawed hand.

chapter 34

It was far from a real pummeling. Dalm Mar Stroph swung his makeshift club at Chiv no more than three times. The blows were inflicted on his head and upper body. Bloodied and whimpering, he yelled, "Stop! He's killing me . . . Chancellor . . . Polk . . . tell him to stop!"

Distracted, I watched as two hovering open-air troop carriers descended down from above. Neither was able to directly land within the compound itself due to the accumulation of dead bodies spread about the site. They ended up setting-down farther away, closer to the tree line. One carrier was packed with Human prisoners; the other with additional Earupitan ground forces. Once landed, the Gap soldiers looked bewildered, finding themselves quickly surrounded by armed Humans. The soldiers were forcibly escorted to the now re-energized holding pens, while the Humans onboard the other craft were freed. More than a few Humans were overcome with emotion. Karen went to console them and explain what was going on.

Thwack! Thwack!

I turned back, finding General Chiv lying on his side, futilely attempting to curl into a fetal position—difficult, since both arms were bound behind his back. He was pleading for the giant to stop beating him with the dismembered arm. I gestured, my hand raised for Stroph to take a break. Kneeling down next to Chiv, I waited for him to glance up. His bloodied face was swollen.

"Are you ready to have a discussion, General? Or should I let Dalm Mor Stroph continue? Seems he's barely broken a sweat. I suspect he could keep swinging that torn-off arm at you all day, so what's it going to be?"

"Just tell him to stop. I'll help you."

I waited several long beats, but when Chiv said nothing, I signaled Stroph to continue the beating. I had no sympathy for the alien—not considering his past crimes against humanity.

"No! There is a command crew of five onboard each one of the Crushers," he gasped out.

I looked up to Vogthner. "Crusher?"

"The large landing vessels. They're referred to as Crushers." Vogthner, now kneeling down beside me, handed me an ear puck. "I believe the individual command crews on each will follow the general's orders."

Taking the ear puck from him, I held it several inches at the side of Chiv's head. It immediately flew from my fingers, repositioning into place over the general's ear. "Contact the command crews, General . . . tell them to stand down. Also tell them they are to report directly to me."

I left Chancellor Vogthner to deal with the arrival of thirteen HovT vehicles, carrying EMS marshals coming in from the Operations and Enforcement Center back in town. He had contacted them on an open channel—apprised them of the current state of affairs. I knew it would be a hard pill for some marshals to swallow, maybe even most. Hell, Humans had been little more than lap dogs to them for close to two years. Having to answer to Humans now would be tough. But those not doing so would face imprisonment, along with the military ground forces currently held within the electrified energy pens. I put Shawn McGee, a.k.a. Spartacus, in charge of shadowing Chancellor Vogthner. Assigned him to take note of everything the chancellor did and everything he said. Trust only went so far at this early stage of things.

Jhally, Karen, the giant Stroph, and I headed off toward the farthest, and for the most part, undamaged Crusher craft. Reluctantly, Stroph left his now pretty much limp and useless *club* behind. I briefly considered bringing General Chiv along, too, then figured with his beaten face, the last thing I needed was the sympathy his looks might generate.

As we climbed the gangway, I asked Jhally, "How familiar are you with these spacecraft? Their capabilities?"

"Familiar enough. For the most part, their main purpose is handling the movement of troops from one spacecraft to another, or transporting them from a spacecraft down to the surface of a planet. The smaller *Minis* load capacity is about two hundred soldiers . . . the XL5 like this one, maybe four to six hundred. Not exactly sure. The vessels are relatively slow and not very maneuverable. Their weapon systems are fair, but—as you've witnessed—they don't compare to what is on even one attacking Shredder."

We entered into what appeared to be a general purpose, no-frills hold area—a staging area for the deployment of troops. The deck held a series of metal grates. Alongside bulkheads were internal curved structural supports. They reminded me of an organism's inner ribcage.

"In your measurements, the vessel is about one hundred twenty feet long by about sixty feet in height. There are four levels above this one, which is Level 1. On Level 2, we'll find barracks and a mess hall. Level 3 is the weapons' deployment center . . . and aft, the drive access."

"And the top . . . Level 4?" I asked.

Jhally said, "The bridge, what we call the Command Center, is at the prow. Farther aft are the officers' quarters and recreational facilities."

Jhally led us across to two frill-less lifts. "After you," he said. Once the four of us stood together on the marred, scuffed platform, he tapped on a side-mounted display and we quickly began to ascend.

"Should we expect resistance from the command crew?" I asked.

"I have no idea," Jhally said. We left it at that.

Twenty seconds later, arriving at the topmost level, we stepped off and into a narrow passageway. As with the hold area below us, and just like the lift, everything here looked merely functional. No frills, no paint, no unnecessary design attributes, and windowless. Hatch doors lined both sides; I assumed each one led into an officer's quarters. Perhaps one was General Chiv's? At the far end of the passageway I could see the open bridge.

"Did you hear that?" Karen asked, leaning-in close to me and looking up. Scanning overhead were a myriad of pipes, cables, and ventilation ducts, plus all the other shit one might find within the darkened realms of an old spacecraft. Then I heard it, too. The unmistakable sound of tiny clawed feet scurrying across metal. I then caught fast movement out the corner of my eye—some*thing*, or *things*, running alongside the deck plates.

"Ahh!" Stroph screamed, doing some kind of hopping around jig as if his feet were on fire. "Get them away from me! Ahh!"

Three small, multi-legged creatures that weren't insects—I noticed they actually had furry faces—but were not small animals either, not with those spidery appendages, scurried up and over the tops of the giant's now dancing feet. They darted about him in tight circles—running this way and that—then, before he could accidentally crush one of them, they sprinted away. They made squeaking noises, which sounded an awful lot like high-pitched laughter. One by one, they disappeared from sight into a narrow bulkhead crevice some twenty feet away. Frantic, Stroph continued to look all about the deck, then scoured the recesses overhead. I already knew the big lizard wasn't right in the head. I also knew I was partially responsible for that.

"What the hell's wrong with you!" Karen barked at Stroph, holding up a hand to her chest. "You scared the crap out of me . . . you big baby!" Annoyed, she looked over at me. "See? This is what happens when you shoot someone in the friggin' head. You turned him into an idiot."

I ignored her. "What were those things?" I asked Jhally, who looked mildly bemused by the giant's antics.

"Gang Pits . . . harmless for the most part, although they do bite. Best to avoid them."

"Where did they come from?" Karen asked.

Jhally shrugged. "We traveled to many worlds prior to reaching Earth. Stowaways, I believe you would call them? Yes?"

"Hmm, do me a favor, Jhally. Once we are in the command center, close up that gangway below. In fact, make sure all the Crusher's gangways are secured. Earth's ecosystem can do without the addition of Gang Pits."

Using crutches, Jhally was the first to swing into the Command Center. I followed behind him with Karen and Stroph bringing up the rear. In the brief moment prior to being shot, I saw six beings waiting for us—their energy weapons aimed in our direction.

chapter 35

Even feeling the explosion of white-hot pain atop my left shoulder, my first inclination was to somehow protect Karen. I dove for her, attempting to tackle her down onto the deck—use my body as a shield—but she was already diving for cover herself. Exposed. I crashed onto the middle of the deck in full view of the armed bridge crew.

Jhally yelled a command in Earupitan, probably something to the effect of: *Hold your fire!*

I managed to rise to my knees. Got a whiff of burning flesh—*my own*. With a quick glance at my shoulder, I saw a scorched patch the size of a golf ball. More of a flesh wound than anything serious, but that didn't mean it didn't hurt like a son of a bitch.

I looked up into the muzzles of six energy weapons, all pointed at my head.

Jhally yelled out again, this time conveying a more

threatening tone. Still, their weapons still did not lower. Back and forth, raised voices continued shouting out—a standoff.

Karen crawled to my side. “You’ve been hit, Brian.”

“I know that.”

“Does it hurt?”

“Yes, it hurts like you wouldn’t believe.”

“Well, buck-up . . . this is no time to be a pussy. Um, I think you’re supposed to do something now.”

I looked up. The command crew, all staring down at me, had indeed lowered their weapons.

Jhally said, “They understand some English, but don’t speak it very well. You should probably climb to your feet now.”

I slowly did so, taking in my surroundings. In contrast to the rest of the battered old ship, this bridge, or control center, was modern and ultra clean. It was also much larger than I expected it to be—maybe thirty feet long, narrowing a bit closer to the bow, and twenty-five feet across from port to starboard. Windowless, the bulkheads were lined with a myriad of advanced-looking technology. 3D virtual projections hovered around what looked to be various crew stations. Small lights flickered on and off at all console surfaces. Other than on the minimally appointed Shredder crafts, this was my first experience aboard a real spaceship. I probably looked a little wide-eyed and awestruck—sort of like a country bumpkin on his first trip into the city.

Jhally spoke in slow, concise English, “Under the authority of General Chiv, you are to relinquish command of this vessel immediately. You, Captain . . . what is your name?”

A uniformed crewmember, wearing a distinctive red sash draped from his shoulder to the opposite hip, said, "I am Captain Guart."

Stroph, taking a big step forward, forcibly yanked clutched rifles away from all the crewmembers. But the captain, taking a step backward, raised his weapon again. "General Chiv . . . he was under . . . ," the captain searched for the right word, "duress. I do not surrender my vessel under such conditions."

Stroph looked back at me, a questioning expression on his face. I nodded.

With remarkable speed for such a large being, Stroph reached out and plucked the rifle from the captain's hands. The captain flinched. Staring up at the giant, I noticed warranted fear in the alien captain's eyes.

"Look, there has been enough bloodshed for one day. Do you not agree, Captain? I see it this way . . . you have two choices: you can either assist us in our mission, or you can join your brethren outside. You know, where your compatriots are being held. Imprisoned within those electrified pens, near that atomizer dome. You are familiar with the atomizer dome, are you not?" I was unsure if they knew the dome was damaged or not, but I could see by their expressions that my implied intention to have them atomized was evident on all their faces.

The command center crew exchanged nervous glances amongst themselves. After several back and forth murmurs, the captain said, "We were never in favor of Earth's invasion. What our forces were doing to Humans."

"Yeah, sure you weren't," Karen snarled, her voice thick

with sarcasm.

Jhally said, "Well, I guess you have an XL5 Crusher craft, Brian. What do you want to do now?"

I took in my surroundings, then eyed the six crewmembers again. "Learn. I want to know everything . . . what the Earupitan's game plan intends. I want to know how far along they are in implementing their Phase II Human eradication program."

Karen said, "And we need to know more about your ground forces; where they've been deployed thus far? And all further deployment schedules. As Brian said, we need to know everything . . . what the entire plan consists of to wipe out humanity."

Jhally, turning to the captain, said, "I, too, wish to know all this. If you lie to us, I will know it."

Captain Guart, seemingly resigned to the new order of things, moved to the closest bulkhead and fiddled with the console. A projected virtual display appeared in front of the command center, spanning the entire forward width of the compartment.

The captain spoke to Jhally in Earupitan. Jhally translated back what was said to Karen and me.

"We are looking at their tactical display feed. Here you can see Earth. Highlighted with red dots are the many OEC marshal stations located within each continent. Earupitan Situational Command ships are represented with blue dots, shown here in Earth's upper orbit."

"And the few green dots, and those big swatches of yellow dots?" Karen asked.

Again, the captain explained them to Jhally, who translated them for us: "The green dots indicate the progression of Phase II . . . the township of Valle d'Aosta, Italy, the township of Armonk, New York, and here, where we are now, Castle Rock, Colorado."

I didn't need the captain to explain the presence of the green dots—I had figured that much out already. They represented the locations where atomizer domes had been constructed and utilized, or were starting to be such as in Castle Rock. I stared at the yellow swatches—huge expansive areas, located on virtually every continent and extending across most countries. Multiple Earupitan blocks of text—alien symbols and characters—provided explanations, or maybe updated logistics, I wasn't sure. "And what is the deployment schedule, moving forward?" I asked. Then frowning I added, "Wait, no way are there enough Gaps here to manage your Phase II endeavor."

"That is true. That's why Phase III was deemed necessary," replied the captain, his voice apologetic. The captain and Jhally spoke quietly together. I could see a pained expression cross Jhally's face as the captain further enlightened him. Jhally slowly turned back to face Karen and me. I sensed his reluctance to share.

"You first need to understand that many millions, even billions, of our kind were killed in the last war on Gahl. Our population dwindled even more in the years since . . . circumstances that involved our females becoming infertile."

"You've already mentioned that to me," I said. "Go on."

"There are only millions of us left. Earth was defeated through the implementation of advanced technology and shrewd strategy. Not due to sheer numbers by any stretch of the imagination."

"So what the hell then are you saying to us? We get it; you don't have nearly enough Gaps to follow through with your original plan to eradicate the rest of humanity."

Jhally didn't answer right away. "The testing aspect in all three townships was well-documented. What you would call *videotaped*. The full horror of Phase III is that it would enlist Humans willing to . . . assist . . . Earupitan forces during this next phase. They will willingly do so. All in order to avoid experiencing a fate similar to that given to the previous, less fortunate, Humans."

"Humans killing humans?" Karen asked, perplexed.

Jhally nodded. "I am sorry. It sickens me that this was ever part of the plan."

Karen said, "Jhally, your brother Chancellor Vogthner . . . I'm telling you, he damn well knew about it too."

"No, I don't think—"

"Sure, he did! He was already prepping someone for a top management position here in town: Ronald Gant, along with his Friends For Friends group. Beyond doubt, there are many Ronald Gant types—similar traitorous Human groups all across the globe. Do you deny that?"

"I don't know," Jhally said.

Karen looked at me, then said, "All the local chancellors of communications . . . like Jhally's brother Vogthner, they have to know. They are part of this *clusterfuck* of traitors."

"I truly did not know this, Brian, Karen . . ." Jhally said, looking crestfallen at me. I decided to believe him.

"I did not know either," Stroph said, exhibiting rare clarity of mind.

"And I believe you, too, Stroph," I said. "But until we know for sure if Jhally's brother is playing us, we have to limit his knowledge and his involvement with any of our plans."

"And what plans are those?" Karen asked, studying the tactical feed.

"Can you call up a general overall display? One that shows the specific locations of all Gap military forces, including the ones in space?"

Together, we reviewed the updated display feed. We learned there were hundreds of craft, already en route from Gahl—Earupitan masses escaping from a doomed planet. And there are scores of military vessels, coming here from Gahl and other sectors within the galaxy—leaving invaded exoplanets that hadn't made the grade.

I asked the captain, "Can you attest to the fact there are a million of your female species within that habitat ship?" I asked, pointing in the direction of Earth's moon.

Captain Guart shot an angry glare toward Jhally. But I already knew the subject of their coveted females was a sore subject.

Karen said, "Wait . . . you're telling me your population is a mere ten million, but only one million of them are female? I guess they are one hot commodity."

None of the Gaps replied.

I asked, "How do we get onboard that Habitat ship? Our original plan is obviously a no-go now."

Jhally said, "Brian, I will not condone any harm coming to those onboard that vessel. As abhorrent as you see us,

Earupitan and Mannarians alike, I will not abide by any plans calling for our extinction."

"And I won't stand by, either, while the Human race is further defiled, soon to be exterminated. You know, as well as I, that the Habitat ship is our one and only means of coercion. Let's just hope a heavy-handed threat will be enough motivation. But I'm not going to lie to you. I'm not playing games here, I'll do whatever I must." I looked at the captain. "Now, how do I get my team up to Solaris Habitat?"

"It would not be permitted. Not even for me. Too well-guarded, too many safeguards in place."

"Would General Chiv be allowed access?"

"Perhaps, but only if granted permission by His Eminence, Overlord Skith."

"And just where is this overlord fella?" Karen asked.

The captain didn't attempt to hide his disapproval of Karen's lack of respect. "He is well out of reach . . . aboard the Situational Command Ship Alcon."

"The defensive armaments on that ship are significant," Jhally added, shaking his head.

"Okay, so we need to have his eminence venture down to Earth for a visit. Tell me, what would be important enough, what would motivate him enough, to do such a thing?"

"His wife," one of the captain's junior officers said. "She already is here on Earth. In hiding, of course."

chapter 36

A klaxon alarm began to chime. Bold symbols and characters began to scroll onto the tactical display. I looked to Jhally to interpret their meaning.

"I am surprised it's taken this long. We are no longer safe here," he said.

"What is it?" I asked.

"The events taking place in Castle Rock have been relayed to their military command. A task force will be dispatched to quell what they are calling a native rebellion." Jhally scanned the rapidly streaming symbols. "Another three Crusher vessels, ships like this one, holding six hundred fresh ground troops, along with ten Shredders, are readying for engagement. We have one-half hour before they deploy, another fifteen minutes, maybe less, before they reach this location."

I said, "We need to get back to my ranch, to our other two Shredders."

"What about all the people outside?" Karen asked. "Many are miles from their homes, some too weak to walk."

I thought about that. Karen, apparently, had reached the same conclusion as me. "Let's get them onboard! Fast!" I addressed the captain: "Do you have a PA system? Some way to broadcast to the compound outside?"

He looked at me like I was an idiot, then gestured to his own ear puck. "Of course."

I quickly realized we should have confiscated those *ear-things* from the crew right off. Now doing so, I said, "Sorry, but we can't take the chance of your communicating with other Gaps." I placed the ear pucks atop one of the consoles after first holding one out to Jhally. "Can you use this?"

"I have my own . . ." Removing an ear puck from his pocket, he flipped it up, close to the side of his head, where it settled into position over his ear.

"Cool trick," I said. I watched as Jhally called up the virtual HUD, quickly tapping on various menu options. Within seconds, the virtual HUD was gone. He then plucked the ear device away from his ear and handed it to me.

"Place it up to your ear. It has Mike Post's updated code . . . so it is Human compatible. Menus are translated into English."

Doing as told, I felt the device swish automatically into place over my ear.

"It is ready to broadcast . . . your voice will be heard by everyone outside," Jhally said.

I nodded, taking a few seconds to organize my thoughts. "Attention, this is Brian Polk. Some of you know me as

Polybius. We need to leave this location immediately. For those of you who prefer to head out on your own . . . return to your homes, your families . . . do so now. Hurry! Others, including the Takebacks, need to get aboard this Crusher ship immediately. The vessel is the one located farthest away within this compound. We are lowering the ramp now. Hurry, we don't have much time!"

Pointing to my ear puck, I asked, "Jhally, is there a way to configure these things for a closed hookup, exclusive to the Takebacks? Especially my pilots?"

Jhally hobbled over to the console with the stacked crew-member ear pucks atop it. First, he reconfigured his own ear puck, via his HUD. Then, one by one, he reconfigured the six others. Pointing then to the captain, he said, "I'm sure you have more of them around. Go get them . . . now!"

The captain moved to the opposite end of the control center near the entrance. Opening an integrated panel, he began handing Jhally ear pucks from a stockpile of about twenty. Jhally reconfigured each one. When finished, he said, "These ear pucks have been disconnected from the Earupitan Prime Network. They have been reconfigured for a closed-comms system. But first, I need to instruct you on how to operate them . . . it is not difficult. I'll start with you and Karen." He handed both of us an ear puck.

It took Jhally about ten minutes to go through the basics of ear puck operations. Since the ear puck HUD menus were similar to those onboard the Shredders, we caught on quickly, though twenty minutes had already elapsed.

I noticed on one of the compartment's display feeds—the one that showed the hold area below—that people were still filing in.

"Jhally, can you pilot this ship back to my ranch?" I asked, not yet ready to trust this crew. Once we were airborne, they might try something harebrained. Like executing a suicide crash into the side of a mountain.

"I am somewhat familiar with this vessel. Perhaps we should keep the crew's captain here, just in case I require assistance," Jhally said.

Jhally didn't look as confident as I would have liked.

"Fine . . . and we'll get Yeager up here in a bit to give you a hand as well. But first things first. Let's all go down to the hold. We'll distribute these reconfigured ear pucks and provide instructions on their operation."

"You sure we have time for that?" Karen asked, looking skeptical. "We need to be long gone before that attack team reaches us."

"We should be fine," I said. "If we're going to survive the next few hours, we need to stay in constant communication with each other."

Jhally, crutches positioned under his armpits, hurried from the compartment. I eyed Stroph. "I'm leaving the captain here with you. Can you watch him for a few minutes? Make sure he doesn't touch anything . . . or try to communicate with anyone."

"Yes, you can trust me, Brian. He will not so much as *pass gas* without first getting permission."

"Okay . . . good to know." Stroph, in spite of being a tad brain damaged from that plasma bolt to the head, *no thanks to me,* had already proven himself willing to go above and beyond to inflict painful retribution upon his own kind—most recently being that of General Chiv. I felt confident I was leaving the control center in good hands.

Armed with energy rifles and our pockets stuffed with ear pucks, Karen and I ushered the five crewmembers from the control center and down the central passageway. By the time we reached the hold area, it was jammed packed. Easily two hundred-plus bodies pressed close to one another.

Shawn McGee, a.k.a. Spartacus, greeted us as we stepped off from the lift.

"I think everyone's now onboard, Brian."

"Need to get these five Gaps out of here . . . into one of the confinement pens over by the dome." I then caught sight of Jhally, already giving instructions to Takebacks on the use of ear pucks.

"I'm on it," Shawn said, as he proceeded to herd the five Gaps through the multitude of Humans and down the ramp. The newly-released Human prisoners were mostly quiet, huddled together. More than a few still seemed to be in shock—perhaps suffering from a form of PTSD—having watched their friends and loved ones marched into that huge dome and not come back out. That would cause anguish to anyone.

Karen practically tripped over Mike Post. They set off together to distribute the ear pucks, providing cursory instructions on their use.

Farther aft, I spotted Donny keeping guard over a slumped-over General Chiv and Chancellor Sleept Vogthner. The latter, catching my eye as I approached, looked indignant at being treated like a common prisoner. I chose to ignore him, inwardly fuming about all his lies and treachery. I was tempted to leave him behind—penned-up near the atomizer dome with the other Gaps.

"Donny, take this," I said, fishing an ear puck from my pocket and handing it to him. "Jhally, Karen, or Mike will show you how to use it. Enemy Shredders are fast inbound . . . along with more Gap troops."

"How soon?"

"Only minutes. But it's imperative we keep in communication with one another."

"Copy that. You want to watch these two?"

"Sure." Before he could head off, I asked, "What's going on with those guys?" I gestured toward the bottom of the ramp where a small army of EMS marshals stood milling around. I noticed none had been disarmed, and they still had ear pucks levitating by the side of their heads.

Donny shrugged. "Hey, I don't know . . . are they our fucking enemies, or new compatriots? You decide, boss . . . way above my pay grade." Donny then hurried off.

Shit!

"You . . . come along with me," I ordered the chancellor, already hurrying down the ramp.

"What about the general?"

"He's not going anywhere in the shape he's in. Hurry up!" I heard Vogthner's heavy footfalls several paces behind me, scurrying to catch up.

The marshals, assembled below, turned their lizardy faces up and stared at me. Dressed in red, blue, and green cowboy shirts—most wearing Stetson cowboy hats—I pointed the muzzle of my energy rifle at Vogthner. "We have mere minutes before an assault team arrives from space. The Crusher full of

Humans needs to be long gone by then. But the big question for me is this: What do we do with you and these others?"

"We go with you! I told you, we've already chosen sides . . . and it's not with the military. I thought you and I were good now. Perhaps even friends."

"Tell me, then, Chancellor, were you lying to me before? About what you knew concerning Phase II and Phase III of the invasion? Explain Ronald Gant and his Friends For Friends cohorts to me; how they were being prepped to work with your military to make up for the Gaps' overall lack of military numbers and enlisted to kill their fellow man, when the proper time arose."

"That's ridiculous! Sure EMS stations were instructed to build alliances and entice Humans into joining Friends For Friends groups to collect intel to avert further subversion. We offered them powerless positions within OECs. But that was as far as it went. Inducting Humans so they could later assist us by killing each other? If that was the plan, I had no knowledge of it. But none of that now is even remotely important. As we've both learned, EMS stations all around the world are to be raided, personnel deemed compromised. I've learned Earupitan Troops are to be deployed immediately, that no more testing is necessary. Hundreds of atomizer domes will be assembled, then reassembled . . . moving from one township, or city, to another. Globally, Phase III translates for both marshals and Humans alike. Both are slated for a quick and efficient termination."

I saw desperation in Vogthner's eyes—as well as in the eyes of the marshals standing below us. *God, I want to rub all their lizard noses into this bizarre turn of events.*

"We're out of time!" Karen shouted from the top of the

ramp. I turned, seeing her and Donny looking more than a little anxious. Then Matt joined them—all three had ear pucks hovering over one ear. Karen glanced up to the sky, her brow knitted together.

I said to Vogthner, "Any minute now an attack force will arrive here . . . Shredders and Crushers full of troops."

He glanced down at the watchful faces just below us. "I have zero doubt that they . . . we . . . will all be executed."

"And you're asking me to blindly trust you? Trust the same aliens that tortured and killed Humans for two years?"

"Yes. We are at your mercy." I took in the chancellor with the bloody bandage around his head and his torn and rumpled business suit.

"We're out of time, Brian!" Karen shouted.

"Tell your marshals to hurry. Climb back in their HovTs and go to my ranch. They can park in the barn. Don't make me regret trusting you, Chancellor."

"I won't . . . and thank you!"

Karen and Wright, our other pilot, were heading down the ramp. "Now, Brian! We have to go!" she exclaimed.

We ran for the awaiting Shredder crafts. HovTs were already leaving the compound. Behind us, I heard the Crusher's big engines coming alive. *Damn, I've cut this way too close.*

chapter 37

I engaged the Shredder's lift thrusters and watched as the outer landscape fell away below me. Karen and Wright, each within their own craft, were also ascending. But the Crusher below had yet to make a move. Perhaps Jhally wasn't as much up to the task as he'd promised.

I heard Karen's voice in my ear: "You want us to stick around, or should we head out?"

"No, you two get going. I'll hang around till that Crusher is aloft and en route."

"Copy that, Earhart RTB . . ."

"Wright RTB . . ."

I smiled at their use of standard U.S. military lingo for *return to base.*

I watched as Karen and Wright's Shredder engines went *hot.* Both crafts shot away—supersonic bullets gone in a blur of motion.

I put my own Shredder into a low-holding pattern. *What the hell is taking them so long?* I contacted Jhally, hoping he'd placed an ear puck at his own ear by this time. "Jhally . . . you copy?"

It was then I noticed Donny below, sprinting away from the Crusher ship, across the compound, toward the atomizer dome.

"Donny . . . what are you—"

Somewhat out of breath, Donny's voice broke in, "We need to snatch back another crew member."

"Why? What's wrong with the captain?"

"Fucking imbecile . . . Stroph . . . he almost killed him. Twisted one of his ears right off his head. Guess there was a misunderstanding."

I found that strangely funny and laughed out loud. I banked into a slow turn, seeing Donny, along with a Gap crewmember, now running in the opposite direction, heading back toward the awaiting Crusher. Right then, something else occurred to me. "Hey, Donny?"

"Yeah?"

"Did you clear the other three Crushers? Ensure that no one was onboard those three ships?"

"Affirmative. Each was cleared—no one on board."

Finally, Jhally had the Crusher lifting off. "Come on . . . move it!" I said under my breath.

The vessel's ramp was still in the process of closing as the ship rose higher and higher into the air. I got a quick glimpse of both Humans and Gaps, tightly packed together, within the Crusher's hold area. As the ship's big engines fully thundered to life, the Crusher headed off toward the south.

Time was up. I had zero time to dillydally here. But I realized I'd be leaving behind three military vessels—for the most part, still operational, ready for the Gaps to later use against us. This was war. You don't leave military ordinances behind for the enemy. I circled twice more, trying to recall the specific instructions Jhally had given me for deployment of the two gravity-disruptor cannons via the HUD. Now activating the weapons system, which interfaced directly with the onboard AI, I watched as the virtual bounding box locked onto the first of my intended targets—the Crusher craft, three hundred feet below me, was now highlighted in bright red. I deployed the forward and aft undermounted weapons systems and selected a destructive level of two (out of three), then manually triggered the firing of both cannons. My Shredder shook as the cannons fired—immense energy blasts struck the selected target. Mid-ship, the Crusher folded in upon itself. The damage inflicted was somewhat less than I'd anticipated. Clearly, these vessels were designed to withstand a big hit. Still, I saw enough damage that I was fairly certain the Crusher would be inoperable and of no further use to the Gaps. One down, two to go.

My ear puck crackled. I heard Karen's exasperated voice, "You better not be anywhere near that compound, Brian."

"Leaving momentarily."

Within another minute I'd targeted and disabled the other two Crusher craft. I found myself constantly checking my HUD for incoming bogies, knowing I was really pressing my luck at this point. Hell, within moments, even seconds,

I could be up against ten expertly piloted Gap Shredders. Ready now to hightail it away, my eye caught sight of another potential target—the atomizer dome. It, too, had to be destroyed, or, at the very least, disabled.

Locking onto this far larger target, I selected level three, the most powerful gravity disruption level. Banking left then right, I swung onto the final approach vector. Moving my sightline from the virtual HUD representation before me, to actual visuals up through the ship's canopy, I noticed the adjacent—and all too close by—prisoner pens. Hundreds of Gap soldiers stared up at me, watching the Shredder as it came around on its final run. Throttling forward, I started my descent. Just prior to giving an order to fire, I altered the gravity disruptive setting from level three back down to level two. Far better than those Gap prisoners deserved, but the thought of stomping life out of hundreds of unarmed aliens just didn't sit right with me somehow. I fired both cannons.

"Damn it, Brian . . . you've got incoming bogies . . ." Karen yelled into my ear puck. I checked my HUD. Sure enough, it was lit up with aerial intruders coming in fast. With no time to view the extent of damage I'd inflicted to the dome . . . or to check on the current state of the Gap prisoners below, I jammed the virtual control ball all the way forward. G-forces thrust me back hard into my seat.

chapter 38

I raced my Shredder, keeping low through the middle of town, even below the treetops. Old-school thinking, probably, that flying below radar levels would somehow benefit me. But no one used radar in this day and age. Least of all the Gaps, I chided myself. Then I remembered our Shredders task beam geo locator units were disabled, so maybe, just maybe, I wasn't being tracked. I reached out to Mike Post for an update.

"Go for Mike . . . what's up, Brian?"

Relieved to find he was utilizing our new closed-comms system, I asked, "Have the Gap marshals arrived at the ranch yet?"

"Everyone's here, I think. Except you."

"Can you pull their HovT TBGUs? The less anything can be tracked—"

Mike cut in, "Bro, this ranch of yours is completely dark.

Told you, I handled that. Looks like a black hole down here as far as the Gaps are concerned. Even their military shouldn't be able to track anything within the perimeter of your property lines. TBGU signals are completely dampened. If a military ship does a flyby directly overhead and gets a visual . . . well, that's a different story. Then we're fucked."

"Copy that."

Upon arrival at my ranch, I found the XL5 Crusher, along with the two other Shredders, had set down in the pasture, while a line of HovTs was disappearing into the back of the barn. No matter what Mike said, I didn't like having our newly formed squadron of Gap ships exposed out in the open like this. I re-circled overhead, keeping an eye on my HUD's tactical display. Tracking the new arrival of military vessels back at the dome compound, I knew I'd cut things way too close.

I set down next to Shredder Three, the one Karen had piloted. Entering the barn, I found a mass of activity. Hundreds of people, along with Gap marshals, scurried about. With multiple voices shouting out, the noise level was extreme, although not quite mayhem yet. Somehow, there was a *crazy* kind of order to things.

A full head taller than everyone around him, I spotted Stroph. Weaving my way through the throngs of people, I reached him and tugged on his sleeve. "Stroph! Hey, Stroph!"

He stared down looking ready to backhand me, but then smiled. "Captain Polk!" he exclaimed, placing a heavy hand on my shoulder. My knees almost buckled under the weight.

"Um . . . where is Jhally? And the prisoner, General Chiv?"

I asked.

"I'll take you. Come!"

He led me toward the east side of the barn, where the corrals were located. Both mares had their heads lowered over their stall doors. Several Gap marshals were patting their necks, scratching behind their ears. I looked down into both enclosures and noticed ample hay distributed on the ground for them to munch on.

Standing by several stalls farther down were Jhally and Karen.

"There you are!" Karen said, as we approached.

Then I noticed General Chiv, sitting on the ground in one of the stalls, his hands and feet bound. As his bruised and bloodied face angled up toward me, his eyes were nearly swollen shut. I *almost* felt guilty about it.

"He's not talking. He's clammed up again," Karen said.

I spotted Mike Post running toward us. Out of breath, he joined our group. "Hey, Brian . . . I really need to talk to you."

"Okay, give me a minute." I approached Chiv and knelt next to him.

"I do not care what you do to me. I will not help you. Kill me if you must. I am done assisting the enemy." He then eyed Stroph, who lurked menacingly at the entrance into the stall.

"You sure about that?" I asked Chiv.

"Yes. I am ready to die for his Eminence."

Stroph grumbled something behind me. "Speak up,

Stroph. I don't think the general here quite heard you."

"I said you should let me tear his arm off . . . let me beat him to death with it."

Karen said, "Come on! Haven't we had enough of that sort of thing?"

Perhaps she was right, but desperate times often called for desperate means. But then, taking a different tact might also work just as well. "So what do you want? We have an expression here on Earth . . . The world's your oyster. So, General Chiv, let's say you could have anything you want . . . the world's your oyster?"

He looked at me, seemingly baffled by the question.

"I see it this way," I said. "We need certain information from you, and we need it fast. The physical location of his Eminence's mate, or wife, or whatever you call her. You have three choices. Choice number one: I'll just kill you, and be done with it. Choice number two: I'll let Stroph pull off one of your limbs then beat you with it until you talk. Or choice number three: you tell me what you know and maybe you get something out of the deal. Besides just letting you go, of course, what other choice, or option, would you like to propose?"

Stroph grumbled something indecipherable behind us.

I said, "You'll have to wait, Stroph. The general can select any one of those three options."

Karen entered the stall, arms folded over her chest. She looked impatient.

"Brian, I really need to talk to you," Mike urged again.

I nodded back, my attention on Chiv. He seemed to be

pondering over his choices.

"A mate."

"A mate? What does that mean? A mate?" I asked.

"He wants one of the females on that Habitat ship," Karen said.

"Really?"

"Ask him," she said.

"You want a wife . . . is that it?"

Chiv nodded. "There are so few females, and so many males."

"Well . . . two males are needed for every female, I do know that much. But even so, the proportion's still off, but . . ."

"I want a guarantee that if you are successful, I'll get a wife."

"Screw you," Karen said. "Did it ever occur to you that females ought to have a choice in the matter?"

"Fine. I guarantee you will have a place in line for a mate. Agreed?" I asked. Glancing up at Karen, I shrugged apologetically. She merely shook her head, rolling her eyes at me.

Jhally and Mike stepped into the stall. All of us stared at General Chiv—waiting for him to come to a decision.

"Eminence, Overlord Skith's mate is already here on Earth. But she is well protected. Much security surrounds her," Chiv said.

"Where?" I asked.

"On the island you refer to as Cuba. Earupitans prefer warm, humid, conditions."

"Cuba is a big island. Whereabouts?" Karen asked.

Outside a small town, called Viñales. There are subterranean caves there, called the caves of Viñales."

"She's living in a cave?" I asked surprised.

"Do not besmirch our maiden sow!" the general barked out.

I was curious what he meant by that, but I'd have let it go for now. "So, what kind of security are we talking about?"

"The Royal Guard . . . two hundred of the Earupitan's most elite fighting force. Also, no less than twenty Shredders have been committed to her safety. The island of Cuba is very well guarded."

"All that to protect a lone Gap female?" Mike asked.

"Gap is a derogatory term," Jhally interjected. "And probably not the best way to phrase things to someone you're asking help from. And a Maiden Sow is not just any female Earupitan . . ."

I said, "General, you're going to have to help us get onto that island."

"Impossible!"

"I'll give you an hour to come up with a few ideas." I stood up, blowing out a breath. I was tired and not feeling particularly optimistic about things.

"Damn it, Brian! Look, the whole planet is being invaded . . . again!" Mike said, sounding more desperate than I'd ever heard him. "I've been up in that Crusher's command center . . . getting familiar with all the tech. Suddenly, their display feeds . . . they came alive! I watched more ships than you can count exit those huge Situational Command Ships up in orbit. It's a major deployment."

We all stared at Mike.

Mike continued, "It's that Phase III thing. Hundreds, if not thousands, of their landing forces are on the way here. You know, more domes to be assembled . . . Humans to be exterminated . . . all on a massive scale!"

"You could have mentioned this a little earlier, don't you think?" Karen chided.

"One more thing, Brian," Mike said, a tad more upbeat.

"What's that?"

"Remember that big robot, back at the dome compound?"

I nodded, not fully paying attention, my thoughts pretty much now occupied with visions of Cuba and the caves of Viñales—not to mention the innumerable invading Phase II space craft.

"Well, I think I can control it . . . like . . . remotely. That is, if you didn't destroy the thing."

I glared at Mike, growing annoyed. "What are you talking about? Who cares about the damn robot? And no, but I probably should have destroyed the thing." I pondered on that a moment, remembering how easily the robot destroyed the M1 tank. Killed Titus and his crew, along with so many other Humans. "You're telling me we can take control of it . . . all the while locking the Gaps out from using it?"

"That's exactly what I'm saying," Mike said, smiling and looking triumphant.

I nodded, even though I felt I was still missing something.

Mike said, "What kind of damage do you think a mechanical beast like that could do once it's unleashed upon that same compound? This time under our control?"

chapter 39

I mentally pictured the compound. For certain, the captive GAP soldiers would have been released from their pens by now. How long would it be before that atomizer dome was back, one hundred percent operational? How long before new ground forces were dispatched to round up every last one of our local Castle Rock humans?

Mike mumbled something I missed.

"Say that again, Mike," I said.

"I'm going to try something . . . hold on," he said, calling up his ear puck HUD. Its quasi-transparent display covered his head and upper torso areas. "I'm going to cross-couple our HUDs together." He glanced up, checking to see who was still standing around in our group. A moment later, Karen, Jhally, Mike, and I, as well as Stroph—were all standing together within a large heads up display.

"What am I looking at?" Karen asked. I felt her bare

shoulder pressing against me. Giving me a bemused smile and a quick sideways glance, she let me know the sudden contact was not accidental.

I asked, "Is this the view from the robot? Are we seeing what it is seeing in real time?" The view was motionless and somewhat tilted, catching the partial aft end of one of the newly landed Crusher craft. The neighboring hillside, a crop of tall pines, showed in the background.

"I'm confused. That robot doesn't have a head . . . certainly no eyes," Karen said.

"Later, you're going to realize how stupid that statement really was, Karen," Mike said. "Needless to say, robots don't actually need heads or eyes . . . this is the bot's front-facing camera feed we're now looking at."

Karen laughed, "Oh, yeah. Guess that was sort of stupid of me."

"So the robot is inactive right now. You've only activated its camera," I said. "To get it moving, how does that work?"

Suddenly, a virtual joy-stick, along with a series of selector buttons, appeared within the HUD. Stroph, a vertical crease forming between his eyes, grunted his approval.

"These are the bot's manipulation controls," Mike explained. "We can make it walk, or pick things up. Shit, we can make it do cartwheels, I suspect, if we wanted to."

Jhally said, "Perhaps it would be best to have the robot fully destroy the dome. Fucking tear it apart, once and for all. Kill as many ground troops as possible before the robot is destroyed by attacking Shredders."

There seemed to be unanimous agreement about that all

around. But then I thought of something else. "Mike, can you show us the feed from the backside of that robot?"

"Hold on . . ."

The visual perspective changed. We now had a much better view of the compound. Ten new Shredders were parked off in the distance, lined up in two perfectly straight rows of five. Beyond them were three Mini Crushers landing craft. Armed ground forces could be seen hurrying down each respective ramp.

"Six hundred new Gap soldiers, plus those being released from the pens. That's an army!" Mike exclaimed. "An army that needs to be dealt with immediately, before they head out to capture more locals."

He was right, of course, though my eyes kept returning to the ten pristine-looking Shredders—lined up like toys on some child's shelf.

"Look . . . there's already a crew working on dome repairs," Karen said pointing

"So, what's it going to be? Shall I unleash the Kraken?" Mike asked, in an announcer's deep growly voice.

Everyone looked to me for an answer. Again, my eyes flashed to the parked Shredders. "Not quite yet," I said.

"Come on, Brian! It's now or never," Karen said.

"Our plan is to do what?" I asked. "Fly our five Shredders to Cuba. Somehow defeat twenty defending Shredders, plus untold ground forces . . . all to get to Overlord Skith's, um—"

"Maiden Sow," Mike said.

"Maiden Sow . . ." I repeated. "She'll be our best leverage dealing with the overlord, who'll help get us access onto the

Habitat."

"Yeah, we already know all that," Karen said, sounding a little too snarky for my taste. "Brian, the odds are shit that we'll be successful. We'll probably all die. But what choice do we have?"

I had no answer for her. "Jhally . . . the marshals over there," I gestured toward the barn's bustling interior, "do you think any of them can pilot a Shredder?"

Jhally shifted his gaze and tilted his large head. All the tall, green-faced aliens wearing red, green, and blue cowboy shirts, were easily notable among the inhabitants. He said, "I think there are at least ten marshals here who previously were in the military and completed flight training. That is . . . prior to them being enlisted into the EMS."

"Wait! So what are you thinking?" Karen asked me.

I pointed back to the HUD feed of the compound. "I'm thinking I want those ten new Shredders. I want to increase our odds of succeeding when we make our little visit to Cuba."

It took the rest of the afternoon, and a good part of the evening to work through a viable plan—one that would involve just about everyone present within my oversized barn. More sketched diagrams were drawn into the dirt floor. What we finally arrived at entailed a combined aerial and ground assault on the alien compound. By no means did any of us hold false hopes that this would be a slam-dunk. Beyond all doubt, we were about to attempt something more than a little crazy; something having ridiculously low odds of success. But at least it was *something*. An attempt. A courageous means for mere Humans, like us, to regain some of what we'd lost over the last two years—our feelings of self-worth.

According to Jhally, and several of our marshals who'd previously served within the Earupitan military, it wouldn't be likely any of the Gap ground forces would be doing much today. Instead, they would start deploying their ground forces, stationed within open-air troop movers, no earlier than first light.

Our attack plan was actually fairly simple. It had only four primary elements to it: one, create a substantial distraction; two, set down our stolen XL5 and deploy our troops; three, order all ground forces to converge on the compound, attacking it from all sides at once; and four, initiate our Shredder aerial attack.

Our five Shredders would be manned by pilots Karen, Yeager, Wright, and me, as well as by one of the other marshals, who supposedly had top-notch piloting experience. Jhally would be piloting our XL5, and Mike Post—controlling the giant robot—would join him there in the control center.

Both Matt and Donny, who shared the most ground assault military experience, would be leading our ragtag army, such as it was, into battle. Donny, currently, was in the process of dividing everyone into smaller squads. Matt was in charge of issuing out our limited supply of energy weapons. Stroph had come up with a few more guns by searching the Crusher, but we were still coming up way short.

I watched as Matt and Donny approached me, both wearing stern expressions. Donny said, "Brian, we only have enough weapons for about half our people. Marshals have their mist-makers, and we have a few dozen plasma rifles . . . but it's not nearly enough to go around."

I nodded.

"We know you have . . . um, a few guns lying about here. Even a few more could make a difference. It'll go for a good cause," Donny added.

Neither Matt nor Donny were ever invited down into my hidden vault. It wasn't that I didn't trust them—I did, with my life—just that the vault was something akin to a sanctuary for me, my own special hideaway. I simply never shared its whereabouts with anyone. But today, that was all about to change.

"Come with me, fellas," I said.

The three of us were about to exit the barn when Karen called out, "Hey, where are you going?"

"Come on . . . you may as well see this, too," I said.

We hurried over to the main house. I led them into the front vestibule and down a side hallway. We passed by a formal sitting room and then my office. I held up at the library's double, ten-foot high, entrance doors. "What you are about to see is not to be spoken of . . . to anyone."

"Yeah, yeah, top secret . . . got it," Karen said, rolling her pretty eyes.

"I mean it!" I exclaimed.

Donny, Matt, and Karen nodded back impatiently. I opened the doors and we entered the library. Dark mahogany shelves, holding thousands upon thousands of hardback books, lined the walls. Ladders moving on track-rails were positioned so shelves fifteen feet high could be easily accessed. Red leather armchairs were placed before a floor-to-ceiling window. A long matching sofa occupied an inset cubbyhole along one wall. The main attraction in the room was a massive stone fireplace, with a huge fire pit nearly tall enough for a full-sized man to stand erect in. All in all, this was a millionaire's library—one no Hollywood movie set could depict any better.

"The Polk family fortune in all its glory," Matt said.

"Yeah, well . . . a lot of good it does me now," I said back.

"So . . . why are we here?" Donny asked, glancing about. He looked uncomfortable being in the room's dramatic setting. "You going to read us a story?"

Karen let out a long breath. In the process of sitting down on the sofa, I said, "Don't sit there," and gestured for her to move aside. I smiled and waggled my eyebrows up and down at the three of them.

"This is stupid," Karen said. "We still have more important things to do."

Reaching around her, I took hold of a mounted brass lantern and tilted it upward and away from the wall. There was a definitive *click.* Suddenly the sofa dropped into a hidden compartment within the floor, and the inset wall slid sideways, disappearing behind bookshelves.

Matt took a tentative step into the empty dark recess and looked down. "I see a staircase."

I reached inside and flipped on a light switch. At the bottom of the descending stairway, some twenty-five feet below us, the now-illuminated three thousand square foot vault was visible for all to see. Hundreds of Army green crates were down there. Some had their tops off, their contents revealed. Colt 9mm SMG assault weapons were in one, Ruger MP-9's in another, and M203F Grenade Launchers in yet another.

Matt leaned over the banister, eyeing an open box of handguns lying at the bottom of the stairs. Whistling, he asked, "Are those Magnum semi-automatic ANT AutoMag IIIs?"

"Uh huh, the very same," I said. "Fires off magnum-caliber rounds from a semi-automatic pistol. Kicks like a mule, but the stopping power . . . well . . . let's just say it's a *bring me to Jesus* moment."

Donny said, "Bro, you've been holding out on us."

"Nah . . . just waiting for the right rainy day when we'd need it all," I said.

It was late, coming up on 0400 hours. Multiple crates had steadily been transported up the stairs by Donny, Matt, Karen, and me from my hidden vault, then hauled outside to the barn. Presently, most everyone was dog-tired, either resting within the XL5 hold, or wherever some free space was found to lie down in within the vessel's upper decks. A small team—both Humans and Gap marshals—had worked well together within the large Crusher's galley, cranking out replicator meals. Others volunteered to distribute the still-warm rations to anyone wanting one.

The barn was nearly empty now. Karen and I sat together, eating in silence on Jhally's old cot. I had no idea what I was eating—I thought it prudent not to ask. It tasted okay, sufficient sustenance for what was to come.

"It's time," Karen said. I nodded yes. Neither of us needed to say that these past few minutes together more than likely would be our last. That whatever *chemistry* linked us probably would never go further. She let me pull her close so I could kiss her lips.

When we separated, I said, "When this is over . . . I think you and Gwen should move in here with me, together."

"Oh, you do, huh?" she said looking surprised perhaps hearing such wistful thinking coming from me.

"I don't know."

She didn't look all that excited about the idea. Well, I had to ask.

"I'd have to speak to Gwen about it. She'd really like that library of yours. And the open spaces . . . the horses . . . and this is way too big a house for just one person . . . I suppose."

Afraid to jinx anything, I stayed quiet.

"I miss her so much. She's pretty much all I ever think about. I was tempted to leave, you know. Hop in one of those HovTs and just go . . . go be with my little girl. Hide out in Utah with her and my parents."

"You could have gone, too. No one would have blamed you. I know I wouldn't have," I told her.

She shook her head. "I'd never be able to look at myself in the mirror. Or into my little girl's eyes without blaming myself. No, win or lose, but probably lose, I'm with you all the way, Brian. I'll think about your offer . . . give me some time."

A few moments passed before she spoke again: "Just promise me, if I die today you'll keep an eye on Matt. He playacts being tough, but he's not like you, or like Donny. More sensitive, he never fully recovered from his injuries."

I nodded. "I promise."

"And maybe you can check in on Gwen, and my parents?"

"Of course."

"Good, I feel better. And I'll make sure Patty and Lucy are watched over . . . if you . . ."

"Thank you," I cut in, "But don't forget about Mort, and the chickens. And of course the fox."

"Oh no, that nasty animal bit me . . . twice! She's on her own."

We kissed again and stood up. "It's *GO* time."

chapter 40

All five Shredder Zion-9 argon boost drives were revving up to flight speed, right outside the barn. Sitting behind me now in one of the Shredders was an Earupitan marshal named Pierce. He supposedly had good piloting training in the past, though perhaps it would be more accurate to say he'd had *adequate* piloting experience. The other four Shredders were manned with both a pilot and a co-pilot, too. Ten minutes earlier, our XL5 Crusher landing craft disembarked from the farm, its hold packed full of ragtag army assault troops—humans and Earupitan marshals alike.

My attention was centered on my HUD, where I could track the various components of the forthcoming attack. Presently, the other four Shredders holding individual two-man teams were rushing down the runway, heading off into the darkness. I could hear Donny and Matt's voices as they barked-out orders.

Jhally and Mike Post, and less-than-accommodating

General Chiv, were seated within the XL5's control center. I heard Mike's voice say, "Polybius, we're on site and I'm about to get things moving. You should now have access to the robot's visuals. You can bring up manual control for it on your own HUD."

"Copy that," I said. I tapped at a combination of virtual buttons and the joystick, with its corresponding surrounding controls, flashed onto my display. "Got it," I said.

"You want to do the honors? Play Geppetto to our mechanical Pinocchio?"

"Yeah, sure, let me give it a try. You're there to back me up if I screw things up, right?"

Two new wide-angle video feeds popped onto my HUD. One hundred eighty degree views on my joystick—one showed the robot's forward perspective, the other a backward perspective. "Pretty dark, Mike . . . is there some way we can lighten things up a little . . . change the light settings?"

"Hold on . . ."

A moment later, both feeds visually improved, the compound's details coming alive.

"Had to initialize an auto-exposer setting," Mike said.

I reached for the virtual joystick and was surprised to experience tactile feelings in my fingers. "Here goes nothing," I said, pressing the *Enable* button for controlling the robot. Immediately, the forward video feed went from one slightly off-kilter to one perfectly horizontal. I watched as the robots two mechanical arms rose up, and three finger-like digits, on both mechanical hands, flexed. Right then, a third video feed popped onto my HUD. A new perspective from some distance away, probably from a camera situated atop one of the Mini Crusher landers. It offered the missing visual component—the robot's present location, relative to everything around it. "Thanks, Mike, that helps."

I pushed the virtual joystick forward and watched the forty-foot-tall robotic machine trudge forward. Next, I spun the robot both left and right, then raised its robotic leg up high, before stomping its metal foot down hard onto the ground. Not too much different, I thought, from a number of console games I'd played as a kid. Getting a better feel for things, I figured it was time to get busy, cause some real mayhem. I moved the robot in the direction of the atomizer dome. A series of tall lights had recently been erected to help out with repairs being made upon the top portion of the dome. Unfortunately, the dome seemed to have weathered my earlier attempt to destroy it far better than I expected.

Audio sounds from the compound were now streaming into my ear puck. Rudely awakened, Earupitan soldiers were pouring out of the three Mini Crusher ships. It was plainly evident to me that no one knew what was going on—how their assembly robot had somehow acquired a *mind* of its own. I had to smile; they were like ants escaping from a disturbed ant hill. Scores of Gap soldiers were running round and round in a frenzy of sorts.

I pushed the joystick all the way forward, forcing the robot to run. As it got closer to the dome, I used the *leap* button, something Mike had showed me how to use earlier. The robot landed hard into the side of the dome, causing the dome to partially fold into itself. Damaged, but in no way destroyed. Off balance, the robot toppled off the dome's wall, landing awkwardly on its rear end. Not sure how to get the robot back up and onto its feet, I signaled Mike. "Mike . . . can you take over control of the robot for me? Get that dome destroyed? Then get to work destroying the enemies' three little Crushers!"

"Gladly," he said.

Hundreds of Gap soldiers, standing around within the compound, gawked at the seemingly out-of-control robot.

I said, "Noble . . . Crazy Horse . . ." Using Matt's and Donny's pseudonyms, "You can commence your attack whenever you're ready."

No one raised a hand. I looked out upon growing expressions of apprehension. Glancing over my shoulder toward the workshop area, I twirled a finger high in the air above my head.

"Copy that, Polybius. We're almost in position. Give us two minutes," Donny said.

"Okay," I said, "we're getting airborne now. Be there in just a few. Oh, and guys . . ."

"Back at you," Donny said, not letting me finish my sentence.

Karen, piloting Shredder Three, was closest to mine—Shredder Five. In unison, we rose higher and higher above the Polk property.

"You all ready to do this?" I asked into an open channel. One purposely set up for our small aerial attack group.

Karen said, "We're more than ready . . . been waiting on you. Hey . . . how about we call our little squadron the NightHawks?"

"As good a name as any," I said. I nudged the control sphere between my knees forward, and instantly felt g-forces pressing me back hard into my seat. "You okay back there, Pierce?"

His gravely voice sounded a bit sickly: "I am . . . fine."

"Just don't throw-up in my Shredder," I said. "Try thinking of something else."

Mere seconds passed before we reached the northern tip of Castle Rock and the alien compound below. The sun, just now cresting over the distant horizon, cast a golden glow on the Colorado landscape beneath us. All five Shredders, our NightHawks, gained higher altitude and moved into a circular holding pattern. Banking, I watched as our four attack teams suddenly pressed in from all sides. The battle had commenced. Bright-blue energy bolts began shooting across the compound, along with sporadic flashes of light from regular gunfire. Two hundred people, mostly Humans, against an estimated eight hundred, highly trained Gap soldiers. But at least we had the element of surprise. I could see that Mike was busy controlling the robot—which was inflicting a good amount of damage. I saw the Dome had been completely destroyed, practically stomped flat. Currently, the robot stood atop an enemy's Mini Crusher, driving its heavy metallic foot down over and over again—denting-in the hull plates on the craft's aft section.

I selected an open channel to reach each of our teams. "Good work, everybody! Time now for ground forces to fall back. Oh, wait, Crazy Horse . . . I see a handful of Gaps rushing toward those parked Shredders."

"On it, boss . . . do your thing," Donny said.

I was about to give the command for my team to attack when Mike asked, "Any chance you can avoid hitting my robot?"

"Seriously? Boys and their toys," Karen said.

Right then, catching my eye, I caught the glimmer of morning sunlight bouncing off numerous distant craft descending lower from high altitudes. Some were heading south, toward Colorado Springs, and others to the north, toward Denver, and farther northwest, toward Boulder. Phase III. The Gaps' plan—eradication of humanity—was now in full swing. Atomizer domes, most likely far larger than the one erected in Castle Rock, would already be under construction. My mind flashed back to Sopravvissuto—the frail old man who walked with a cane and lived somewhere in northern Italy—a half a world away. How worried he'd been about his daughter who lived in an adjoining small town—and how I had stopped him from speaking her name aloud. She was, of course, long dead now. As were thousands of others, rounded up and forced into one atomizer dome or another. A deep sadness came over me—moisture filled my eyes.

I said, "This is for you, Sopravvissuto. For you and your daughter! Shredders . . . attack now!"

chapter 41

Captain Guart sat quietly within the stolen XL5's control center, biding his time until the moment was right. He felt sick. All thanks to that crazy maniac, Dalm Mor Stroph, who had literally ripped his ear off. He used an extended claw to poke and probe at the bloodied mess at the side of his head.

Guart watched as the traitorous Mannarian, hobbling around on his crutches, along with the scrawny Human male, who went by the name Mike, completed their dirty business—destroying the atomizer dome. He watched the video display above as five human-piloted Shredders began their aerial attack.

They really should have secured my hands behind my back—instead of in front, he thought. From his visual perspective sitting on the floor, he could see what they could not. The one plasma pistol their repeated searches had missed. Secured to the underside of the communications console, not five feet distance from where he sat, he could see the weapon plain as day.

The Human, Mike, sure was a clever one. First thing he did was to command that robot to smash its mechanical fists down onto each one of the three Mini Crusher's communications arrays. Captain Guart doubted any distress calls could have been transmitted in time. No, that would have to wait until he was able to regain control himself. He just needed them to turn their backs to him at the same time. He only needed four, maybe five, seconds to scurry across those few feet to retrieve that hidden weapon.

Guart watched as Mike maneuvered the assembly robot with more finesse than he thought possible, especially for someone of such a barbaric and inferior race.

Mike laughed out loud as he instructed the robot to stomp and kick at another section of the mini lander. Soon it would soon be little more than a heap of scrap metal. *But then it happened.* Jhally hobbled over to Mike's side to watch the display, set high up on the bulkhead. He watched as the robot continued to destructively flail its metal limbs as if possessed by daemons.

First his left foot and then his right, Captain Guart slowly brought both feet under him—positioning himself into a low crouch. A spring set to be sprung, he raised his bound hands before him—and leapt.

Both Jhally and Mike, clearly startled by the commotion behind them, spun around. But it was too late. Guart already had pulled the weapon free from the hidden holster. Close to them now, he aimed his pistol at the traitor first, shooting Jhally in the chest. As the Mannarian dropped lifeless to the deck, Guart re-aimed, firing at the Human. Mike, attempting to dive for cover, took the plasma bolt into the back of his head. He, too, dropped lifelessly onto the deck.

chapter 42

With my Shredder taking point, we were coming in low and fast, one after another—the first of our strafing runs. It was then that I noticed the robot had gone perfectly still—as if it was frozen in time—with one of its bit metal fists poised high up over its head. *No time to worry about that now.* I triggered both wing-mounted plasma guns and began mowing down Gap ground forces there within the compound.

What I didn't expect to see was incoming bright green energy bolts shooting up at us from two of the three Mini Crushers. "Incoming!" someone yelled over our comms. As we all took evasive measures to stay one piece, I said, "Night-Hawks . . . you know what to do."

Streaks of bright green plasma fire was now crisscrossing the morning sky all around us. I engaged my Shredder's gravity disruption system and felt a vibration as the two canons lowered and locked into place from their respective aft and forward fuselage compartments.

"Brian! They have a lock on you!" Karen's voice squawked into my ear puck.

Already seeing a series of energy bolts tracking my every movement and closing in on me, I immediately banked left and then right and then left again—but I was a millisecond too slow. The tip of my port side wing exploded—flaring bright white followed by a trail of bluish flames—it was a direct hit but hopefully not a catastrophic one. I continued to fly as wild and erratically as possible, keeping my virtual control sphere always on the move. All the while, I watched as the onboard AI was attempting to lock onto any number of potential ground targets—each passing by beneath my craft in a blur of motion. I jerked the controls hard left as multiple energy streaks came within inches of my canopy—illuminating everything within the cockpit in a sickly shade of green. Finally I heard and saw on my HUD I had a target lock. It was one of the Mini Crushers below. I fired both canons then immediately pulled back on my control sphere to get some needed distance and altitude. With a quick glance over my shoulder I saw the aft section of the Mini Crusher was a flat as a pancake. Like angry circling bees, the four other NightHawks were dispatching devastating hell fire onto the compound below. Most startling and grisly were the hundreds of partially visible Gap corpses—hard pounded deep into the ground—as if the very foot of God had stomped down with a hellish fury. I listened to the other pilot's excited cross talk. I heard Karen's voice as she yelled, "Got them! Hold your applause folks . . . all in a day's work."

By this time, incoming plasma fire went from sporadic to non-existent. All three of the Mini Crushers had been decimated. What remained of the enemy ground forces had been ripped apart by our NightHawks plasma fire. The enemy had been defeated. I maneuvered in low, passing through black plumes of rising smoke. I saw that the robot was still oddly immobile—still frozen in time. "Jhally . . . Mike, how about a status report?" I waited several more moments and said, "Come back, status, guys? The comms channel stayed quiet. The other pilots were now holding back with their chatter.

I was surprised to hear Chancellor Sleept Vogthner's distinctive voice come over the comms channel. *Wasn't he still being held captive himself within the hold? Stroph must have brought him and General Chiv up to the bridge to get them ready for the next part of the plan.*

"I'm sorry . . . both Jhally and Mike are down. I repeat both Jhally and Mike are down. Shot by the prisoner . . . by Captain Guart."

Stunned, I was having a hard time piloting my craft. I squeezed my eyes shut. Oh, God, I felt dizzy. Both, in their own way, were family. . . . *No, I can't go there . . . I can't let this derail what I have to do today. Suck it up, grieve later.* "And the murderous fucking captain?" I asked.

"Dead . . . He's been decapitated."

I didn't need to ask. Obviously that would be Stroph's unique handiwork. *Good.*

Vogthner continued, "But not before the Captain had gotten off a distress call. We have incoming aerial forces coming in from both the south and the north."

I verified as much on my own HUD. Shredders headed this way. Too many to count. Fortunately, my NightHawks were already setting down and letting out their copilots. Two of them were dashing across an open field toward the awaiting dual rows of enemy Shredders. I'd almost forgotten my own copilot that was still seated mere feet behind me. "You still with me back there, Pierce?"

He cleared his throat, "Yes, yes I am."

I brought my Shredder down—probably faster and more dangerously than prudent. I opened the canopy and waited for Pierce to climb out onto the wing. "Best you hurry, Pierce," I yelled over the loud engine noise. "As you heard, we're expecting company."

I waited for my canopy to close before asking, "How much time do we have, Chancellor?"

"Not much . . . maybe three minutes."

I caught a glimpse of Donny helping a limping Matt there amongst the remaining friendly ground forces. *At least these two friends had survived the day.* But we'd lost at least half of those we'd arrived with. A heavy price to pay for acquiring five additional Shredders. Men, women, and Gap marshals, were filing up the ramp and into the XL5's hold.

I heard Karen's soft voice, "Brian . . . hey, I'm so sorry . . . I know how close you were to both—"

"What the fuck!" I said it aloud, not meaning to so rudely cut her off. But it was the robot. Suddenly, it was moving again. And it was walking toward the XL5.

"Brian?" Karen said sounding a bit miffed.

"Just hold on a sec, Karen."

One by one the NightHawks continued to lift off around me. Our squadron of five was now ten. But my attention was still on the robot.

"Umm, Chancellor, is that you controlling—"

Another voice came on the channel, "No, that's me. I think we should keep the robot. Fuck, the thing was a rockstar out there . . . did you see it?"

"Wait . . . Mike? Is that you? You're supposed to be dead!"

"The way my head hurts, I feel like I should be. I guess the lowest of the three settings on a mistmaker pistol is a kind of stun level. But if you could see the back of my head, it's scorched and as bald as a baboon's ass—"

"And Jhally? Is he okay too?"

I waited for several long moments.

"Well, he's alive . . . still breathing. But he's unconscious. He'd been a good bit closer to that asshole captain."

Apparently, Mike had put the robot into some kind of automatic hibernation mode. Currently each appendage segment was retracting into the main torso becoming a perfect rectangle. A side panel on the XL5 slid open, revealing four extending armatures. Within moments the rectangular block of metal was being hoisted up and pulled into the awaiting compartment. The XL5's lift thrusters came alive and the big landing vessel began to rise amidst a flurry of swirling small rocks and dirt.

Ten Shredders and one XL5 Crusher vessel headed south-east—toward the island of Cuba.

chapter 43

We were cruising along due south at an altitude of twelve thousand feet within a standard military Vic, or V, formation with my Shredder Five in the lead position. Karen, in Shredder Three, was flying slightly behind and on my port side, while pilot Yeager, in Shredder Four, was off to my starboard. The XL5, being piloted by a marshal familiar with the vessel's helm, was situated within the middle of our eleven-vessel squadron. Four times we had altered our course to avoid flying directly over new dome military compounds—most still seemed to be under construction, but some looked to be almost complete. *Ready for business.*

Tapping into the Gaps' frenzied communications chatter, it was clear that we'd certainly stirred the proverbial pot. Yes, not only had the Castle Rock military encampment been attacked, but, somehow, *inconceivably*, had been completely wiped out. Hundreds of ground forces killed. Multiple Crushers destroyed; Shredders were possibly missing. But the most surprising turn of events was the Gap high-command assumption that the uprising had solely been the work of the local, traitorous, EMS marshals, only justifying his Eminence, Overlord Skith's earlier decision to annihilate all EMS personnel across the globe. Apparently, lowly Humans were not deemed capable of such a brazen and triumphant act. We had picked up on one very crucial bit of information—that his Eminence, Overlord Skith, was currently in high orbit onboard the Situational Command Ship Tasthmal 8. His most prized possession, the Maiden Sow, was assumed to still be in the Cuban subterranean caves of Viñales. All incoming hails were answered with terse audio-only replies that this squadron was on a special mission for his high Eminence. General Chiv cannot be bothered with mindless inquiries at the moment.

I reflected on my most recent communiqués back and forth with Vogthner. Jhally was still unconscious onboard the XL5—possibly at death's door. But I'd detected little emotion in the Chancellor's voice. Were things so different with these Gaps that the potential loss of a close family member, a brother in this case, was of such little consequence? I reflected on the loss of my own brother, Glen. A brother who, like so many others, had been summoned into a local OEC building and was never seen again. I hadn't considered it much before now, but there was a good probability Sleept Vogthner, the Gaps' local chancellor of communications, had been directly responsible for Glen's death. Perhaps he'd even been there during my brother's final moments of life. It would have been so easy these past two years to be utterly consumed by hatred. Up till now, I'd steered away from going there—seeing how those kinds of spiraling emotions had destroyed the lives of those still living. But now, thinking about Glen, seeing more and more of those vile domes taking shape below us—*hatred* had come a knocking again. It would be up to me if I answered that door.

The plan was to fly right into Cuba's airspace as if we were under direct orders to do so. And we'd still be counting on General Chiv's clout to get us as close in as possible. We'd need to be careful with any visual communications though—his bruised and swollen face would be hard to explain if inquiries were made.

Up ahead was the tip of Florida with the Atlantic Ocean off to the left and the Gulf of Mexico off to the right. Then I saw the first of the shipwrecks. No less than ten U.S. Navy vessels in various stages of destruction sat along the southern shoreline—a once magnificent aircraft carrier, two battle ships, a frigate, and several destroyers—each had the telltale spans of hull that had been grotesquely flattened, characteristic of the gravity-disruptor cannons. Our squadron went quiet.

As we progressed farther south, the deep blue waters of the Atlantic were slowly being replaced by the aqua blue waters of the Caribbean. The Florida Keys islands came next—it was here the first of several great oceanic cruise ships lay crushed and sideways upon sunny beachheads. Undoubtedly, decomposing Human remains were still among the wreckage—no atomizer domes had been built two years ago to deal with such things.

My HUD *dinged* as a new visual feed from the XL5's Control Center popped into view. I saw a Gap marshal standing at the helm and Chancellor Vogthner manning another console. Stroph's hulking presence could be seen lurking in the background and Mike Post was closer in, seated with his scorched bald spot in full view at the back of his head. Donny was just now escorting—*more like manhandling*—General Chiv into view. Donny plopped the general down hard into an open seat.

I asked, "How's his uniform look?"

Donny looked up and around as if trying to find a camera.

"I'm ninety degrees to your left," I said.

Donny spun the general's chair around, giving me a full straight-on view of Chiv's face. I cringed. "Ugh, he looks like someone took a baseball bat to him."

"Close enough," Donny said sending an irritated glare at Stroph.

"I see you've repaired his uniform, cleaned the splotches of blood from his jacket."

"We grabbed a new one from his quarters," Donny said. "Pretty nice digs by the way."

I said, "General Chiv . . . do I need to remind you that your life ends the second you call for help, or do anything to warn the Royal Guard there is anything amiss?"

Chiv didn't answer right away. Then I saw a clawed hand, one the size of a dinner plate, descend down onto his shoulder—obscuring the fancy epaulet there.

"Does my friend Dalm Mor Stroph need to give you a little reminder?" I asked.

"No need for your ridiculous threats," the general spat. "At this point, my execution would be a forgone conclusion. Earupitan High Command does not take kindly to failure. I will do as you ask." He glanced down at Stroph's hand.

"Please have this freakish marshal remove his hand from my shoulder."

As if on cue, an incoming hail chimed. Mike said, "Royal Guard . . . air command. Should we accept?"

"It's now or never . . . what's the worst that can happen, other than us being blown out of the sky. Put him through to General Chiv," I directed.

chapter 44

No less than thirty vessels, an assortment of Shredders and other just as dangerous fighter crafts, rose up from below, surrounding our NightHawks squadron from all sides.

"We're totally screwed now . . ." I heard Mike murmur into my ear puck.

A stern-looking officer with close-set eyes and wearing a dark red, visorless cap, one that reminded me of the caps worn by U.S. Navy Sailors—back when there were sailors—and back when there was a U.S. Navy. Although only the top portion of his upper body was visible, I could see an angled sash across his chest—adorned with an assortment of shiny medals and colorful ribbons. I assumed he was high up within the Earupitan Royal Guard. Although his angry sounding words were spoken in Earupitan, I could guess what his demands were. Fortunately, I had Vogthner whispering into my ear puck providing a translation.

"Halt! This is a restricted airspace. You will identify yourself and progress no further!"

General Chiv's battered and equally angry face appeared on my HUD sharing a split-screen feed with the Royal Guardsman.

"How dare you speak to me in such a tone!" Chiv said with Vogthner's somewhat delayed translation. "I have a mind to put you on report. Now tell me who it is I am addressing, and be quick about it," Chiv demanded.

The guardsman's beady eyes scrutinized Chiv's appearance clearly curious to know the reasons for his facial injuries, but also not comfortable interrogating a senior officer. "I am Colonel Haing and I apologize, General . . . no disrespect was intended. Even so, this is a restricted—"

Chiv broke in, "Are you a complete idiot? Who do you think dispatched this squadron? We are here on the direct orders of his Eminence, Overlord Skith, himself."

"His Eminence? Why have I not been—"

Again, Chiv cut him off, "Are you so clueless you know not of the rebel attacks in the North American sector? The total defeat of our Earupitan ground troops at the Castle Rock encampment?"

"Well, yes, General, we have heard . . . well, in truth the information has been sketchy at best."

"Let me ask you this, Colonel, are you not concerned with the Maiden Sow's welfare? Would you have the overlord's wife slaughtered when a surprise attack befalls this location?"

"I assure you, General, there is no more secure location on this planet."

"I see. Perhaps you are right. I will instruct my captain to simply turn this squadron around. Perhaps Overlord Skith will be fine with a mere Colonel countermanding his orders."

Listening to Chiv's superior and snarky tone, I had to give it to the Earupitan general. He was selling this bullshit like no one else could.

"Again, I apologize, sir. Perhaps if you would allow me simply to verify his Eminence's orders? Just a few minutes while we confirm his wishes."

"By all means. It is only your career, or what is left of it, that is at stake. And I am certain that by you transmitting this highly classified information onto an already compromised Earupitan comms system . . . revealing the whereabouts of the Maiden Sow would be of little concern to him. Maybe while you are at it, you should put out a general announcement across all comms channels for all, friend and foe alike, to tune into."

Colonel Haing looked to be in physical pain. "Sir . . . what is it you wish me to do, General Chiv?"

"Exactly what I said, "Get the Maiden Sow up and about. Have her things packed and ready to go in ten minutes. She's being transported into space to join her husband where she can be far better protected."

The Colonel grimaced hearing Chiv's stinging words. "I assure you. She will be ready. Please . . . my Adjunct Fighting Squad will now escort you in."

Only now could I see the distant landmass of Cuba rising up along the distant horizon. Mike provided our HUDs with an updated logistical feed. It looked like the little town of Viñales was about one hundred and ten miles due west of Havana. We would be there in mere minutes. Looking around, I had the distinct feeling our Shredders were being highly scrutinized by our alien escorts. I wondered if they were they capable of scanning our vessels—perhaps determine our Human DNA? Or had Mike contrived some kind of shielding for such a thing?

One of the alien vessels, a kind of small warship, veered closer to mine. I could almost make out the contours of the Gap's lizard-like profile—could he see me with the same clarity? Sure, our canopies were tinted, but were they tinted enough?

"I don't like this," I heard Karen say. "He's like looking right at you, Brian."

I turned and looked over my shoulder toward her—could see her Shredder Three right off my port wing. "I think we're okay . . . I mean, I can't see you. Not really. Not with the amount of glare off that canopy. There's nothing we can do about it anyway. It's not like we can hide ourselves."

"No, but I can fire before I'm fired upon," she said.

"Just cool your jets, girl . . . nobody's firing at anything, yet. As far as the Gaps are concerned, this is just a routine encounter. And there isn't a one of them that would believe a Human was capable of flying one of these birds."

"Uh huh . . . ," she said, not sounding remotely convinced.

Mike cut in, "Here we go. I've forwarded the Gaps' landing zone parameters to your HUDs.

As we crossed over Cuba's landmass, I marveled at how green and lush the countryside was. Approaching the town of Viñales, I saw the terrain had turned rocky and mountainous with a muddy river coursing through a narrow valley. The nearby town itself was basically a narrow lane bordered on both sides by a few rickety shacks. Directly south of the town was a large circular area about a half-mile in circumference, completely void of vegetation. Upon closer examination, though, I saw the land had been brutally stomped down—creating a kind of indented span of darkened earth. The adverse effects of multiple gravity-disruptor cannons doing their nasty business. I tried not to think about the scores of indigenous wildlife killed for the lone purpose of procuring a suitable landing pad.

Our squadron of NightHawks set down in unison with the XL5 positioned closest to where a darkened, triangular-shaped, crevice dominated the facing of a rocky hillside. This was the entrance to the subterranean caves, I assumed. I instructed the other pilots to keep their power plants going—be ready for a fast getaway if the need arises.

A half dozen of the Royal Guards' spacecraft set down along the outer perimeter of the landing pad—doing so in a way their armaments were pointed inward toward our NightHawks squadron.

"They have requested the general's presence . . . within the cave," Vogthner said. It's some kind of protocol. The Maiden Sow must be presented with a high-ranking escort."

"No . . . I don't trust Chiv any farther than I can throw him," I said. "Once he's inside that cave, all bets could be off. You'll have to go with him."

"Me . . . who's wearing a torn and bloodied business suit?"

I thought about that a moment. "Captain Guart . . . he was about your size, I'm sure he had more than one uniform."

"I'm also Mannarian . . ." Vogthner added.

"I don't care. Hurry up and get dressed. I want your ear puck HUD activated so I can see everything going on in real time."

I hadn't noticed them prior, but now I did. There were multiple teams of Royal Guard sentries moving behind that dense foliage within the surrounding jungle. It made sense that there would be.

It was another ten minutes before I saw the XL5's gangway start to lower down to the ground. A moment later, General Chiv, Chancellor Vogthner, and an armed Gap marshal that I recognized, who was also wearing another crewmember's uniform, all strode down the ramp and headed off toward the cave's entrance. I could see Vogthner's activated HUD—a bluish translucent dome situated over the upper portion of his body. I took note of the transmitted feed within my Shredder's Heads Up Display—I both heard and saw everything the chancellor was hearing and seeing.

I watched as Chiv, Vogthner, and the marshal were met by a contingent of seven Earupitans. Colonel Haing bowed slightly as General Chiv and the others approached.

"Welcome to the caves of Viñales," the colonel said, eyeing both Vogthner and the disguised marshal, but Chiv made no overture to introduce them to him.

They all continued down a wide and meandering pathway. The farther in they all went, the more breathtaking the surroundings became. This had been a popular Cuban tourist attraction at one time—the lighting was dramatic, hidden spotlights splayed here and there onto the massive and jagged stalactites above. "As you can imagine, we are on a tight schedule, Colonel," Chiv said impatiently.

They walked for what I guessed was about a mile—far enough that I was beginning to get concerned I'd lose Vogthner's HUD transmission.

Dark, ominous, clouds were rolling in overhead and within minutes it had started to rain. Soon it was a torrential downpour so extreme it was nearly impossible to see out my canopy. The constant drumming of raindrops made it hard to hear what was being said deep within the cave—not that much discussion was going on at present.

"Hey, Brian, seems you've got a lookie-loo coming up on your six," I heard Mike say. "An armed sentry meandering through the squadron."

"I'm surprised you can see anything through this downpour," I said.

"Yeah, well the XL5's optics can pick up infrared signatures."

Then I saw him. A shadow of a figure moving around off to my right down below. "Shit . . . I think he's climbing up onto the wing," I said. "Without the sun's glare, he'll be able to see right inside my canopy. And see my all too human-looking face."

The dark figure stepped closer. I could now see he had his rifle slung over one shoulder. He loomed over me and was looking directly at me. He swung his head a little to the right and then left—as if by repositioning his perspective it would give him a better vantage at what he was looking at. *Fuck!* He was leaning in now, bringing his dripping wet face closer in to the canopy. He was cupping his hands around his eyes as to better see inside the cockpit—*to better see me.*

His eyes went wide with astonishment as realization took

hold. As he now saw exactly who it was that was piloting this Shredder. A Human. An enemy.

chapter 45

In that split second I stared right back at him—incapable of stopping this train wreck of a catastrophe, knowing there was no way to keep this looming sentry from calling out in frantic alarm. Like a frenetic drum roll, the rain continued to pour down. And then, oddly, there was another dark form standing right behind him. I leaned forward and squinted my eyes, as if that could possibly improve the visibility outside. Perhaps in that moment the rain had let up, just a little, or perhaps a tad more light had pierced through the thick cloud bank above. But in that moment, I saw him. Shawn McGee—Spartacus. The Krav Maga MMA mixed martial arts master who was a full foot and a half shorter than this towering Gap. McGee moved fast. I watched as he thrust a foot down hard at the back of the sentry's lower leg—buckling the knee joint. A lightning fast uppercut slammed the alien's chin up high. This was followed with a kind of sideways chopping motion to the Gap's now fully exposed larynx. All movements were fast and efficient. As the sentry staggered, both hands now clutching at his crushed air pipe, McGee unleashed a spinning back kick that not only lifted the alien up off his feet, but propelled him right off the Shredder as well. I caught a glimpse of a toothy grin before the Krav Maga master leapt from the wing and then was pulling the dead sentry through the mud by the nape of his collar. The rain was pouring down so hard now that unless you were staring directly at the XL5's gangway, you wouldn't have noticed the darkened shapes ascending up into the ship's hold.

"Did I really see that . . . or did I imagine it?" Karen asked.

"No, you saw it. Let's just hope nobody else did. And that the sentry isn't missed prior to us getting out of here."

"Copy that," she said.

I shifted my attention back to my HUD and the dark cavern. I wasn't completely sure what it was exactly I was now looking at. Someone, or something was approaching Vogthner and Chiv's position.

I heard Mike's voice over the comms, "What the fuck? So this is the Maiden Sow? She's like, enormous."

I caught glimpses of her bulk as she passed beneath overhead spotlights. Creamy white in color, she was basically an overgrown, segmented, maggot. A maggot with a small head that, surprisingly, was reptilian looking. She was easily seven feet tall and ten feet long. Basically the girth of a fully grown hippopotamus. How her six short, spindly legs supported so many hundreds of pounds was a mystery to me. Each of her approaching labored steps was accompanied by strained sighs. And then there was the loud flatulence—farting sounds that kept perfect cadence with each of her labored steps. Coming up the path behind her, were multiple hard-case trunks that had been piled high onto a kind of hover-sled. Two Gap guardsmen were necessary to maneuver the sled while keeping the cases from toppling off one side or the other.

Most surprising was her voice. It was soft, high-pitched, and had a kind of sweetness about it. I didn't need to have Vogthner's translation to know she was apologizing for her slow pace, or maybe her flatulence, or both.

The hand off was uneventful. The Maiden Sow was accompanied by Colonel Haing and his Royal Guard as far as the cave's opening.

Colonel Haing said, "If I may ask . . . will the Maiden be returning to us anytime soon, General?"

Chiv, already heading out into the rain, didn't bother turning around, only saying, "I wouldn't count on it."

Vogthner and the marshal had taken over the precarious steering of the hover sled while Chiv and the Maiden Sow, now walking side-by-side, sloshed forward through the mud. By the way the General kept looking over to her, seeing his peculiar expression, it was becoming more and more apparent that he was quite taken, enamored even, with her.

"Shit!" Mike said. "Okay . . . we need to get this shit show on the road. Earupitan chatter is all a buzz about us. High command is now aware that both Humans and EMS Marshals were responsible for the Castle Rock attack. And their equivalent of an all-points bulletin has just been issued for our NightHawks squadron."

"So . . . has the Royal Guard here, Colonel Haing, put two and two together yet?" Karen asked.

"No . . . but they may be getting suspicious. All the more reason to get that monumental slug to hurry things up."

I watched as they continued to move painfully slow up the ramp. Halfway up they had to stop so she could rest. I saw the Maiden Sow huffing and puffing there, trying to catch her breath. My eyes kept flashing over to the surrounding trees where untold hundreds of Royal Guardsmen might just start shooting at us at any moment.

"Screw it. It's now or never. Donny . . . Matt, get whomever you need to help bring everyone on board. Go! Hurry! Mike . . . get that ship airborne!"

chapter 46

With our spirits lifted, the NightHawks rocketed up through Earth's stratosphere at a sharp, nearly straight up, angle. Truth was, I half expected our previous good fortune to be dashed at any moment. Enemy Shredders could show up on our HUDs—blips on our displays—following behind us in close pursuit. Or perhaps innumerable space fighters could have been deployed by one or all of those high-orbit Situational Command Ships—ready to obliterate us in a matter of seconds.

The sky darkened as we progressed higher from the mesosphere and into the thermosphere. It occurred to me I had absolutely no idea how to fly this craft in space. Would the controls respond far differently in a weightless environment? Was there something we were supposed to do prior to reaching Earth's low orbit—maybe a switch to flip?

I selected a closed channel on my HUD controls. "Mike, any chance Jhally has come around yet?" I asked.

It was a full minute before Mike said, "Sorry, man . . . just checked. Got him situated in an officer's quarters. He's breathing. But no real change."

I tapped at a few more virtual buttons until a wide angle feed of the Control Center came into view. I saw General Chiv was back at the helm along with the same marshal who had escorted him into the cave.

Mike said, "The plan . . . um, is still to head directly to the Moon? That Solaris Habitat thing?"

"Affirmative."

"There will be defenses. Probably a shit load of ships."

"Undoubtedly there will be," I said closing the channel.

Apparently there was no magical switch I had needed to flip, as it was now completely dark outside my Shredder's canopy. I said into our squadron's dedicated channel, "How about this? We're officially astronauts."

The view truly was spectacular. A million twinkling stars against an obsidian backdrop. The moon as bright as a lone headlight on a deserted night's street, some two hundred thirty-eight thousands miles away, beckoning us onward.

I hailed Karen. "Go for Karen."

"What could be better than this?" I asked.

"Hmm . Maybe just one thing . . ."

"Yeah? And what's that?" I asked.

"Me sitting there with you . . . on your lap."

I liked the sound of that—

"Incoming!" Came Yeager's booming baritone voice.

I scanned my HUD and, sure enough, we had incoming

bogies not only coming from Earth, but up here in space. Well, it was bound to happen. It was only a matter of time.

"Talk to me Mike, what's their ETA?"

"You're pretty much looking at the same thing I am. The little general here says we all need to throttle all the way forward. We may be able to maintain our slight head start."

We all did as suggested and our individual spacecraft shot forward. The subsequent g-forces pulled me hard back into my seat.

I saw that Vogthner was hailing me. Out of habit I said, "Go for Polybius."

I saw the Chancellor standing within the crowded hold area. Bodies huddled in close all around him. He shifted his position and the Maiden Sow came into view behind him. She was speaking to a group of five Marshals—their rapt attention, more like infatuation, made me smile.

"The Maiden Sow has relayed to me she is feeling a little ill. She's requested we alter course for the nearest Situational Command Ship . . . so she can deal with some, um, personal issues."

I noticed that the other Humans there in the hold were giving the female Earupitan a wide birth. Clearly, the oversized gasbag was making the air in that hold toxic. "Tell her you asked and I, apologetically, had to decline the suggestion."

He nodded.

"I'm fairly sure you knew what my answer would be. Was there anything else, Chancellor?"

He nodded. "Perhaps this plan of yours is . . . not a sound strategy."

"And why is that?"

"You must have already considered the fact . . . you will, most certainly, fail. Any attempt on the females aboard that habitat . . . Brian, the wrath you will incur—"

I chuckled at that. "Either way, we would die. What difference does it make?"

"You are correct, Brian. Death would be the end result for you and this attack force, me and my marshals included. But I assure you, harm any one of the females, and it would not be quick. Remember, my kind is well versed in the application of pain. Unimaginable pain."

"I'm aware of that, Chancellor. As I'm sure my brother was, too . . . during the long hours of torture he endured prior to his own execution. I'm not going to ask if you were there, or if you were the one responsible. Knowing that would mean I'd have to kill you. Both Donny and Matt, there with you in that hold, would leap at the opportunity to carry out my orders. But you still might be useful to me."

I killed the Chancellor's channel and tried not to think about failure. His use of the word *plan* gave far more credence to our actions than they deserved. I'd been pretty much winging things since the start, making decisions based solely on my gut. *Plan? What plan?* What were we going to do once we got to the habitat vessel? Saddle up to the front door and knock? Ask to come in for tea and crumpets?

Mike's face popped into view on my HUD. "Two things, no wait, three things . . . first, a fucking armada of warships is closing in on us as we speak. Second, critical levels of methane are making the air in the lower decks unbreathable. And three, none other than his Eminence, Overlord Skith himself, is on the line waiting to speak with the commanding officer of this squadron."

"You could have led with that last one, Mike. But this is good; I've been waiting for him to make contact. Go ahead and put him through."

"We all want to see this," he said.

"That's fine," I said. "Put it on an open channel."

It took a few moments and then there he was, the most powerful individual in all the Earupitan Empire. He spoke first. His English was impeccable. "Ah, so you are the one they call Polybius."

"That's right, Overlord . . . nice to make your acquaintance." I could see he was barely holding it together. Seething. While Human faces flush pink when they seethe, Gap faces, instead, turn a factor of shades of darker green. That and his breathing looked forced—was labored. He was clearly about to blow a cork.

He said, "A fleet of Earupitan warships is nearly upon you. You will not achieve your goal . . . to come anywhere close to our sacred Solaris Habitat. Halt your progression now . . . while I am still feeling amiable and willing to discuss things."

I furrowed my brow—making an exaggerated thoughtful expression. "Well, . . . I don't really think I want to do that. I figure we're all dead anyway. We'll just continue on our way and see what happens."

"Do you know how easy it would be . . . destroying you, your little convoy of stolen ships?"

I shrugged. "I imagine, pretty damn easy." I snapped my

fingers. "That's how quick." I looked at him. Can your kind do that, snap your fingers?"

"Do not play with me, Human. I assure you, Captain Brian Polk, you will not win. You will be made to regret all your actions moving forth."

I had to smile at that. "The thing is . . . your Eminence, to play this game you actually need to have something to bargain with. Look at my face. Hell, look at any Human's face today. We've lost everything. You've taken our loved ones from us, our friends and family. You've taken our fucking planet from us. So we'll be satisfied with something relatively inconsequential."

He raised his nose and waited for me to continue.

"We'll be satisfied hurting you. You, individually, and, if possible, your kind . . . collectively."

He scoffed at that, waiving a dismissive hand in the air.

"Say, Mike, can you provide the overlord that feed of the hold area? Let him see his wife, his Maiden Sow, being seduced by more than a few, highly infatuated, EMS marshals?"

"You got it, boss."

The now split screen feed showing the hold area was perfect. The Maiden Sow seemed to be holding court to no less than twelve marshals. I let him glare for several more moments before saying, "My plan is to raffle her off. Do you have such a thing where you're from . . . a raffle? You know, where some lucky bloke's name is drawn from a hat—"

"I know what a raffle is, Captain Polk. Harm her, and I will make your last moments alive—"

"Yeah, I got it, beyond agonizing."

I looked up and around, surprised to see we were quickly closing in on the Moon. There were hundreds of vessels keeping pace with us. True warships—big substantial starships—undoubtedly each with countless canon muzzles directed toward us, toward me.

"What's it going to be, overlord? And by the way . . . she's been asking for you. Doesn't seem to realize the gravity of the situation. Maybe I should just tell her. Tell her that she's just not that important to you? That she, unfortunately, along with the rest of us, will soon to be blown to—"

"What exactly do you want?" He yelled.

His eyes were wet with brimming tears. His face looking resigned to whatever I would ask. But I knew her lone life would not be enough to get these fucking lizards off our world.

"We're approaching the habitat," Mike said in my ear.

I took in the massive vessel. And it was truly beautiful. Clearly a feminine design. A wispy rainbow of variant undulating hues. Soft pinks and baby blues beneath flowing bands that were as bright and golden as our sun. Contours of the habitat were comprised of gentle lines—never a harsh angle. We moved ever closer while the armada only seemed to grow in numbers.

"What I want, Overlord Skith, is entry into that habitat."

"That . . . is impossible. Will never happen . . . not ever. So do as you will with my wife. Which pains me to say. But even if I gave the command to allow such a thing, it would be ignored. For right there lies the very future of our species."

Mike said, "Um . . . Brian, I've found the front door. A kind of flight bay entrance." As the somewhat spherical shaped structure revolved on its axis, I saw what Mike was referring to. A rectangular opening large enough to receive twenty XL5 ships simultaneously. It shimmered a bright aqua blue—glowed as if it were electrified.

The overlord said, "That access portal you are scrutinizing is, of course, shielded. It is an impregnable energy field . . . one capable of withstanding more firepower than this entire armada could produce. An energy field that can only be disabled from someone on the inside."

I didn't doubt everything the overlord was saying to me was anything but the truth. So I looked elsewhere. Interestingly, as much as the structure looked almost ethereal and not solid, I saw, now being in such close proximity, that it was an illusion conjured artificially by use of projected imagery. An elaborate light show. Hull plates comprised the outer skin of the structure. Hard to see, sure, but there were cable runs, and junction boxes, and antenna arrays—all the kind of advanced and intricate technology any space vessel of this complexity would require.

"So we are at an impasse, Captain Polk," the overlord said. "I am not without sympathy for your species' plight. Yes, the Earupitan's have made mistakes. We are responsible for unspeakable acts of cruelty. Brian, I assure you . . . none of you will be harmed if you surrender—"

"Save your breath, your eminence. Let us in to that habitat, only then can we talk."

Karen said, "Brian, he is right. This is a standoff and how long can we sit here? Another ten minutes I'll be peeing my pants. Maybe we make a run for it . . . head back to Earth? Hide?"

But I was still looking at all the little inlets and outlets—all the many contours that made up the outer surface layer of the habitat.

"Mike, ask whoever is at the helm right now how close he can get that XL5's starboard hull to the habitat."

Chiv himself got back to me. "Right up to it . . . but why bother? The habitat structure is shielded in its entirety against incoming fire. Missiles, lasers, plasma bolts, all would be thwarted."

"How about something moving a whole lot slower. Like an assembly bot?"

chapter 47

General Chiv stared back at me expressionless. Then he said, "The shielding may not attempt to repel such an action, especially since the robot is, essentially, the same Earupitan technology. I imagine similar bots are used for ongoing hull maintenance processes or necessary repairs."

"Look, General. You've been far more helpful than I could have expected you to be. You more than proved that down in that Cuban cave. So I just want to assure you, I have no intention of hurting the females of your kind inside that structure. That is not my intent, far from it."

"I believe you. It would be impractical for me not to. I completely understand the concept of . . . a bargaining chip. But I am not assisting you out of the goodness of my heart. Or any kind of new found morality. No, you made me a promise, Captain Polk. One that I expect you to keep. Remember . . . the wife of my choosing among any of the one million females aboard this habitat."

I heard Karen murmur something undecipherable in my ear. I'd forgotten I'd been talking on our squadron's open channel.

"No . . . that wasn't the deal, General," I said emphatically. "What I said was that you would be guaranteed a spot in line for the females to consider, not guaranteed a female of your choice."

I turned my attention back to the issue at hand. "Mike, there's what looks to be some kind of large access panel about twenty yards to the left of the flight bay access."

"Okay . . . yeah, I think I see it. Maybe fifteen feet by fifteen feet . . . a square."

"That's it. Have Chiv position the ship right in front of it."

It took a good five minutes for Chiv to get the XL5 properly oriented then slide in close like a boat drifting into a dock.

Mike looked nervous. "This little stunt of ours has caused every one of those warships to power up their weapons systems. And his Eminence . . . he's back on the line, demanding to talk to you."

"If you haven't noticed, they're being extremely careful not to fire directly toward the habitat. Let's just hope it stays that way. Go ahead and put the overlord through."

"You are playing a dangerous game, Captain Polk," the overlord spat. Your close proximity to the habitat is unacceptable! Move that Crusher vessel away and do so now!"

"I assure you, my intentions are guileless. Look, exposing one flank to the enemy is far preferable than exposing both. Or have you forgotten about your wife's safety so soon?"

"Do not test me, Polk! You have one minute before I

commence firing upon your vessels."

"Fine, I'll speak with the captain of the Crusher. See if he can push us off a bit." I muted the connection to the overlord.

"Mike . . . how fast can you get that robot dispatched onto the outer hull of the habitat?"

"Already on it. Getting the big guy dispatched, as you put it, is mostly an automatic affair. I'm watching as that block of metal is sliding out on guide rails right now."

I watched from the cockpit of my Shredder. Hopefully, there was no way anyone would be able to see what was happening on the other side of the XL5.

"Thirty seconds, Captain Polk . . . do not force me to fire upon you."

"You do know, your Maiden Sow has a gun pointed at her head. You fire, we fire."

Mike said, "Okay, the headless monstrosity is unpacking himself. Appendages are extending."

"Can't you move the thing along faster?" Karen interjected.

"No, it goes at its own speed."

In a brilliant flash of light, something exploded nearby.

"Shit! We just lost Shredder Eleven," Mike said. "Marshal Pierce was the pilot.

"Connect me to the overlord," I said forcing myself to stay far calmer than I was actually feeling.

Before he could respond I said, "You reptilian fuck . . . I want you to watch as I have your wife's two front appendages blown off."

Back came the split-screen video feed with the view into

the hold. "Donny . . . go ahead and shoot her front legs off!"

"No! Please . . . I am sorry we fired upon your vessel. But please . . . back your Crusher away from the habitat. That is all I ask. Then we can resume constructive negotiations."

"So . . . you want me to hold off on shooting the worm lady, Brian?" Donny asked.

I let out a long over dramatic breath. "Have you ever heard the phrase, an eye for an eye? Or a tooth for a tooth, Overlord?"

His mouth opened but no words escaped his lizard lips.

"A dear friend of mine just went up in a ball of fire. The loss I'm feeling . . . there needs to be reconciliation."

"So you do want me to shoot her legs off?" Donny said.

"No!" the overlord screamed. "Please tell your man NOT to shoot. Please!"

Mike said in my ear, "Bot's having a tough time opening that access hatch. Are you sure it even is a hatch?"

I wasn't sure at all.

Overlord Skith was practically rambling now. ". . . you have to understand, nothing will keep my forces from defending this habitat. Defending the one million precious beings held within. I did not order that Shredder to be fired upon. Just have your captain ease away from the structure. That is all I ask. And please. Do not fire upon my wife."

Another bright flash and another Shredder was destroyed. Cold fear ran though my veins. I swung a look over my shoulder to see if Shredder Three was still there—if Karen was still alive.

"Oh, god . . . that was . . . pilot Wright's Shredder," Karen said barely holding back a sob.

"Fuck it, I'm taking the legs," Donny said. I saw two bright flashes within the hold's video feed. I knew Donny well enough he typically didn't bluff. And he very much did know what an eye for an eye meant.

Overlord Skith was screaming now. His words no longer coming out in English, but in high-pitched Earupitan gibberish.

I said, "I didn't give that order to fire. You see, my men will do anything to protect their own. I think you know what I mean, don't you, your Eminence?"

Mike cut in on my comms, "He's in."

"Repeat that . . ." I said.

"The headless horseman is inside the habitat. I'm controlling him remotely as we speak. Any idea where the switch for the Bay's force field is?"

I had no idea. Above the continued blathering of the overlord, I heard Mike asking the others there within the Control Center. No one had any clue. *Shit! Shit! Shit!*

I said, "Mike, go ahead and get that ship pulled back a bit from the habitat. I don't want to lose anyone else out here."

"Copy that."

"And get me a feed from that robot."

"Copy."

I now had multiple video feeds coming into my HUD: the XL5's Control Center, the hold, the overlord wiping tears from his eyes, and a jittery front view perspective of the robot.

"Thank you for repositioning the Crusher," the overlord said in a barely audible, raspy, voice.

"You're welcome, Overlord Skith. How about I check on the condition of your wife?"

"Oh, yes, please."

"Donny's smiling face came into view within the hold's feed." I shook my head, *asshole.*

"My man is a renowned terrible shot, Overlord Skith. I believe your wife is fine."

I watched the robot's continued search—more accurately Mike's continued search.

There was sudden movement within the Control Center's video feed. Another large Gap had entered the compartment. I watched as the Gap physically shoved Mike right out of his seat—hard enough that he went sprawling onto the deck. There was distorted yelling back and forth.

"What the hell is going on!?" I barked aloud.

Taking a closer look, I had to smile. It was none other than Jhally, who was supposed to be lying on his deathbed, and who was now answering my question.

He said, "The control panel is nowhere near where Mike was telling the robot to look for it."

My jaw fell open as I watched the robot start running within the large flight bay. Ships of all kinds, some smaller warships similar to those nearby aiming their weapons at us, as well as a number of Shredders, parked one after another along the outer perimeter of the bay.

"There it is," Jhally said.

I said, “General Chiv . . . once that shield comes down, how fast can you scoot that Crusher of yours inside?”

“Fast enough,” he said flatly.

I said to the rest of the NightHawks, “Prepare to move, everyone. Fast! Diddle-daddle and you die.”

And then it happened. The energized aqua blue flight bay shield blinked off. The XL5’s big maneuvering thrusters immediately came alive and within four seconds the Crusher was accelerating toward the opening.

That’s when the Earupitan armada of warships unleashed total hellfire upon us. First one, then another, and then another of our NightHawks Shredders exploded. The XL5 slid safely inside to safety. Karen, Yeager and myself wasted no time—we flew as countless plasma bolts crisscrossed all around us. In a matter of three seconds, my Shredder took no less than five indirect hits. My portside wing disintegrated right as I entered the flight bay. Karen’s Shredder lost its tail section in a blaze of green energy bolts. Yeager, coming in right behind us, didn’t make it. His ship exploded just as he cleared the flight bay entrance.

My ruined ship crashed hard down onto the deck and proceeded to slide sixty yards, all the way across the flight bay. Dazed but unhurt, I slid open my canopy. Karen was already leaping down from her Shredder’s wing, onto the deck. Then the flight bay’s energized shield came back online—all incoming enemy fire, suddenly stopped.

Ten feet away, the towering robot loomed high above us, motionless. Armed men, women, and Earupitan Marshals were already streaming down the XL5’s ramp. I spotted Donny and then Matt—both were in full combat mode—both barking off orders to our remaining Takebacks. Moving as quickly as they could manage with Jhally's arm draped over his shoulder, Mike helped the injured Mannarian traverse the sloping gangway.

We were all, close to two hundred of us, looking around at our surroundings. The voluminous flight bay spanned hundreds of feet from one side to the other and continued on deep into the bowels of the habitat. High above us, hundreds of feet up, I could see a myriad of hanging catwalks and pedestrian causeways. Clearly, this Solaris Habitat was immense.

Jhally, with Mike's help, moved directly toward the far-side bulkhead. There he began tapping at an integrated console. Immediately, a virtual 3D projection came alive in front of him. Jhally shook his head, then turned toward me. "This isn't good."

chapter 48

"Talk to me," I said, approaching Jhally and what appeared to be a virtual schematic of the ship's interior now suspended in the air.

Jhally said, "There are twenty primary levels that make up this habitat, all of which are above us. Each level is independent of the others with its own dedicated power grid and separate environmental sub-systems. And each level has its own dedicated security forces . . . the barracks, a central armory, and an integrated weaponry to repel the advancement of hostile intruders. Each level contains a centralized bio-vault where the Earupitan females reside. Those vaults are about as impregnable as anything I've ever seen." Jhally looked at me, his reptilian features revealing more than just the accumulation of stress and worry from the past few days, but something else as well—*resignation.*

I tried to ignore the constant pinging sound in my ear puck—the overlord was hailing me again. Finally, I opened the channel. "Your Eminence?"

"You will find any future escape from that flight bay impossible, Captain Polk. And you will find access to any other areas of the habitat impossible. Whatever your intentions were, Captain . . . you have failed miserably. And while you pose no threat to our cherished female Earupitans, you are marooned. Only if you surrender now will I be able to spare your lives."

"Oh, really? You'd do that for us . . . let us go? Just like that?"

"I said spare your lives, I did not say anything about granting you your freedom."

"I don't know, I imagine we could live fairly comfortably here in this bay for quite a while. There are food replicators on the XL5, and probably on the other ships in here, too. I think we'll just sit tight here for the time being. I'm okay knowing we have blocked access for any of your other vessels to enter the flight bay . . . so you won't be making any deliveries any time soon."

The overlord said, "Let me tell you how things will progress from here, Captain. Sooner rather than later, Solaris Habitat's security forces will storm that flight bay. Prior to that, though, the surrounding atmosphere—your breathable air—will be flushed from the compartment. You likely have already noticed that the temperature has dropped significantly. It won't be long before you will be forced to stay cloistered within one of the space vessels where there are controlled environments. So you see, Captain Polk, you have already been defeated, you just haven't come to terms with that fact yet. I'll give you two hours to surrender. After that, you will be solely responsible for the deaths of those same people you are trying to protect."

Irritated, I cut the channel.

"So how many Gaps are we talking about here?" Matt said from behind me.

"One hundred of the overlord's most highly trained soldiers," Jhally said.

I looked back to see Matt and Donny. Both were standing with their arms crossed over their chests. Donny shrugged, giving me a *it's a no big deal* expression.

"That's one hundred security forces on each level. Two thousand total." Jhally emphasized.

I thought about everything Jhally was saying. I watched as more warships passed outside the flight bay's energy field. There would be no escaping this vessel. We either succeeded here today or we'd die trying. *But how do we succeed breeching not just one heavily fortified habitat, but twenty? And do so with a fighting force that is untrained and one-tenth their number!*

"Unfortunately . . . there's more," Jhally said. He pointed up to the slowly revolving projected schematic. There are eight lifts that allow access between the various levels." He looked away from the projection and stared deeper into the depths of the flight bay. "There . . . you can see four of the lift access ports at the far end of the flight bay. You can also see that not one of the lifts are even down here. And, Brian," Jhally paused for effect, "there are no adjoining stairwells like you would have within a high-rise building on Earth."

Two hundred rebel souls stood in silence, waiting for me to magically come up with something that would contradict Jhally's dire accounting of our situation. I saw Karen rubbing her bare arms. It was getting colder in here. What I wanted to do was find some hidden place, a corner here or a nook there, to just think things through. Instead I turned to all those that had followed me here. Karen returned my gaze and, remarkably, offered me a bemused smile. Donny raised his brows questionably and Matt stared impatiently at having this prolonged delay. I moved into the crowd seeing big Randy and his mother. She scowled and said, "Time for you to man up, boy . . . don't be such a pussy!"

Shawn McGee placed a reassuring hand on my shoulder and nodded with confidence. "You got this, man."

Some here had been saved back at the dome, others were members of my original Takebacks group. Not one of them was unarmed. I recognized some of the weaponry from my own armory, but there were also plasma rifles and mistmakers too. I continued to move amongst this pathetic rebel force. A rebel force that had, *somehow*, accomplished more than anyone else. More than the armies of all the great countries on Earth. But perhaps the overlord was right. Perhaps all our actions to this point had been for naught.

"Just give me a second," I said to no one in particular as I strode away from everyone. I kept going until I was another thirty yards deeper into the bay. I stopped and looked up—took in the technological wonder of such an amazing spacecraft. I looked all around me—at the numerous and impressive parked spacecraft that loomed tall nearby. I tried to ignore the fact I could actually see my breath now—condensation of the moisture in the cold air. We were all going to die here and there was nothing I could do to avoid that outcome. Maybe I should reconsider the overlord's offer—what choice did I have?

And then I started to chuckle. A chuckle that soon turned

to laughter. Concerned faces stared back at me and that seemed funny too. My giddiness subsided and I wiped the tears from the corners of my eyes. I found Mike staring back at me. I gestured him to come join me. He did as asked but his expression mirrored the others. He thought I had totally lost it—the pressure had gotten to me. *And we were all fucked.*

I placed a hand on Mike's shoulder just as Shawn McGee had done minutes earlier. I gestured to the flight bay around us, "Tell me, what do you see, Mike?"

He shrugged and let out an exasperated breath. "A prison?"

Murmurs from the others came back in agreement.

"And those craft all lined up over there?"

"Shredders . . ."

"And those big ones down there farther into the bay?" I asked.

"Looks like three of the smaller Crusher craft and another XL5 like this one," he said gesturing to the XL5 he and the others had arrived here on.

"And Mike, what is this thing here?"

"You mean the robot?"

I nodded.

"Well . . . it's a robot." He shrugged. "What's with the twenty stupid questions?" He looked at me, annoyed. And then, slowly, he smiled as realization crept in. "Those Crushers. They probably each have a collapsed assembly bot within—"

I cut him off, "Mike, would you be able to control those bots same as you did this one?"

"With Jhally's and a few other's help, yeah, sure."

"Can you make them climb?"

I watched his eyes as he took in all the little nooks and crannies that spanned the surrounding bulkheads. Mike looked up. "That's probably some kind of reinforced metal plating up there. Might be a challenge for the bots to break through," he said.

"Okay, how about we make them a trap door then?" I said, gesturing to the neat line of Shredders.

It took close to an hour for us to make the necessary preparations for battle. Most everyone had withdrawn into the warmth and higher oxygen levels within the XL5. The rest of us struggled within the now quickly dissipating atmosphere of the flight bay.

Mike and the small team he had assembled were busy awakening five assembly bots—bringing them out of their hidden Crusher craft compartments, awakened from their hibernation modes. One by one, they began to take shape there upon the flight deck—great metal leg and arm appendages expanding outward from their massive barrel-like torsos. It wasn't long before our army of five forty-foot tall headless giants stood motionless before us. Next, Mike instructed his team on how to control and maneuver the mechanical beasts.

Karen, now wearing someone's oversized coat, was spending her time sprinting between the various Shredder crafts determining which were operational and then getting them flight ready—going through a kind of pre-flight checklist she'd come up with.

Jhally, Donny, Matt, and I pretty much stayed huddled around the habitat's projected schematic. For some reason this same level of information was not accessible within the XL5's command center. We were all finding it hard to breath and the temperature had dipped into the low thirties—close to freezing. Donny had come up with an ingenious way for one of the robots to be solely dedicated to the transferring of our fighting forces up to the levels above. Seems there are open compartments within the torso of the big bots that are about ten foot wide by eight foot high.

"We can squeeze, I don't know . . . maybe teams of fifteen or so in there at a time." Donny said. "The roof of XL5 seems to be about the right height. We'll have the teams enter through the access panel there on the bot's lower back area."

There were nods all around.

"Unfortunately," Jhally said, "the compartments are not pressurized, so both temperature and the lack of atmosphere will soon be an even bigger issue."

I had started to notice movement high up above us. Soldiers were scurrying along the catwalks—undoubtedly taking up positions to fire down at us.

"They are wearing vac-suits . . . with helmets. Our time is quickly running out," I said.

More nods all around.

I heard Karen in my ear puck, "I have three Shredders operational . . . I think. Good news, cockpits are getting nice and toasty. We going to do this, or what?"

Before I could answer, plasma bolts rained down on us from above.

chapter 49

The integrated control panel to Jhally's right erupted into a shower of sparks. Streaks of bright blue energy careened off the deck plates and nearby bulkhead. We all ran—fortunately, we knew what our respective jobs were. On my way to my awaiting Shredder, I hailed the XL5's command center. "Get the ship's guns activated. Return fire!"

I was now helping to support Jhally, his crutch had dropped somewhere along the way. The alien was struggling to breathe now—his seven-foot-tall body mass required a hell of a lot more oxygen than that of a Human. All three of the awaiting Shredder's argon boost drives were cycling steady and loud. Karen had left the closest two craft for us. Plasma fire from above continued. I was thinking we were fortunate that we hadn't been hit—no one's aim up there seemed all that great. Of course, that's precisely when Jhally was hit in the shoulder and I was hit in my right calf. My lower leg felt as if someone had jammed a white-hot poker into it—fortunately, it still supported my weight. I continued to push and shove Jhally up onto the closest Shredder's wing.

"I'm fine . . . go!" he yelled down to me.

I ducked and ran beneath his craft and sprinted, as best I could with my injury, to my awaiting Shredder. Within seconds I was seated and cursing at the canopy to hurry up and close.

"Hey, handsome," I heard in my ear. I looked to my right and was just barely able to make out Karen's face within the cockpit.

"You ready to do this?" I asked.

"Sure. Piece of cake. See you on the other side."

Lift thrusters engaged, Karen's Shredder was rising up within the flight bay. Jhally's craft was next and then mine. I stole a quick look out over my starboard wing and saw one of the big assembly robots was positioned right up close to the XL5. Mike had it stooping down a bit—like it was taking a crap. Donny, on the Crusher's roof, was ushering people and a few Gaps, one who was unmistakably Dalm Mor Stroph , into the bot's open compartment.

"I'm taking these fuckers out," Karen said over our comms.

"Have at it," I said, poised to do the same. My wing guns came alive as I strafed a horizontal line of plasma fire across one of the lower catwalks. No less than ten Gaps were hit—two of which were propelled right off the catwalk—arms and legs flailing as they plummeted to the flight deck below.

This was part of our plan. Karen and I would clear the walkways and catwalks of enemy shooters, while Jhally concentrated on breaching the flight deck's ceiling using his gravity-disruptor cannons. He was now flying upside-down now—fuselage belly angled toward one of the predetermined weak points we had selected earlier.

"Show off," Karen said.

Boom! Boom! Boom!

I actually like the unique thunderous sound those big canons make when engaged. Karen and I continued to take pot shots at the catwalks, although most of them were already ruined or had fallen down to the deck below. Enemy fire was down to a minimum.

Jhally was circling above and was upside down again. *Boom! Boom! Boom!*

"How's it looking, Jhally? Having any success?" I asked.

"Not so far. I'll make another run at it, but you and Karen may need to assist me."

"You know how I love blowing shit up," she said. "So don't be shy asking."

Jhally made three more runs at the same ceiling location before chiming back in, "We have a breech!"

I could already see it. The bay's ceiling looked as if a massive fist had punched a hole right up through it. There was a gaping ragged hole with surrounding bent up metal shards. "Good news! But that may still need additional pounding to enable our bots to crawl up through. Jhally, why don't you get started on another access while Karen and I take turns expanding this one."

"Copy that," Jhally said.

It took another ten minutes before the three of us had four ample-sized breeches situated close to the side bulkheads.

Oxygen levels were already bad when we'd started this operation, I could only imagine how bad it was for everyone now. Two of the robots were now scaling the bulkhead walls on opposing sides of the flight bay. One was halfway up, the other a little lower.

I hailed Donny.

"Go for Crazy Horse. Good work breeching the next level, Polybius."

I smiled at his return to using our code names. "I take it you're in one of those climbing bots?" I asked.

"There're twenty of us. Packed in here like sardines. Let me tell you, Stroph's got some mean body odor going on in here."

"So oxygen levels are still okay?"

"Yeah, must have been those holes you guys poked into the upper floor. Temperatures and atmosphere seems to be normalizing."

"Copy that," I said. "Hey . . . good luck up there. I'm landing now. Will catch the next ride up."

"Copy . . . see you topside," Donny said.

I heard the channel close and wondered if that would be the last time I'd ever hear my friend's voice. I then heard a familiar ping in my ear. I saw it was Overlord Skith. I ignored his hail. By the time I was climbing down onto the flight deck, I saw that both Jhally and Karen were already moving toward the XL5's open ramp. Jhally was hopping on one leg while holding onto Karen's shoulder for support. Heading after them, I grimaced in pain. My own leg was giving me trouble. Looking up, one of the bots was in the process of wiggling through one of the openings made by Jhally. I heard gunfire suddenly erupted up there—bright flashes of plasma fire strobing down through the opening. Two more robots were climbing the side bulkheads leaving just one remaining by the XL5.

I saw Matt was standing on the roof signaling me, "Hurry up . . . that fight's not going to wait for us, man!"

Minutes later we were standing within the robot's dark and claustrophobic hold compartment. Somewhere along the line, the plan had deviated some—pretty typical for such a loosely made plan. All of the robots had taken between twenty and twenty-five passengers on up to the next level. Karen was standing right next to me and I could feel her nervous energy. One of her feet was tapping nonstop. She, like the rest of us, was ready to jump into the fight. We all had our HUDs activated and we were watching through multiple video feeds as the events transpired on level one above. I took in the jittery feeds provided by each of the robot's forward cameras. Jhally would make his way to the XL5's command center. Mike and his team were doing an admirable job remotely controlling the big machines. Once in a while someone would propel a robot into a bulkhead or one would stumble, but that was to be expected. One thing that was immediately apparent was that the robots were a bit too tall for the confined space—each was required to hunch over a tad, to avoid hitting the bulkhead's ceilings. But all in all, these mechanical beasts were tearing through the habitat's first level like raging bulls running rampant through a china shop. The areas that I could see were beautiful spaces made of natural elements—wood and glass and even stone textured walls. Now all were being turned to rubble.

The security forces were relentlessly firing upon the bots nonstop. But mistmakers and plasma rifles showed to be ineffective against the hulk-like brutes.

Our own robot abruptly began to jerk and sway. Although I couldn't see much inside our jammed tight compartment, I could tell a good many of us had toppled over—some cursing obscenities in the process.

"I think we're climbing up through the breech hole," Matt said.

I took in my HUD's numerous activated video feeds. Enemy fire had not only subsided but seemed to have ceased completely. The level was in a total shambles.

"Polybius, you copy?" Donny said over comms.

"Loud and clear . . . status?" I asked.

"Robots have destroyed about one tenth of Level One. This place is huge. My team, as well as the three others, are all feet on the deck now. Bots are off on their own. We're holding up for your bot to arrive. Okay, there you are . . . see you coming now."

I heard a pinging in my ear. The overlord's near constant hails still coming in. But I wasn't ready to talk to him just yet.

The compartment jostled around some more and the next thing I knew, the bot's back panel was open and light was streaming in. The fresh air filling the space around us was also a welcome change. Mike had lowered the robot in such a way that it we only needed to jump down four or five feet onto the deck.

The video feeds hadn't done justice to just how much damage had occurred here.

"I almost feel guilty," Karen said, looking around.

Matt handed her a rifle and then one to me. "Any word on locating this level's bio-vault?" he asked, knowing I was getting comm feeds from all the teams.

We had to literally step over innumerable Gap dead bodies from the security forces. Bodies that had been crushed and flattened into dented deck plates. A gaping, split-open helmet revealed half of a Gap's face. I looked into the poor bastard's lifeless eye. "Not the best way to go," I murmured.

By the time we joined up with Donny's team, we'd progressed through the remnants of the soldier barracks, a canteen or mess hall where not a chair or table was left standing, and one bank of elevator lifts—which was pretty much destroyed.

Donny raised his chin, "Hey." His team of twenty or so merged with Matt's team of twenty-five.

"Hey," I said back. I held up a hand, "Hold on a sec, Mike is hailing me."

Mike sounded exasperated, "Holy shit . . . looks like combined forces from, um, Levels Two, Three, and Four are storming in from above. They're using one of the few still operational lifts. Spartacus' Team 2 has already engaged the enemy."

"Where are all the other robots?" I asked.

"They're already a half-mile away. I'm going to take yours . . . your team will need to hoof it. No time to wait to load you all inside again."

I heard the assembly bot come alive behind us. Heavy footfalls shook the deck as it ran past—now seeing the hunched robot plowing through the debris, I was glad these things were on our side.

"We need to hurry," I said, and sprinted off after the robot doing my best to ignore the pain in my calf.

chapter 50

By the time we reached the battle, our side had taken serious casualties. Our robot was lying in a heap across the deck. Its metal hulk was already being used for cover. Ducking low, I marveled at the sheer breath of the opposing plasma fire. Blast strikes were erupting everywhere. It would be impossible to get shot off the way things were. I saw Spartacus off to my left, hunkered down with several other Takebacks. His left cheek was scorched into a blackened crust. Keeping low, I made my way over to him.

"Shawn! What happened to the robot?"

"They brought along some kind of electromagnetic pulse weapon . . . it toppled the son of a bitch in one second flat!"

That wasn't good. Without our bots, we were toast.

We ducked as the man standing directly to Shawn's left crumpled to the deck. A shot to his forehead had killed him instantly.

"We're going to be picked off one by one . . . we need a Plan B, Polybius."

I hailed Mike, "Tell me our other robots are still en route."

"I could lie to you and say they were. Enemies got some kind of—"

"I know, I know, an EMP weapon."

"One seems to be partially responding to our commands. It can crawl, a little. No sense of balance. The gyros no longer—"

"Ask Jhally if he's found any of the vaults yet."

"The bio-vaults?"

"Yes, ask him . . . to hurry."

Another body slumped to the deck and then another. A woman screamed.

Jhally came on the line. "I think I found it. It makes sense, really, where it is situated—"

"Jhally!"

"It's actually very close to your current coordinates, Brian. The whole inner section, a massive allotment of floor space within the habitat *IS* the vault."

I took in my surroundings, then scrutinized the nearby bulkhead. It was slightly curved and went on and on into the distance. It did indeed seem to a part of the habitat's supporting superstructure.

"Any idea where the door is?"

Mike was back in my ear. "Jhally's trying a few things with the robot. Here's the thing . . . there is no door. I guess it's part of how the Gap females are kept safe. Safe from enemies and their own kind as well. So the vault only opens when the time is right . . . when they're released on Earth."

A plasma bolt came so close to my head, that I could smell my own burnt hair. I ventured a quick peek at the enemy line. They were approximately one-hundred-fifty feet away. They, too, had taken cover behind a barricade—but one that looked to be designed for just that purpose—not a dead robot. From what I'd seen, very few of the enemy was down, while we were being taken out far too quickly. I leaned back and saw Karen and Matt were lying prone on their bellies. Both were firing their rifles through open gaps below the bot's legs.

"Do you see it yet?" Mike asked.

See it? No, but I certainly heard something. Looking behind me I saw it. The lone remaining robot. And it was running full out. Hunched and menacing-looking—a bull making its final charge.

I yelled into the open channel, "Fire! Fire! Fire! Give them everything you've got . . . distract the Gaps!" *Don't let them even think about using that damn EMS!*

We all did just that. This was no longer the time to be careful. To hide. I was the first to stand and hold the trigger tight. The stock of my rifle jerked back over and over into my shoulder as I unleashed a hailstorm of plasma fire into the enemy line. The others around me soon were right there with me—all standing. Donny was the first to start yelling. Not in pain nor in fear. It was a fucking war-cry. And then he was standing atop the robot and shooting down into the line. One by one we all joined him—not a one of us released our triggers. Not a one of us wasn't yelling at the top of our lungs. While some of us fell in those few seconds, the rest of us did not falter—we killed a lot of Gaps.

And then the charging robot was upon us and quickly moving past us. From what Mike told me later, it hit the bio-vault's wall at close to eighty miles an hour. A two-hundred pound freight train of kinetic energy colliding with a bulkhead made of some kind of hardened dura-steel three feet thick—but it was no match for the robot's impact.

It was akin to an earthquake—a ten on the Richter Scale. Not a soul was left standing. A seismic wave coursed through the Solaris Habitat causing it to strain and grown as if experiencing physical pain. Dust and debris filled the air. I laid there on my back looking up—wondering if at any moment the very bones of this vessel were about to collapse into itself. I rolled onto my side and then managed to slowly get onto my knees. Off in the distance, I saw Karen getting to her feet. I breathed a sigh of relief.

But I hadn't expected what happened next.

At first there were just a few of them. They were smaller than I expected, no larger than your average house cat. Then they were everywhere. Hundreds, no, thousands upon thousands of them. Running here and there. Like hairless white bunnies, they were skittering and hopping around all over the place. Clearly they were ecstatic at being freed. I smiled—a chorus of funny squeals filled the air.

I heard Jhally speaking in my ear. "Captain Polk?"

"I'm here, Jhally," I said, laughing as one of the little creatures has somehow leapt onto my shoulder.

"Apparently, we have located the females."

"Really? These are the females? They're tiny . . . they don't look anything like that Maiden Sow thing."

"It's because they are still quite young, they are called norps."

I tossed the little norps onto the deck and got to my feet. I peered over the robot to see what was left of our enemy. I shook my head. Apparently, our charging robot had been directed to trample them on its trajectory toward the bio-vault. All were dead. The wall behind them was gone. I did see the bottoms of the robot's feet still visible though. That and countless more juvenile norps hopping here and there.

An all too familiar pinging sound was accosting my ear. Overlord Skith most definitely wanted to talk. This time I answered his hail. "Overlord Skith . . ."

"Captain Polk . . . I beg you, please. Do not injure any of them. They are literally the future of our species. Oh . . . I think I can hear them. Oh, what a beautiful sight that must be . . ." His voice trailed off. "Anything. I . . . We . . . will do anything. You have won. You have beaten us. Just please, do not harm them . . ."

"We'll talk, Overlord. I promise. But right now, I have some other business to take care of." I broke our connection.

As I limped toward her, I saw that she was already sprinting toward me. Hair flying wild behind her, this amazing woman was a true warrior. She leapt high into the air and right into my open arms. I spun her around and around, and she laughed out loud. I pulled her in close and breathed her in. I could feel her wet tears against my cheek—or perhaps they were my own. Now, with her lips close to my ear, she said, "You know I love you, Brian. But I have to be honest with you . . . I never thought this would work. Any of it! I'd simply chosen to spend whatever little time I had left doing *something*. And I did it for Gwen . . . I wanted her to know her mother was one of the ones who had fought back." Her voice cracked and laughter had turned to sobs. I held her tight as she wept—as we both wept.

epilogue

Seventeen months have passed since those fateful few days spent on board the Solaris Habitat—just a stone's throw from Earth's ever-watchful moon.

As a good faith gesture, we released ten percent of the norps back to the Earupitans—in conjunction with the last of their Situational Command Ships leaving Earth's high orbit in search of their future home world. Communications between our species would remain open. Over time, additional norps would be released back to them. Earth would use that time to build adequate defenses based on the mostly Mannarian technology left behind, along with the help of as many Mannarians as chose to stay. The plight of the OEC Marshals is ongoing. Even in light of a number of them being instrumental in the eventual ousting of our interstellar invaders, Humans have found it hard to forgive and forget. Hell, who hadn't lost a loved one at the hands of one local OEC station or another? Any remaining Earupitans have all been imprisoned, including Dalm Mor Stroph and Chancellor Vogthner. Their past crimes were just too egregious. All now were relegated to, perhaps not surprisingly, the only place on Earth nobody put up much of a stink about them inhabiting—Chernobyl, Ukraine. Apparently, any residual radiation stemming from the 1986 nuclear power plant disaster has had little effect on Gap physiology. *Time will tell.*

But Earupitans and Mannarians are not equal—at least in the eyes of humanity. And while I had never found their appearance all that different from one another, that didn't seem to hold true for most Humans. While almost all Earupitans still inhabiting Earth are now living in Chernobyl, not so with the Mannarians. And I think I had something to do with that. As it turns out, my Takebacks have taken on nothing less than *hero* status. The story of one Human and one Mannarian, once enemies and later friends, who repaired first one, and then four other Shredder craft—it was the start of a rebellion that would change the course of history. A history where humanity would no longer be the lowly subjects of a cruel Earupitan Empire.

In seventeen months much has reverted back to the way things were prior to the invasion. Cell phones are back, as well as the internet and cable TV. Countries have reestablished borders and boundaries. The United States of America is back in full form. Somewhere along the line, we even picked up another five states. And, of course, politics has reared its ugly head.

At present, I'm spending a good amount of my time bringing Polk Ranch back to its full glory. At most recent count, we have eight hundred head of fine Aberdeen Angus cattle roaming those fertile plains off beyond the big barn.

The *we* I'm referring to, of course, refers to me and my wife, Karen, and of course, our daughter, Gwen. Jhally is here, too; he pretty much runs the place since I'm often pulled out of town for one thing or another. Seems there's a grassroots effort growing to have me elected as the next U.S. President. *Go figure.*

The End

Thank you for reading *The Hidden Ship*. If you enjoyed this book, PLEASE leave me review on Amazon.com—it really helps!

To be notified the moment all future books are released—please join my mailing list. I hate spam and will never, ever, share your information. Jump to this link to sign up:

http://eepurl.com/bs7M9r

Acknowledgments

First and foremost, I am grateful to the fans of my writing and the ongoing support for all my books. I'd like to thank my wife, Kim, she's my rock and is a crucial, loving component of my publishing business. I'd like to thank my mother, Lura Genz, for her tireless work as my first-phase creative editor and a staunch cheerleader of my writing. I'd also like to thank Kimberly Peticolas for her amazing, detailed editing work. Others who provided fantastic support include Lura and James Fischer, Stuart Church, and Eric Sundius.

Check out the other available titles by Mark Wayne McGinnis on the following page.